BRANSON'S COUNTRY

"KANE"

BASED ON AUSTRALIAN ACTOR
TONY BONNER

JANETTE ANDERSON

Published in the USA by:
BearManor Media
P O Box 71426
Albany, Georgia 31708
www.bearmanormedia.com

ISBN 1-59393-352-5

Printed in the United States of America.

Dedicated to
Anthony F. Bonner
without whom this book would not be possible,
with love

CHAPTER 1

The serenity of the warm Australian summer afternoon lay undisturbed. Undisturbed, that is, until Kane Branson appeared. Finding his quarry in the old French chateau was not easy. Disposing of him was.

"Hey, mate? You said the guy was an old friend. Didn't look like he knew you to me," stated the young and innocent valet. Sweat poured down the valet's forehead and nose. He tugged at his white shirt collar; the starch irritated his skin. He shuffled in his shoes and scuffed the soles on the tarmac driveway.

"Humph. Watch and learn son. Watch and learn. Then, one day you won't be valeting for these arse-holes. Here." Branson waved the promised $50-bill in front of the valet's nose and he could smell the freshness of it.

"I thought you were kidding. Thanks, mister. Now, I can take my girl-friend out on a proper date tonight."

Stuffing it into his back pocket, he continued, "So, what's the other part of the joke?" he asked while looking up at Branson with respect.

"Joke? Oh yeah. That's what I said." Branson looked towards the entrance of the chateau.

"The guy whose car I just fetched, well… he'll see the funny side of it. Give him a minute to get the Mercedes into the right gear. He just needs the right…" and Branson paused.

Branson removed the overly starched collar and black tie and tossed them onto the green grass of the chateau grounds. Sliding out of the spare valet jacket, he handed it to the astonished young valet.

From the top of the driveway, the explosion rocked the slumbers of the afternoon. The sparkling new Mercedes ignited into a flaming ball, showering the rich Australian gentry that Branson despised. The Mercedes' occupant departed for a better life.

Branson smiled, causing a few lines of maturity to furrow his brow. Charlie, the other attendant, stared at his companion.

"You're not what you seem, are you?" the boy stammered, almost becoming afraid of the man next to him.

"The hell I'm not. Been nice knowing you; and hey, thanks for going along with the joke," Branson retorted to Charlie in an offhanded way.

Branson laughed and walked across the lawn behind the Chateau to where his chrome and graphite-gray behemoth stood waiting. He vaulted one-handed over the four-foot, steel-spike fence. His Harley-Davidson with its 115-horsepower engine stood
gleaming in the sunlight. Branson swung his leg over the Australian flag, which he had specially emblazoned on the gas tank.

Without a backward glance, he fired up the bike and took off down the path. Each gear took him higher into the speed he liked. Gusting winds whipped against his face as his lungs inhaled the salt air.

Far below him, the panoramic views of the beach still managed to take his breath away. As usual, Branson steered the bike down the twisting, tree-lined hill, his body one with the machine. At an insane speed, he headed toward the junction. The wind ballooned through his white shirt and caused his long blonde hair to fly out behind him. Surely, this was justice. Maybe this was even freedom of a sort. This… was Branson's Country at its finest.

At the crossroads, he screeched to a halt. Branson parked his metallic ride. Leaning back in the saddle, he reached in the back pocket of his tight black pants and pulled out his cigarettes. Next, he struck the match against the bottom of his boots, to light up the cigarette. He inhaled deeply. A nasty habit, but one he had abused of late. He took a long drag on the smoke.

Branson looked at his fancy gold Rolex and began counting the seconds. Fingering the watch's bracelet, he turned it over and read the inscription. This reflecting brought back memories. His thoughts were disturbed by the sound of distant sirens. The noise became louder. Countless police cars flew past him. Branson watched closely as a couple of unmarked cars sped by. The driver idly glanced at him while Branson waved.

"One, two, three, four…"

The Australian Federal Police cars screeched to a halt with their tires burning rubber. One of the unmarked police cars turned and headed back towards Branson.

"Five, six…"

He finished his cigarette and squashed the stub between his fingers.

His hand revved the throttle. The next thing Branson knew, the unmarked car decided to stop.

"What the hell are you doing here, partner?" Officer Lord asked while banging his hand on the side of the car door. "No, don't tell me. I don't think that I want to know. Buchanan is gonna have my head for letting you here on your own. You know I have to hang with you," Deputy Lord said.

Deputy Lord had been Branson's partner for seven years. He respected him because he had seen him go through hell and back and still be able to stay part of the force. In Branson's eyes, he was also babysitting him. Ever since…ever since six months back.

"You wanna tell me what you're doing here, dressed like that?"

Lord climbed out of the car and shut the door. Younger than Branson by some twenty years, he admired his boss, but sometimes not his ethics.

"Dirt biking," Branson flippantly replied.

Lord leaned against his black sedan.

"Sure. In a white shirt and black dress pants. I don't think so." Lord, looking back up the road, inquired cautiously. "Know anything about the chateau?"

"Yeah," answered Branson, staring at Lord. His blue eyes penetrated clear through to a man's brain.

Dan Lord rose. "What?"

Branson repositioned himself on the flying machine.

"That Chateau's a damn good place to get barbecue," Branson said cuttingly with a mischievous wink toward Deputy Lord.

From naught to seventy was Branson's usual speed. Today was going to be no different. He left Lord standing in the dust.

"You goddamn son-of-a-bitch. You're gonna get us both thrown out of the AFP," yelled Lord getting angry at Branson's speed.

Next morning, Branson woke to the sound of a family screaming in the adjoining apartment, seeming as if it was coming from the balcony. This type of scenario was becoming commonplace in his neighborhood. He pushed the crumpled sheets from his naked body and reached for the cotton robe, which he kept on the chair. Slipping into the robe, he pulled the belt around his waist. Branson brushed his bedraggled hair away from his eyes. Then he shuffled across the room.

He opened the glass doors and moved out onto the concrete block.

Branson stretched in the morning sun. On the patio table sat a glass of whiskey from many days before. The glass held half liquor and half rainwater. There was that damn noise again. Loud and long, the neighbor could be heard screaming at the kids. He looked over the top of the concrete divider and onto the adjoining patio.

"Hey, you, can you shut the hell up?" Branson yelled in the direction of the disturbance.

"Why don't you mind you own goddamn business? They're my kids. I'll shout when the hell I want to shout. And, I will shout at whomever I want to shout at!" came the reply.

"The hell you will. You better keep it down or the landlord will turn you all out on the streets."

"Yeah, that right mate? Who's goin' to tell them... you? The drunk from next door."

His neighbor was right. In the past, he had been the drunk from next door. However, this was no longer an accurate description of him. That was then and this was now.

Branson reached back through the glass doors and pulled the Glock 9 Millimeter out of its holster. "I'm telling you one more time...mate. Shut the hell up. One last chance. You keep it down... keep it quiet. If you can keep those kids in line, we'll forget about the disturbance," he said as he pushed the hair from his eyes once more. Absentmindedly, and with automation, he picked up the drink and took a swig of it. The sour mesh whiskey was foul and he spat it out with disgust at himself for not paying more attention to what he was drinking.

"Stick it all straight up your ass mate," the rude tenant and overbearing father yelled back.

"That's what I thought you'd say."

Branson reached over the divide and leaned into the balcony. He could see the kids and the wife with her face black and blue. He'd never noticed them before. Maybe he had and he hadn't cared till now. Maybe before now, he had not been sober enough to notice the rest of the man's family, or any of his neighbors for that matter.

Ever since his wife died, he had been a real self-absorbed jerk and he was not destined, at least for the moment, to change that.

"This change your mind?" He pulled the gun level with the man's raging face.

The man found that staring eye to eye to Branson's Glock was not good for his stomach. He threw up where he stood.

"Now you goin' to shut the fuck up, or what? Maybe you'd rather I go and get you evicted. On the other hand, maybe you didn't even know I was the landlord. Okay, so now we both know where we stand. I'll warn you about this once. Leave her and the kids alone and don't hurt them anymore. If I see bruises on them after today, you're history. Better yet, maybe I should call Child Well-Fare and have them come look at the bruises that you put on your wife and kids. Would you appreciate that? At that point, you'll have me to deal with, as well as them. Branson waved his free hand towards the wife's face pointing at the fresh bruise. "You understand me?"

The guy nodded.

It was at that moment, Branson realized what he was doing. He'd raised a gun to his neighbor. Here he was, one of the law's finest and he was threatening his neighbor, out of hate at the world, for losing his wife. Was this what had become of him? The gun gleamed in the morning sun. Branson caressed it. The Glock had a job to do, and so did he. He spat on the concrete.

Thinking back to the events of six months ago was almost too much for him. One by one, five men had taken turns raping his wife that night while he lay in a drunken stupor in his nightly hangout. Maybe he should have used the gun on himself afterwards. Not a bad idea, even now. First, he had an operation to finish…an operation he had code named 'Sage.'

Sage Jay had been the mother of his beautiful daughter. A daughter that they also named Sage, whom he hadn't seen since she'd left for the big city a few years before her mother's death. A daughter Branson intended to find wherever she was; and whatever it took to find her. Getting even for his wife's sake was the job most important to him now. Then, he could solely concentrate on locating young Sage Branson. For now, he had to get back to work before he no longer had the force to be his cover while he continued his dirty work after the explosion.

Closing the patio doors, he set the gun down on the bedside table and headed for the shower. He turned up the heat as high as he could, trying to wash away the memories of the last few months. Water ran down his fifty-two-year-old body. Six feet and two inches tall, tan and slender, Branson came from good stock. He rubbed soap onto his torso while standing under the spray. He turned slowly in the shower, his muscular body never flinching as he turned the temperature from hot to ice cold.

After working out and exercising most of his life, he had managed to keep his body taught and lean. Flipping his head back, his blonde hair hung down his back. Undercover for so long, he wore it Branson-style: always long, rough, ready and unkempt.

The shower had been a special place for him and his wife. A place they had often made love. Now he was alone, and he hated it. Closing his eyes usually did him no good. He could still see her beautiful face. It haunted him day and night. Those brown eyes and those round red lips. He turned off the water and climbed out, water dripping from him. Branson wrapped a huge black bath towel around his waist and looked in the mirror. Dead pools looked back.

"Damn. This shouldn't have happened. Why me? What did I do to deserve this?" He banged his fist on the dirty glass of his vanity cabinet.

Self-pity was not becoming to a member of the Australian Federal Police. He dressed in tight blue jeans and a black wool sweater. Slipping on his shoulder holster, he made sure it was hidden beneath the leather jacket. He sat down on the unmade bed and pulled on his snakeskin boots.

Branson looked around. Clothes strewn on the floor, several days' dishes stacked in the sink, trash more than a week old; the place missed his wife and so did he. Swinging his leg over the Harley, he powered up the bike. With one push of a button, the side door swung open and Branson steered smoothly out into the road. The door closed, leaving behind his old way of life. He stepped into the other world of Branson's Country.

CHAPTER 2

Kane Branson was known in the turf that he covered. Drunk or sober, he was a man that people feared. He had ten notches on his gun in twice as many years…twenty years, ten notches; ten accidents, accidents that had been unavoidable…until now.

After Nam, Branson graduated from the police academy with honors. For years, he'd been on the AFP special drug team, a job that occasionally took him across the ocean and oftentimes, away from his family. His rank earned him the respect he gained from his co-workers, and Branson's file was full of commendations and honors. A crack shot with any weapon, a master of the martial arts, he was a one-man demolition squad.

"Morning, partner. Bunch of paperwork in your office. Two or three urgent matters need your attention, and Buchanan wants to see you." Deputy Lord said the last sentence quickly.

Branson peered over his shades at Deputy Lord hovering in the doorway. Lord watched Branson, uncertain if he should broach the subject of the day before. Wherever Branson went, he was supposed to go also. However, since Sage's death, Lord had seen a dramatic change. He knew Branson drank. It was common knowledge. The department overlooked it, because Branson got results, and in his department, results counted. Branson had his ways, and no one questioned them.

"Kane, about yesterday?"

Branson removed his shades and looked up from the desk. "Yeah?"

"I was just wondering…well, goddamn, we both know who barbecued the guy and…"

"And what?" Branson's sultry eyes dared him to speak his mind.

"Nothing. Buchanan's waiting for you. He's hot. You better get your butt in there."

Branson continued flicking through the files on his desk. He was aware that Lord was still watching him. The way he took out the next person would have to be subtler. Putting his own deputy in the line of fire just was not a good thing... fire from Commander Buchanan. It wasn't the department's battle…only his. This was personal. They had failed where he would succeed.

"Close the door on your way out," suggested Branson.

Branson knew where to find his next victim and he knew his hangouts. What he didn't know exactly was what he was going to do when he caught up with him. He sat back on his leather seat, contemplating his mission. He stared at the walls. The one full of citations was near a window that looked out on dreary buildings. The gray buildings continually reflected his mood. Six months was not enough time spent grieving after twenty five years of marriage. There had been many women before her, but when Sage Jay came along, he never strayed from the path. Age forty-two was far too young for her to die. Sexual brutality and an overdose had caused her death. The official death certificate had said, 'overdose.'

The glass door reopened.

"Boss, Buchanan said now!" He hesitated. "You okay?"

"Yeah, fine. Just thinking." He closed the files on his desk.

"About what?"

"What the hell do you think?" Branson looked dismayed.

"Oh, yeah, right." Lord stepped out of the way.

"Okay, so I'm going," Branson said while following his deputy to the door.

"Sit down, Branson. Cigarette?" Commander Buchanan's face showed no expression.

"Sure," Branson said, with his trademark lack of respect to Buchanan, and leaned back in the soft leather chair.

"Look, we all know that losing your wife has been hard on you. Especially the way that she died and all." Buchanan tried playing at good cop first.

Branson leaned forward. His hands thumped down hard on his boss's desk.

"You don't know a fucking thing. You think you know. You all think you know. This department couldn't even bring the five people that were responsible to justice. That's how much you all knew." He paused merely for breath.

"Stop right there! You're way out of line, Agent Branson. I'm trying to be nice here." Buchanan was fast losing what little patience God had given him. "Believe it or not, I do understand. I understand that your revenge is going to get the department into a whole lot of damn trouble. We have enough problems with the media thinking that we're all a bunch of cowboys without you messing up."

He stood up. "I'm not gonna mess up, I'm gonna…"

"Branson shut the fuck up, now! Listen to me, or get the hell out of here and stay out. You understand me?" Commander Buchanan may have only been a small man, but what he lacked in stature, he gained in guts. "So get your butt back in that chair and listen to me."

Branson sat down. Only because he'd never seen Buchanan this angry and he wanted to see exactly how far he would go with his threats.

"I'm listening."

Buchanan moved round the large oak desk and sat on the corner.

"That's better. First, I know full well that it was you yesterday who made dinner with Pierce's Mercedes. Secondly, I have a new assignment for you."

"What, playing crossing guard at a kindergarten?" interrupted Branson.

"That's it, Agent." Buchanan stood up. His voice was filled with anger. "You're out of here! Forget it. You tow the line, or you really are out of here. Who the fuck do you think you are? Damn you, Branson. You think you're still the hotshot you once were? Maybe you are. But you have to do this our way, and you know I mean the department's way… or no way at all."

Branson stood up and headed for the door, his face totally unreadable.

"The U.S. is about to file charges against Miles Stratton." The commander was using everything he knew in order to get his agent back on track. "Stratton is in Australia now, but he may try to return to the States. If he's here, so are the other two men. King and Stevens will be close to him."

Branson stopped and then slowly turned.

Seizing his opportunity, Buchanan continued, "The department knows the fifth man. The one named Walker who smuggles heroin. There's a witness, but the person won't come forward until Walker's in prison." Buchanan watched Kane's facial expression. He continued, "I'm going to give you a chance at finding Walker's compound. Next, I want you to link Stratton to Walker's operations. Just make sure you break up this damn big drug ring. You'll have help from U.S. Marshal, Reese Wade. She, shall we say, has a deep-cover relationship with Stratton. Wade will contact you in her way and help anyway that she can."

"I don't work with anyone, let alone a damn woman!" Branson retorted.

"You do now. Well, you're booked on the night flight from Sydney to Brisbane. One last thing, on the same flight is the witness. For God's sake, make sure you don't mix the two up. Here's the folder with the photos and all the information you need now. All I ask of you is that you stay in touch. The rest is up to you, except the U.S. would like Stratton back alive if possible."

Branson's look was slow and deliberate. As Branson looked at him, Buchanan saw a look in his man's eyes that he never wanted to see again.

"You're sure Stratton is here in Australia?" His voice was almost a whisper. Deep pools of anger burned holes in his boss's face. "In my country? You're sure?"

Buchanan nodded his head. "Yeah. Go home. Pack a bag. A car will take you to the airport. This group has never seen your face, unless your wife had pictures with her that…"

"No." He stopped.

Buchanan cleared his throat. "You're going in undercover, and this time you can do it your way. One last thing, the witness that I mentioned is a woman who was working with Walker. Get her back here. I have a feeling you know how."

"Oh, yeah. I know how. Hell, I know exactly how. Hope she's a looker."

Branson left the room with a slam of the commander's door.

Buchanan had omitted to tell his agent one very important piece of information. He smiled to himself and sat back in his plush commander's chair pushing a button on his phone.

"Lord, get yourself in here, now. Your partner is on his way to Brisbane. You are not. You'll keep tags from this end."

Branson pulled out the only suit he had. He chose it and a couple more pieces of clothing that would give him the desired affect of a drug dealer.

If he needed more money than he had on him, he'd send for it later. Sitting down on the bed, he picked up his wife's picture to reminisce yet another time. He pulled the photo from the frame and pushed it into the lining of his case, piling his clothes on top. Somehow, on this particular evening, it felt as if his wife's photo would bring him some good luck.

As AFP, he was licensed to carry guns onboard most flights. As Branson, he was licensed to carry what he needed to get jobs completed. His reputation showed that where the police had failed to do their job, he would not fail.

Traveling by car was not in Branson's repertoire. When he traveled, usually it was through the courtesy of Harley. His uneasiness was apparent to the driver. Branson lit up a cigarette.

"Sir. Mind not smoking in the car?"

"I do mind," he replied, but put the cigarette out anyway. Looking through the tinted windows, he realized that he had an additional problem with the raindrops blurring his vision. Thinking back, he remembered that it had been raining the night of his wife's murder, too.

"Honey, I'll be late. You go on over to the party without me. I'll meet you there. Yeah, one of the guys is getting married this weekend. Just gonna have a quick drink. I'll meet you there by nine, promise. Wear that little black dress that's my favorite. Hey, honey." He paused. "I love you." He had gingerly hung up the telephone.

Sage Jay had been ready to go by eight. At eight-fifteen she had walked out of the apartment. By ten that same night, she was found dead at the airport.

In the cells late that night, Pierce described how he had picked her up. Sage Jay had been waiting for a cab outside of Branson's home at 116 Del Rio Place. Pierce had driven the cab and had picked up fares from that address before. Instead of taking her where she wanted to go, he had driven her out to the old airfield where his buddies were waiting.

From the front of the cab, Sage Jay had been handed a can of fruit juice. She had joked with him while drinking down the juice. Sage Jay had no way of knowing the drink had contained Gamma Butyl Lactone. Pierce had known that it did. He also had known how she'd be feeling by the time he got her to the airfield. The drug was one that was easy to purchase at local health food stores. It was also know to be a great basis of a dietary workout supplement, and an excellent date rape drug. He figured they could use a woman; and if they couldn't as a team, he sure could.

Marketing heroin on the streets was the group's game, and that particular night, a big time drug dealer, named Walker, came to the small town on the outskirts of Sydney. His car was waiting in the hangar to take them all back to the Sydney airport. By the time the cab arrived, two of the guys were high on booze and tablets.

Pierce pulled into the lot and flashed headlights. King came out to help him.

"Got us a good one - real pretty." Pierce's sinewy fingers wrapped themselves around the woman's limp body. "Funny thing is she doesn't know where she is."

"Goddamn, Pierce, can't you get a woman by fair means?" Walker's eyes followed through. "She is pretty though. Let's get her inside. Stratton is here and he'd probably like a turn. You know how he likes the pretty ones," and he laughed.

Inside the room sat Walker's pilot, Stevens, who was entertaining the big time Los Angeles drug baron, Miles Stratton. They were making plans to set up a shooting gallery, when Pierce brought the woman inside. Walker cleared the table with one swoop of his arm and they brutally laid her on it.

She tried to focus, trying to scream the whole time. Shaking her head left and then right, with her eyes bulging out, she still could not use her vocal chords. She felt them take her clothes off and then they had taken them away, leaving her naked. In her head, and her heart, she screamed for Branson. No one heard.

Each man took turns raping her. Miles Stratton took two turns with Sage Jay.

"Yeah, she's good." He rose up and zipped up his pants. Then he noticed her breathing. It was labored, which worried him. They didn't need her dead.

"How much of that stuff did you put in the drink?" Miles screamed.

"Tablespoon, maybe more. I dunno. Wasn't paying that much attention when I made the damn drink for her. Why? Don't matter does it?"

"You stupid bastard. She's stopped breathing." He was feeling for a pulse.

"Can't have…"

Stratton's fist came up and hit Pierce full on his chin. He slumped down by the table out cold.

CHAPTER 3

Back at the bar, Branson had drunk far too much, and as Lord drove him to his house, the call came over the radio.

"Anyone in the airport strip vicinity goes…now. Backup needed."

It wasn't their job to answer regular calls. But something made the pair head that way. By the time they arrived, only Pierce remained. The others had flown the coop. A guard from the hangar had found her along with an unconscious Pierce who had told the story and laughed in the jail cell.

There was never enough evidence to prosecute. The case stayed on hold…but not so with Branson. It would take time to come to grips with the fact that her death was not his fault. He had no way of knowing it would happen, but he did have a means of putting it right, starting with the man who picked her up. Now, here he was with a shot at another.

After a half-hour drive, the car pulled into the waiting zone at the airport. The driver opened Branson's door. Branson stepped out, dressed in a black suit, his hair trimmed to collar level, moustache and beard combed. Carrying his black leather suitcase to check-in, he handed it over, and sat down to wait for the flight. An imposing figure in shades and dark suit, he crossed his legs and watched.

Looking around the lounge, Branson saw an impressive array of people. But he had the feeling he was not alone. In the corner sat a cop that he recognized from his own precinct. Branson moved to the window and looked out toward the tarmac. In the glass window, he could see the reflection of the man watching him.

Branson headed for the men's room, and moved to a urinal. Finished with what he had to do, he crossed over the tiled restroom floors and looked in the mirror. Washing his hands twice, Branson dried them on paper towels. The door opened and in the mirror, Branson could see the man from the AFP behind him. Branson was ready. He spun around and his hands circled the cop's throat. His grip was strong as he pushed the guy against the bathroom wall.

"Who sent you?" he demanded. "Was it Buchanan?"

Branson pulled tighter on the guy's neck muscles. His captive struggled, no match for Branson. He tried to force the hands from around his neck and failed.

"Yeah," he murmured.

Branson let go. The man coughed and spluttered.

"Goddamn, Branson." He rubbed his neck. "Buchanan was only looking out for you. Thought you might need some support. No need to rip me apart. Just wanted to make sure you made the plane," he said while straightening his suit.

"Yeah, well, I don't need support. I have my own plans and you don't fit into them. Get the hell out of here. Tell Buchanan not to try this again. The next guy might not be so lucky. While you are at it, give him a message for me."

Branson doubled his fist up and hit the guy in the face. The AFP man fell backwards. Blood spurted from his mouth.

"What the fuck? Why'd you go and do that? "

"For letting me see you following me." Branson wiped his hands down the man's jacket, and left the men's room.

The agent wiped the blood on his sleeve and a smile spread across his face. "Buchanan was right. He hasn't lost his touch," he muttered.

As he boarded the plane, Branson showed his papers to carry weapons legally.

"Sir, your seat number?"

"Twenty-six A."

"Straight down the left aisle and over by the window," the brunette flight attendant with the royal blue suit on said. She gave him an admiring look. He acknowledged her with a wink, as he was grieving, not dead.

"Excuse me. Think you're in my seat."

Branson looked at a young woman standing over 26A. She was maybe twenty, twenty-one, pretty; hair pulled back in a ponytail and had on too much make-up. She reminded him of his daughter. Young Sage had been close to that age when she left home. She couldn't handle the life her father led. A bitter argument had brought about her angry farewell. Despite efforts by everyone to find her, she hadn't surfaced. The girl sitting in 26A could be her sister.

"I'm sorry. It was empty and I didn't think anyone would mind." She gathered up her bag and jacket and blinked at him with soulful eyes.

"My mistake. I'm actually supposed to be in 26B," Branson replied.

As he sat down, his jacket caught on the armrest. The girl could hardly miss the gun. Her eyes widened.

"You some kind of cop?"

"What if I am?" he replied.

"Oh, no reason. Just curious." She popped the gum in her mouth, a habit Branson had always despised.

"Let's just say, I'm in the business." Sounded good.

"You protect people?" the girl asked as she fidgeted in her seat.

"Yeah. Why, do you need some help?" he asked.

"No." She teased while sizing him up.

He leaned back in the seat, fastened his seat belt, closed his eyes, and waited for takeoff. Someone tugged on his arm, causing him to open his eyes.

"My seatbelt seems to be stuck." The magazine that had been placed across her lap fell to the floor.

She looked pitifully at him. Branson had the distinct feeling she was flirting with him and this amused him.

Reaching across her lap, he said, "Pull the straps from under you."

"Yeah, that would help, wouldn't it?" and she tugged on them. "They're stuck. Can you help me?" The gum popped on her face.

She *was* flirting with a man old enough to be her father. He also had the feeling she wasn't as innocent as she made out. Branson forgot about sleeping. Maybe he'd flirt back. Been a long time since he'd seriously tried.

"So, where are you heading?" Kane asked, as he pulled the strap from under her backside.

"Brisbane." She popped again.

"Yeah, I figured that much, as that's where this flight is heading."

"Goin' to a small ranch outside Brisbane. About forty or fifty miles away from there; You?"

Branson took notice, but ignored her question. "Any particular reason?"

"Yeah, my pa has a business there. Where you goin'?" she asked again.

"Same as you, Brisbane." He was cool.

She looked sideways at him. "Yeah, even I figured that. Then where? You got business? Guess you have, if you're carrying a piece."

Nice thinking.

"Want to know a secret?" he asked her.

She leaned in his direction and he looked into her face, winking at her.

"Normally, they don't even let me on planes on my own." He smiled.

She laughed. "My pa could probably use a man like you; and really, I need protection…don't you think?"

She fluttered her eyelashes at him, pulled her purse onto her lap, and fumbled in the purse while he watched her.

It might be the men that needed protection, Branson thought to himself.

"What does your father do?" he asked. Suddenly there seemed to be a connection to the young woman.

"I think you're a cop," she stated.

"Would it matter?" he asked playfully.

"I'll think about that," and she rolled her eyes at him.

"Yeah, you do that. And while you are busy thinking; do you want a drink?"

The girl sat upright. "What kind of drink?"

"Maybe something to put you in a good mood," and he rested his arm on her shoulder.

"Mister, you flirting with me?" She pulled the lipstick from her purse and bright pink lips creased her face.

"Maybe. Been around guys for so long, I'm just glad to be talking to someone who doesn't have a dick. You don't do you?" He looked her up and down.

"Think you can see that for yourself. In fact, no, I don't have one, but I've had a few." She replaced the lipstick in the purse and turned her eyes to him.

His eyes followed her legs clear up to her face. The young woman was attractive, very much so. Her short skirt led to promise, and her cleavage taunted him. This was getting tricky. He viewed his flying companion closely. Was she the witness he was to be looking for? It all seemed a little too convenient. He did know she was like a Venus flytrap waiting for its next victim. Those baby blue eyes and that full round mouth…he tried to steer his thoughts away from the obvious. He failed.

"By the way, never found out your name," she said.

"I never did tell you, but it's Kane."

"That your first or last name?"

"Both," he replied.

"Well, Mr. Kane Kane. You gonna buy me that drink or not?" the Venus flytrap asked.

"Depends, I guess."

"On what?"

"What I get in return," he replied.

"Think you know the answer to that. You married?"

 Branson bristled. "No. You?"

 She laughed out loud. "Shit, no."

"So, you want to have a few drinks? By the way, you know my name. What's yours?"

"Yeah, right." She put her hand out to him. "The name's Kelly, Kelly Walker."

"Pleased to meet you, Kelly Walker. Very pleased, indeed." Holding onto her hand, Branson knew what he had to do. His job had just become more interesting.

"You like older men, Kelly?"

"Yeah, 'specially when they come packaged like you."

 He hadn't lost his touch after all.

CHAPTER 4

It was pitch dark when the flight landed. In the airport terminal, a lone figure waited. Deputy Lieutenant of the U.S. Marshall Service, Reese Wade, pulled her thin trench coat around her slender body. It was chilly for an Australian summer night. She wore black pants and a white sweater. Although it was against the law for a U.S. officer to carry a gun in Australia, she could feel her gun strapped secretly and close to her chest. Reese was no rookie cop. At thirty, she'd managed to win many commendations. Her job was her life.

Leaning against the seats, she waited for Flight 220. It arrived on time. One by one, people filed off the plane. Noises began to crescendo. No Branson. Reese, looking at her watch, wondered if she had the right flight. Where was he? She paced the floor of the terminal.

The passengers that had come off the ramp of Flight 220 all went separate directions. Some of the passengers were hugged by their loved ones; and, some of them were greeted by what appeared to be only slight acquaintances. Soon, the area seemed almost abandoned again and the noises died down. It was as if the passenger unloading had not occurred at all. What was left on this drizzly late evening was Reese laying low in the shadows. Kelly and Branson walked toward her location.

Coming down the unloading ramp from Flight 220, Branson asked Kelly, while helping her with her carryon, "You need to make any calls?"

"Yeah. I'll find a pay phone. You got money?" Kelly was dressed in a black short miniskirt with a silver blouse tucked neatly inside. She wore black strap-up heels that had silver sparkles glowing on the straps. Hard to miss a woman dressed like that in an airport.

He rummaged in his pockets and produced change, while looking at her. Handing Kelly the money, they touched hands. He'd make sure of that. As they entered the lounge, Branson placed his arm around her shoulder.

Reese had taken to leaning against a wall while reading a newspaper. With an ever-so-slight movement, she peeked out to see a man and a woman coming toward her from about thirty feet. She recognized him immediately from the file she'd been given; but thought Branson was supposed to be on his own. Something must be going down. She slipped back into the dim shadows of the terminal waiting area. From behind her newspaper, she watched them go by. Reese placed a call on her mobile phone.

In a different area of the airport… "There's a phone over there." Kelly pointed to the bathrooms. "You stay here and I'll go call Pa."

"What are you going to tell him? Don't you think he'll be a little bit suspicious of me being with you? You're up for the witness protection program and then I go and turn up here with you?"

"But Pa doesn't know the reason you're here. One thing he does know though is that I have a thing for older men. I'll tell him that some other guy tried to pick me up on the airplane and that you saved me! I still can't believe you're a cop. You just don't look like one." Kelly eyed him up and down noticing the Armani suit he wore.

"As long as he thinks like that, we're fine. Remember what I told you on the plane? I'm here so that I can take your father back, as well as being here to protect you," Branson lied.

"Do we get to finish what you started earlier?" she brushed against him. Kelly was the type of female that brushing up against men was part of her job. She did it well.

"Where are your morals?" Branson asked Kelly.

"They were beaten out of me," she said while pulling the band from her hair sensually. Once she had the band removed, she lifted her chin and looked Branson straight in the eyes combing her hair with a couple of her fingers.

"Yeah, right," he was good at following the game through when it came to people's reactions.

Branson lit up a cigarette, and then suddenly realized there was a 'no smoking' sign behind him. Although he was slightly frustrated from not being able to smoke, he snubbed out the cigarette and looked around him. One of the things that stood out most to him while he surveyed the dimly lit terminal was a woman, not known by him, standing in the shadows. In a flash, he had noticed that she had moved out slightly. Now he was able to get a little better look at her. It was then, that Branson realized he might know her.

When she passed closer to a lighted area, he became sure that he recognized her from Buchanan's description. Slowly, he removed his shades from his eyes, folded them, and secured them in his top pocket. Branson had been wearing his shades, believing that the shades were a fashion statement, for a good ten years. No one had bothered to tell him that he looked better without the glasses. He pulled them out again and replaced them on his face.

Reese slipped back into an area where she was slightly hidden behind some flight information screens.

Approaching him Kelly sang out, "All set. Told Pa you'd be flying with me. One of his guys never showed. Got himself killed by one of your damn cops. So, you're with me. Asked all about you. Told him you were fine. You are fine, right, Kane? I mean can you pass in his line of work?"

She chewed her gum and pulled her skirt down with her hands. All the time, she had her eyes on him. Her slim high heels made her look older, but she was still young.

"I'm with you, darling, you know that. I can pass since I have worked so much in the drug scene all these years. It's not exactly my best department, but then I'm slick in all of them, you know? So what's next, Kelly?"

He leaned back against the pillar that was holding up one of the large television screens. She was his ticket inside the scene all the way. He knew he had to get her back to Sydney with him in order to testify. Without her cooperation, her father might be impossible to land. One out of two wasn't bad.

"Chopper is going to meet us in an hour. You want some coffee? Didn't think much of that stuff on the plane. Let's look for some real gutsy stuff and get some food in us. Want to… are you at all thirsty?"

"Sure, but I have to make a pit stop first. Why don't you get a table in the coffee bar and I'll join you. Be back in a few minutes."

"Where are you…oh yeah, the men's room. Okay, I'll go and get us some seats. Pa will send someone to get us. We won't have any trouble getting away from here."

He watched her walk away, her saucy little backside in full swing. He wasn't sure how he was going to handle all that he had on his mind. Waiting until she was out of his sight, he made for the bathroom.

Walking out of the bathroom, Branson turned quickly to his right. Reese had suddenly appeared and was standing beside him.

"Got a light, mister?" her quiet, seductive voice, asked.

"There's no smoking in here."

"I know that. Let me introduce myself… Reese Wade at your service… I am the person you're supposed to meet. Or did someone forget to tell you. And who the hell is that?" Reese asked pointing towards Kelly. She did not exactly expect to find Branson with a woman and especially one who was extremely pretty. Damn women with long brown hair and slender long legs just irked her to no end. She tried hard to wave and send a smile towards Kelly, but ended up scowling instead.

"That is Kelly Walker. She is our ticket to us nailing her father who is the latest on the most wanted list. At this time, she's under my protection. It took some convincing, but she managed to get her father to let me go with her. Someone somewhere likes me. All I have to do is …"

"Please. Spare me the details. Then what? You're going in alone? I've heard about your reputation, but that's a little dangerous, even for you." She tossed her hair backward, with a quick movement, and at the same time, gave Branson a stare that only confident and proud women can accomplish and still appear attractive.

Branson returned the stare, he, too, showing confidence. If he'd met her in another situation, he would probably have been interested enough to ask her for a date. She was definitely more his kind of woman than Kelly was. Attractive, bright, mid-thirties, but right now, paying attention to her would just put her in his way.

"You plan on making it a threesome?" he laughed.

"Funny. She's young enough to be your daugh…" Reese stopped.

"Yes, you're right, she might be. But she's also the key that I need. Kelly says we're going to a place outside Toowoomba. You ever seen the place? Know where it's located?" he asked.

"I'll find it. Buchanan filled me in on most things. You want me there?"

"Yeah. Give me your mobile number. Don't come in unless I call you," Branson instructed her.

Reese raised her eyebrows. "You're the boss. Just be careful in there. You know this is a dangerous mission. These guys are renowned killers and known to be rough."

Branson turned in time to see Kelly walking back out of the bar. "No, lady. Can't you see it's time for me to get moving?" He turned away from her and headed toward Kelly.

Reese lowered herself in order to pick up her purse, which caused her to look as if she was hiding her face in her royal blue trench coat. Next, she beat a path to the ladies room.

By now, Kelly could see Branson walking towards her. "Where the hell you been? Coffee's cold." The bubble popped on her face.

"Some sheila tried to bum a cigarette. Let's go back in the bar. Kind of chilly in this lobby." He glanced back to take a last minute peek behind him, only to find that Reese had vanished.

As they walked past the coffee shop, the gift shop and the newsstand, conversation became easier for them. By this time, they were more relaxed with one another. As long as they didn't get too relaxed, Branson thought he'd be fine.

Brisbane Airport was cold and desolate at this hour of night. Maybe it was because it was late and he was tired. Branson thought about having some more coffee. He needed something *more* than coffee, but he needed his senses about him. After all, if he was going to go straight into this hornet's nest, he needed to have his wits about him.

First, he had to take something that Walker cherished the most. The way Kelly had responded to him that would be easy. Walker didn't know his own daughter was changing sides and turning on him. Come to think of it, why was Kelly changing sides?

Maybe this had been a setup from the start; maybe not… he dismissed the idea, but was sure that he needed to be careful just the same. Branson was also convinced that he would have to take Walker out… not take him in… it was going to be interesting. Nevertheless, he was Branson and capable of almost everything!

"Pa," she yelled, waving him down. "Pa, over here."

A tall, heavy-set man in a crumpled raincoat entered the bar. His belt was wrapped around him in a slovenly fashion. He smiled and a gold tooth gleamed. Behind Walker, came the muscle, not particularly heavy. The pair headed toward the table. Branson clenched his fist by his side.

"Pa." Kelly, seeing her father, smiled and rose from her chair to greet him. She threw arms around the big man. She was a good actress.

Walker returned the hug, his fat hands clasping her arms. Branson remained seated, but still managed to appear cordial.

The hired goon moved in behind him and stood waiting for orders. It was late and the bar was empty. They were alone.

"And you are?" Walker turned to Branson, with his big physique protruding in front of him. Obnoxious and arrogant, just like the rest of the drug lords he had taken down.

"She already told you. The name's Kane and I'm sure you'll check me out. And before your goon here frisks me, yes, I'm carrying." Branson pulled his jacket open, slightly, to show his weapon.

"That it?" asked Walker. "A Glock 9 Millimeter?

How'd you manage that on the flight?" Pa also chewed gum.

"How the hell do you think?" Branson was a master at playing the badger game.

"Pa, he looked after me on the plane. Some scumbag tried to pick me up, and Kane here stopped the guy from getting to your little girl. Can he please come with us?" she pleaded.

"You want him to come with us, or you want *him*?"

Walker looked at Branson.

The girl giggled. "If we can take him with us, I can have both. Please, Pa? You're always looking for men such as him. I told him it was okay."

Walker studied Branson with an experienced eye. "Okay, let's go, but you stay where I can see you at all times. I'm a man short. Thought only the special cops had guns on planes." He also knew if he said yes to what his daughter wanted, she'd hush her whining and they could get on with business.

"They do. You're looking at one… that's what I am." Branson never flinched. Kelly looked surprised.

"Yeah, right. Don't look like any damn cop I ever knew, so I put in a telephone call from the chopper and you did check out under Kane. Some hotshot from the south, out to make a name in this line of work. How come you only have one name?" demanded Walker.

"Easier to remember me by. Never said I wanted to work for you. I want to work with you. Have some ideas. Heard you were running drugs through from the east. I have contacts. I also have a price," Branson exclaimed.

Walker's face creased in a smile.

"Seems you've done your homework. How'd you find all that out?"

"Like I said, I have my contacts." Branson was precise and to the point.

"I bet you do. We should talk."

Kelly stared at Branson wondering how this plan of attack had originated. Was he what he said he was?

She picked up her overcrowded purse. Kane grabbed the rest of the luggage. Walker smiled an evil grin. His daughter seemed to have the man under her spell. Not unusual, but this guy was older than the rest, and very different. He was quite possibly dangerous and too much trouble too; so he made up his mind to keep his eyes on him. As soon as possible, he was going to have one of his goons get more information on the guy Kelly had picked up.

The group climbed inside the chopper under the noisy propeller blades. It took off in the rain, which caused some turbulence. Packed tight inside with luggage and people, the chopper flew low. Branson could feel the twenty-one year old girl's body next to his. Opposite him sat Walker. Branson had the feeling that Walker was only bringing him along for his daughter's pleasure.

His assignment was clear. The Federal Police wanted the entire heroin drug ring shut down. His part of the deal was now looking like it was going to involve killing Walker. The department wanted him to take down the whole ring. He stared back at the man.

Thinking back, the idea of Walker having been with his wife was unbearable for him. His mind was momentarily blinded by hatred; however, Branson was a pro. Kelly wiggled beside him causing his thoughts to return to the present.

"Hate flying in this thing 'specially in the rain. Like sardines. How much farther, Pa?"

"Not much. Maybe you shouldn't have come, Kel. I needed you near me, so I could keep an eye on what you're doin'. Hated to leave you behind, but you'll be fine with this new playmate of yours, now won't you?" His tone was sarcastic as he leered at Branson. "Course we wouldn't want the same to happen to him that happened to the last one, now would we?"

"No, Pa. We wouldn't," she said while lowering her head.

Kelly's father was a few years older than Branson. His hair was graying and he was rough-cut with a gangster-type walk. Being a known felon, he had a list of crimes a mile long, including extortion, rape, drug dealing, and murder.

"And what are you doing threatening me?" asked Branson.

"He shall… let's just merely say, the man had an accident. Brakes went plum out on his car, poor bloke." Walker laughed as he spoke. "Yeah, that he did. He was much younger than you are, Kane. Now Kelly's doin' what she's best at."

"Damn, Pa. You don't have to scare this one, like you have the others." Her shrill laughter ripped through Branson.

Branson glanced at her. She seemed nervous as far as he could tell.

The chopper lurched in midair.

"Damn you, you bastard… watch where you are going. I can't believe you. You are a real class act! Why in the hell don't you watch what you're doing," Walker yelled at his pilot.

Walker was a nervous passenger, often requiring a small shot of booze.

The chopper landed on the dirt runway. Sodden by the rain, the compound was awash. Lights stood out in all four corners and Branson could see cliffs to one side and a dense forest on the other side. They disembarked.

Ushered to the main building, Branson followed behind the group. He looked around the place, which was somewhat crummy, as he thought it would be. On one side of the building, were four bedrooms. On the other side, was something resembling a kitchen. These rooms didn't interest Branson. All he wanted was to find where the heroin was manufactured, nail Walker, and then get the hell out. Didn't he?

"Kelly, you take the room next to mine. Kane, Stevens will show you where to put your things. In the morning, we'll meet up and have a talk. Kelly, you stay in your damn room tonight. The last thing we need now is to have to go chasing you down. You understand me?"

She cracked her gum with her teeth like she had been doing it for years. "Yeah, I understand you. I promise to behave. Anyway, I'm too tired for anything else." She turned to look at Branson while running her fingers up his sleeve. Kelly said, "See you tomorrow, Mr. Kane." Her eyes glowed at him.

Stevens. Two birds with one stone. Branson should have realized that the pilot would be one person and one only. Walker would stick with that same guy.

"Come with me."

The gaunt man who had helped kill Kane's wife led him away. The guy coughed as he walked, which made it hard to concentrate on what he was saying. This guy really had the look of a heroin addict: bloodshot eyes, thinning hair, and slow deliberate movements. He would be an easy one to pick out of a crowd, especially if he wouldn't stop that damn hacking. Walker was a different story. They reached a door.

"This one's yours. We meet in the kitchen at seven... You be there. No excuses, you hear. Night."

Branson entered the room, which was a hovel compared to the other rooms he had seen at the compound. At this point, nothing much was fazing him. Dumping his bag on the chair, he took his jacket off and lay down on the bed. He pulled his gun and laid it by his side, just in case. The knife he decided to leave safely in his boots. So much for a long day, at least this one was over.

Light streamed through the window. Branson sat upright on the bed. It took him a few minutes to figure out where he was. The rain had stopped. Swinging his legs over the filthy bed, he pulled off his boots and suit pants. He quickly changed his clothes and stowed the bag, along with its contents, in the closet. The gun he kept with him. Stepping outside the room, Branson made his way to the kitchen and began fumbling around looking for something to drink.

"Mornin' Kane. You sleep well?" Her eyes scanned his body. "You look just as good in jeans as you did in that suit you wore last night. Like *my* jeans?" she asked him turning her backside toward him.

"Yeah, nice. Your pa awake yet?"

"Don't know. Why?"

Branson slid his fingers into her back pocket and pulled out a bright yellow scarf. He would have been blind not to see it dangling. "This hanging out for some reason?" His hand slid onto her backside taking the scarf with it. He let his other armrest gently around her waist at her backside.

"Yeah. For the very reason you took it."

"You're still just a kid." He let go of her.

"Am I? That's not what you said to me on the plane. Or, were your words last night just to pacify me until you got here? What the hell are you playing at? I nearly pissed myself when you said what you did at the airport."

Branson coughed.

"You want to find out how much of a kid I am?" She ran her tongue sensually over her lips and then grinned.

He turned away very aware that they were not alone. "Want some coffee?"

Taking the hint, she said, "Sure, why not?" Picking up her cup, she left the room, frustrated that her flirting was not gaining her more ground than it had so far.

"Morning, Kane. So, you said last night you had a price. You never said what that price might be, even if I was interested," Walker said. "My daughter, well, her you can screw with all you want. But, don't you go getting too deep into my territory or get your nose into my money or I'll kill you. You hear me, this I promise you."

It took all Branson's strength to control his temper. He clenched his hands around the cup.

"Think you got the story wrong, Sir. Your daughter's not my prime target, you are."

Walker calmly sipped coffee from his cup. "Very clever. You think you're some kind of big shot, don't you? Kane, from the south… ten hits, multi-talented, expert in firearms, and wanted in the States for drug offenses. I also hear you even have a reputation with women. Did I miss anything?"

Branson sipped the coffee. "Nope, you just about covered it all; and, my price is seven percent and I still get to screw your daughter as part of this fucking deal."

"You're insane and you know it!" He thought for a moment. "Five percent."

"Seven, and the girl. I know you need a buyer for some of the stuff you have here. I can supply that. Word is, you have too much of the stuff on your hands and you only have one major contact from the States."

"How do you know so much? Even with your charm and good looks, you would have a hard time finding all that out. Unless…"

"Unless, what?" Had he pushed it too far? "You know a man named Pierce?"

Walker's eyes shifted uneasily. "Yeah, you?"

"Did some business with him. He told me," Branson lied.

Like a gift from above, Stevens appeared through the door.

"Want me to take him out to the grounds?" Stevens asked Walker.

"May as well." Walker turned to Branson.

"Seven… and your daughter gets thrown in the deal, too." Branson set the empty cup down on the wooden table and followed Stevens out the door.

CHAPTER 5

"Something not right with that guy. Something, somewhere," Walker murmured.

He helped himself to eggs, sausage, and bacon, twice over.

Branson looked around the grounds. Glancing up, he noticed that the guards were holding AK 47's and were dressed in all-black commando uniforms. Walking over near the truck parked by the gates, Branson got close enough so that he could see several kilos of pure China white. The drugs that were sitting there had been bagged. Inside the bags, the China white had been covered with coffee grounds to help ward off the custom department's drug sniffing dogs. The stuff would soon be exported if he didn't do something to stop the process. There was so much of the white that he couldn't even begin to place a value on it. If he could stop it, he would save hundreds of people from having to be subjected to even more of the shit being on the market.

"Want to try some?" Stevens asked.

"Never do the stuff..."

"No, it's just little girls that you do then?"

Anger flared in Branson. "And you, what kind of women do you like?"

"Older women. Ones that submit easily," he retorted and laughed an evil howl.

Branson looked away. He had to before Stevens saw his disgust. Stevens' time would come. He went back to one of the bags and looked at the heroin. Branson picked up the bag, and slid his fingers inside a small opening. He ran a fragment of white across his fingers. He sniffed enough to put a buzz in his head. If he didn't, Stevens might just end up becoming suspicious enough to tell Walker.

"Okay, seen enough, and now I've tasted plenty.

This is some good quality stuff. Tell Walker, I like."

"*Mr. Walker* to you. That a problem?"

"No problem." He began to feel sick. It had been a long time since he'd touched the white and now here he was completely convinced it was quality stuff.

At lunch, Walker joined them. Kelly sat opposite Branson and expertly slipped off her slick black heels. She moved her toes up the inside of his leg. As she spooned the food to her mouth, her eyes focused on him while she licked the spoon. When she finished with that, she turned peeling a banana into an art form. Piece by piece, Kelly removed the peel, letting each peel fall gently to the side of the banana. Raising it to her mouth with the ease of a real pro, she licked it slowly at first, and then her lips closed around the top.

Branson had caught a different sort of buzz from watching Kelly and her antics. Maybe tonight he would take Walker's little girl. After all, she wanted it to happen and so did he.

First, he had to contact Wade. The surveying had paid off and there had been plenty to see. This drug ring was far more advanced than the AFP had first thought it was. Maybe getting some help busting them wouldn't be such a bad idea. He'd need Reese inside the compound within a day or two.

There were only so many ways he could get her inside, without alerting the goons as to whom she might be. He smiled at the girl, acknowledging her attentions and squirmed around trying to get his white Dockers adjusted. Kelly's father was too busy eating to notice their playing around, nor would he care if he had noticed.

"Excuse me. I need to go back to my room." Branson pushed his chair away from the table.

"Why is that, big guy?" Walker didn't even miss a beat.

"Need to get something from my case. Do I have to ask your permission?"

"Yep." Walker carried on eating without ever looking up from his plate.

"What the fuck for? I'm not a servant here."

"Remember, you're only at this table because my daughter wants you here." Morsels of food sprayed out of his mouth.

"Yeah, and for my contacts." Branson's disgust and anger intensified.

"That too," replied Walker, and continued to fill his overstuffed stomach. Eating seemed to be for him, another way to show his power.

Back in his room, Branson closed the door; made sure the lock was secure and lit a cigarette, hoping to clear his head. He lay back on the dingy pillows, inhaled deeply and watched the smoke rings float into the air. He counted…one, two, three, four, five, and six. There was the expected knock on the door.

Hearing the knock, Branson swallowed hard and prepared himself for the evening. Unlocking the door, he slowly inched the door open about two inches and said, "Kelly, come on inside."

She pushed the door open another couple of inches and then leaned against it. Gently, she curled one of her high heels, at the foot of her slender leg, inside his room and then stuck her head inside with a big grin appearing on her face.

"You just going to stand there half in and half out?" Branson said walking over to the sink to fix them a drink.

"Do you want to wait until later tonight?" she asked getting straight to the point.

"Why wait?"

Slowly and deliberately, he removed his jacket. Sliding the gun holster down his shoulders, Branson then placed it under the bed, but within reach. He never took his eyes off the girl. Kelly stared back at him. Who was he bluffing? Was he going through with it because he wanted to and felt completely driven to do this; or, simply because it was his job?

Closing the door, she walked slowly and deliberately toward Branson. As she waltzed toward him, she unbuttoned the top button of her blouse and began kicking off her heels in a fashion similar to a stripper. Excited, he looked up and grinned at her.

"You want me? I'm all yours." Her voice was low and sexy.

She undid a few more buttons of her silk blouse. It seemed to pour off her. Pursing her lips, she flashed her blue eyes at him. The flirt was in full swing and he realized now that he had a need for sex. Kelly was right there in front of him and he wanted her. However, since she was a key witness, it was now up to him to protect her. He backed away from the closeness. To not appear rude, Branson walked back over to the bar to finish mixing the whiskey.

"Something wrong with me, Mr. Kane?"

"You don't have to go through with this, Kelly. Not now."

"Don't you want me?" she whispered.

She was too tempting. He slid his arms round her waist and pulled her to him. Warmth instantly invaded them. Looking down into her eyes, he placed his hand on her half-opened blouse and undid the final set of buttons. Her breasts felt firm and round against his chest. Looking down, he noticed on one, she had a tattoo of a beautiful purple and pink butterfly.

Kelly saw him look at the butterfly and watched his face finish to a full grin. All Kelly wanted was a fun roll in the sack. Before arriving for their visit, she'd used some cocaine. So many times before, cocaine had been the booster she'd need before entering rooms to entertain the men. She was more than sexually aroused, and the sight of him enhanced that feeling. At sixteen, she had been hooked…on dope and prostitution. But, if she had not come from a half-ass refined, family she was sure she would have been more of a slut than she was already becoming.

Branson let go of her already warming body, and turned the key in the top lock of the door. Taking her in his arms, he bent his head and kissed her for at least a full minute. The feeling of her breasts against him aroused strong sexual desires that were beginning to be irrepressible. He slid his hand down inside her jeans until he reached the moistness that lay there.

"Holly shit little lady, you feel as if you've already had me; don't you believe in underwear?" he murmured.

"Only gets in the way." She could smell the scent of cigarettes on his breath, which only seem to attract her to him more.

She was so cool that it scared him. One of the things Branson liked about Kelly was the fact that she did not complain. At this point, things were looking too good to still be true. Was she setting him up? He kissed her again, this time with meaning. Kelly rubbed her foot up inside his pant's leg and used her toe to get that special grin back on his face. She was a pro and it showed. She moaned as his fingers caressed her. Kelly pulled his sweater upward and then gasped at the sight of his chest hairs and the muscles.

"Oh my, you do work out don't you?" Suddenly, leaning forward, she kissed the dark blonde hair on his chest. His face nestled into her hair and he closed his eyes. The girl's silk blouse slipped to the floor. The silver of it blended in with the gray carpet of his room. Branson pulled back.

"How long?" he asked Kelly.

"How long for what?"

"You been on drugs?"

"Long enough. My pa introduced me to them. Some of his special friends helped me to lose my virginity at fifteen. Surprised? Don't be. You knew what I was when you invited me in here. I ain't no angel, just a butterfly. In fact, you could call me 'Madam Butterfly' if you have a mind to; and you… Who are you?"

"Just a cop, no one special. I'm just here to look out for you and make sure Walker gets taken in where he belongs." He lied to her.

"Maybe, maybe not. There's something more you ain't saying; I can just feel it. I didn't come here to chat; you want to finish what you started? From the cut of your jeans, it looks like you have the same thing on your mind that I do." She undid his belt. "And you asked me about underwear."

Branson took a second to breathe and asked Kelly, "You take precautions?"

"Hell, yes," she lied. "You think I want some brat hanging onto my skirt? Got a lot more living to do yet. And no, I don't have any diseases, if that's what you're wondering; or why you are hesitating. I get regular checkups and stay clean. Promise, you're safe on all counts."

"Yeah, I want to finish. Don't you?" he replied.

She couldn't help but look at his body once more. On a chain around his neck hung an 'S.' Kelly grabbed the chain with her right hand and fingered it.

"Not your name. Whose?"

"You ask too many damn questions. Why the third degree all of a sudden? You want to get laid or what? Simple yes or no."

"By you…yes." She answered softly wrapping her arms around his waist.

Branson was gentle with her. For a reason, he did not understand right then, he felt a sudden surge of protectiveness towards Kelly Walker. Pushing the strands of hair from her face, he touched his mouth to hers. Kelly's sparkling blue eyes closed tight for the enjoyment yet to come.

When his lips touched hers, Kelly stifled the feelings that were sparking inside of her. This guy wasn't any ordinary John. This guy was special and it wasn't only his looks that made him special. His kisses were like nothing she had ever tasted before or probably ever would again. Warm and longing, sensual and real. How in the world was she going to keep from messing this one up?

He moved her towards the bed before she even realized it had happened. Ever so slowly, she felt the dank sheets come up to meet her body. In the sunlight, he could see her young breasts. Her thin waist was almost too much. His eyes glanced down and she bent her legs to encourage him.

Kelly was good. She'd had enough practice. Oddly enough, Branson was better. When she felt Branson enter her body she cried out and said, "Take me now."

"Did I hurt you?" His breathing was hard. In fact, his breathing usually settled faster after sex than it was now. Was it Kelly?

She lay under his weight. "Nope," she responded looking as if she didn't know if she should hurry and get dressed and leave; or, if she should just relax and stay awhile.

He felt her tears on his body.

"Kelly, don't cry. Please don't cry. It had been so long since…"

"No, it wasn't that."

She turned her face away.

"Then what? What did I do?" He really wanted to know.

"You made love to me."

He understood then.

She lay in his arms, and for a few seconds, she forgot about being a hooker. Realizing he, too, had forgotten he helped her to relax with him. Kelly got out of bed first. She faltered as she spoke.

"Pa will be looking for us. We need to hurry or he'll be trying to kill you."

He was getting to her. Something like he intended. Wrapping a blanket around his waist, he helped her back into her clothes. Slipping the skirt and blouse back on was sensual for him also.

"You want to meet again tonight? Wait 'til Walker…I mean your pa, is asleep. You know your way to my room."

Kelly zipped up her black miniskirt and strapped her tie-up heels back on her small feet. Branson finished by buttoning the blouse buttons nearest her wrist, while they looked each other in the eyes.

"Cigarette?" He lit up two and handed her one.

"You don't have nothing stronger?"

"You don't need it." He stood up. "Why do you think you do? Makes you feel more powerful? Gets you going? You're a pretty girl with a great body. You shouldn't have to use drugs for that. A real man should be able to do that for you."

Branson held her by the waist, realizing that her necklace had caught in his pocket. Reaching in his pocket, he pulled it out saying, "Kelly, I want to tell you… all you need is the right way out of this lifestyle your old man got you stuck inside."

"With you and the witness protection program?" she wiped her runny nose on her sleeve.

"Maybe. Think about it. Think also that you should get the hell out of here before he does come looking for you. I know he said I could have you, but I have a feeling your pa changes his mind a lot. Would I be right?"

She turned toward the door, looking back at the man who had finally caused her to feel half-decent, and said,

"Right. And we don't want to make him any wiser than he is already, or neither of us will get out of here…alive that is. Kane, what's in all this for you?"

She surprised him. No, sir. Kelly may be what she was, but she did have a brain that she was capable of putting to good use. Now, he wasn't so sure he wanted to lose this girl. He was unprepared for this as he had planned on it being full-blown business. Now, here he was getting full-blown confusion instead. Not too many hours' back, he had been reflecting on making love to his wife, Sage.

"Not a damn thing." He turned away.

"Kane?" At the same time, Kelly was feeling an emotion stronger than lust and more moved than she had ever known. For the first time in many years, she wasn't feeling cheap and used. Instead, she felt cared for and near to someone's real emotion. She was not ending up feeling thrown away as usual.

"Yeah?" Branson asked her.

"You should have seen some of the men. I needed the drugs to get me through…well, you know what I mean," Kelly looked down at the floor.

He moved towards her and lifted her chin with his fingers. "Like I said…right man."

Branson, with politeness, opened the door for her.

"Where you been? Walker's been looking for you. You and the girl; you been fucking?"

"Watch your damn mouth." Branson's look was enough to stop Stevens. Plus, his fists appeared clenched and ready to brawl.

"Okay. I get the message. Don't matter to me mate. Got my own whore in this place. Walker keeps a whole bunch of them. Kind of a sideline of his."

"Is that so? Well, you watch your mouth when referring to me and my business, you hear!"

Acting as if he had not heard Branson's threat, Stevens continued, "Gets them from town and brings them in here. Right now, boss wants you to go watch something outside in the yard. Follow me." Stevens led the way without even looking to see if Branson had followed him.

They picked through the sheds to the yard way out back. Branson looked at the people working in the grounds. Again, he glanced up at the guards. He was way outnumbered. There had to be a way for him to get Walker on his own. If only he could manage to get, Reese Wade inside there also. He was thinking of ways, when his brain was suddenly thrown into another gear.

"Mr. Kane. How nice of you to join us. I have something for you to watch that I think you'll find very interesting. See that son-of-a-bitch by the wall? Well, that guy tried to take one of the whores away with him. Don't mind how many of the girls the men go with, but they aren't allowed to go away with them. Get my drift?"

"Yeah, I get it. You're dealing in prostitution. Really don't understand what's that got to do with me?"

Branson repositioned himself to gain more control. His anger was causing him to sound more caring than he wanted.

"Just a warning. So you know what will happen if you get any ideas about taking Kelly away. This guy used to be one of my guards. Watch," he commanded.

Branson, who had seen most everything, looked at the man hanging from ropes on the wall. The guy's arms were stretched full above his head and his legs were tied down to the ground. His was face contorted with total fear. The henchman stood in front of him. In his hand was a knife, red hot with a sharp blade. The henchman held it close to the man's eyes. The victim shrieked in terror.

"Shut the fuck up, Watson. You're sounding like a baby. You knew the rules. I want you to see what you did to the girl. Don't think she got off without punishment. Stevens, go get her. And, while you're in there, fetch Kelly, will you? Maybe she'll find this interesting, as well."

Branson viewed the compound walls. Aside from going over them, he was able to determine that there were only two ways to get out: by chopper, or out through the huge gate. Someone could take a truck and crash right through it. First, he had to get Reese inside there and then he'd blow up the sheds. Soon. Buchanan had been right. This issue was departmental, not personal. Kelly arrived and stood between Walker and Branson.

"You wanted me, Pa?"

She glanced at Branson and he gave nothing away. Walker put his arm around her shoulders and slid his hand down her arm grasping her flesh. It sickened Branson to see Walker treat his daughter that way, but saying something now, would only give him away. Walker was making a point. Kelly flinched. Branson noticed. He glanced back to the wall. The man was still hanging, awaiting his doom. The guy's eyes seemed the most likely target. On the other hand, maybe Walker would shoot him in the crotch, or both.

Stevens reappeared with a bunch of girls, sixteen, maybe seventeen years of age. "Thought they should all watch. This will keep the sheilas from getting any ideas 'bout running off." He wiped his bony nose on his sleeve and announced, "And here's the little lady herself. Still thinks she's something special," he laughed hysterically.

The girl stepped out into the afternoon light. Long blonde hair, under-nourished, she stumbled in the sunlight and tried to focus. Her face was bruised and bloody. A ragged dress covered her body. She looked up at Walker who pulled the unkempt hair from across her face and then she turned her head toward Watson.

Branson turned and in slow motion, he saw the girl's face. Fire exploded inside his brain. Uncontrollable rage surged through every vein. Kelly saw it but did not know how to react. She looked back at the girl. A little older than the rest, early twenties, there was something sweet and recognizable about her. Had her father done this to her? Had he actually stooped to badly beating upon this woman? She looked back at the man she'd slept with and noticed the veins standing out in his neck. Then she glanced back to take another look at the girl. One thing was clear. It was certain that this creature didn't know where she was.

"Watson, take one, long and final look," ordered Stevens while nodding to his henchman.

The screams brought Branson back to reality, screams of someone losing his eyes. He couldn't lose control now. Now more than ever, he had to get a game plan. His mission had grown more important with every moment.

Thinking this caused him to clench his fists by his side. Next, he turned toward Walker, but caught the girl's eyes instead. She blinked through the swollen sockets that housed her once-beautiful eyes. Blinking again, she struggled to focus on the man nearest her. Her mouth moved, but there were no sounds. She recognized him and he, her.

"Take her out of here. Put her in one of the spare rooms and clean her up. I'll visit her later. Oh, and I'll finish the job over there." Walker strode to Watson.

Suddenly, he grabbed a knife from his belt and very slowly slit Watson's throat from ear to ear. Walker only grinned and slid one hand down his large abdomen. A dead man hung from the wall. Blood spilled from his gutted throat. Kelly, shocked, could stand no more.

"Mr. Kane, would you take me inside? Kane, get me out of here." Begging and tugging on his sleeve was all that was left at the moment.

"Yeah, let's go." He grabbed Kelly's arm. "Let's go to your room, maybe we'll even get us a drink."

"Or something stronger?" pleaded Kelly.

Stevens looked suspiciously at them. "I'll take you."

"You do your job, Stevens. Kane will take me back," she stated.

"Better not be seen getting too friendly with that guy. Your pa may have decided to work with him, but your pa's still in control here. Send him out here in thirty minutes, no more. Or your pa may have to pay him a visit, and I'll pay you one too."

Kelly was revolted by the thought. "Yeah, right. He'll be back."

Branson entered his room to try to get the image of the girl's face out of his mind. He couldn't wait for Wade. Tonight he would take out Walker. Kelly followed him and closed the door behind them.

"Kane…Kane. Look at me. What is she to you? Answer me, damn it!"

She sat on the bed pouring him a drink, and then parted her legs to offer him what she had. There was a deep darkness in his eyes, which frightened her, but he also excited her. Without planning it, his eyes traced her bodyline. He knocked the drink from her hand, pulling her violently to him.

"Get your clothes off."

She followed Branson's orders and his eyes never faltered in their commitment. Watching every move she made, he pushed her down on the bed and roughly made love to her. He wanted to hurt Walker, to strike back at him and his hatred. This was the only way… until later that night, when he planned to kill Walker.

Kelly lay there and let him do all that he wanted. He entered her brutally with vengeance on his mind. Never flinching, she clung tightly to the bedrail. Somehow she knew the pain he was experiencing. He lay back on the pillows, while she leaned across him and touched the 'S.'

Branson grabbed her hand.

"She's your daughter, isn't she? I heard Stevens call her Sage. That's why you have this 'S' around your neck. Did you know she was here?"

"No. I didn't." He looked into her eyes. "I came here to protect you." He rolled over onto the side of the bed, stepped out and pulled his black jeans on his satisfied body. "Fuck, that's not why I came." Running his hands through his disheveled hair, he said, "I came to kill your father, and you, little butterfly, just got in my way."

CHAPTER 6

Reese Wade had the nagging feeling that she should be doing something besides waiting on Branson. In her motel room in Toowoomba, she called Commander Buchanan.

"Sir, he hasn't reported in since the airport. Had a girl with him when he got off the plane. She's Kelly Walker. Yes, Walker's daughter. Oh, you knew that." Standing by the window, she jerked back the shades peering through the dark at the rain. "He met her on the flight. I don't know any more details. Except, well…never mind." The word *tart* popped into her brain. "Should I wait here or go down in on some pretext? Is he carrying a phone? In his boot? Does he always carry things in his boot? I forgot. He's Branson."

She hung up and sat down on the bed. Tomorrow she would get in the car and go find him. *Hell, why wait?* She picked up her car keys and closed the door to the seedy motel. Running through the summer rain, she struggled to open the car door, climbed in and drove out into the night. Reese got five miles from the hotel. The rental car spluttered to a halt. The gas tank read empty.

"Damn!" She smacked her hands on the steering wheel.

Climbing out of the car, she dropped the keys in the mud. The rain poured down. She didn't hear anything except that. Opening her umbrella, she stuck her head underneath.

"Need some help, lady?"

Reese Wade looked up. In front of her was a tall, skeletal man that sent chills down her spine. He'd scared her half to death.

"No…yes. I didn't hear your car. I dropped my keys." She fumbled on the ground.

Stevens leaned down and ran his hand through the mud. He made contact with the steel and then handed her the keys.

"Thanks." She turned away.

Stevens put his sinewy hand on the door. "Haven't seen you around before. You new in this area?" was his remark while he looked her up and down. "What you doing out here miles from anywhere?"

"Haven't been here before. Stupid car ran out of gas."

Seeing his tired eyes, Reese thought she could see the telltale signs of a heroin addict. Chances were, he might know where Walker's place was in a small area like this.

"Where's the nearest place to get gas?"

Stevens laughed. "Ain't no station round here. I know of a place nearby." He looked around him. "I can take you there."

Toowoomba was inland, and she'd figured the operation wasn't far from there. Wade was sure that he was talking about Walkers'. Had to be. She seized the opportunity.

"Can I get a drink?" She hesitated. "I'm kind of cold and thirsty." She could just about see his expression.

Had she acted too quickly?

He hesitated. "Sure. You can get anything you want, lady. You an American?"

She put her hand out to him. "Yeah and I'm on vacation. Name's Reese… Reese Harris."

Stevens spat on his hand and then swiftly wiped it on his rain soaked jacket.

"Pleased to meet you, darling. Lock your car and come for a ride with me?"

"Sure, why not?" Closing the umbrella, she made sure her appearance seemed relaxed while walking with him to his car.

Now there was no doubt they were going right into the lion's den. He opened the door of his beaten-up car and in they went. She purposely let her skirt ride up. Stevens gave his approval with a swift pat on her rear. Reese was inside.

Stevens drove fast despite the rain. Being in the business he was in caused him to always be in a hurry for his boss, much less for himself. His arm rested on the leather seat behind her head.

"You said you were visiting someone in town, Mr. Stevens?"

"Yeah, and it's just Stevens. A friend needed something."

His eyes darted back and forward like a caged animal.

Bet they did. "Must be a good friend to come way out here on a night like this."

"You know how these things are. Money to be made and you got to go places to get it made."

His hand slid down onto her shoulder where it rested for a while. Reese's flesh crawled. His clammy fingers touched her skin. He felt like death, but still she showed no outward reaction. The drive seemed like an eternity to her and to make it seem to go faster, she tried to smile and make small talk to deter his advances.

As they drew close to the compound, Stevens flashed his headlights. For once, Reese was beginning to get scared. What if Branson wasn't in there? How the hell would she get ever out again? This was a gigantic risk and one she hoped she would not regret taking.

The gates opened, the car passed through and then it stopped at the house. Stevens got out first. It was then, that Reese was glad that she left her gun in her car. He opened her door and her legs swung outside the car, slowly first, one foot touching the ground, then the next. Stevens licked his lips, his pallor changing just slightly.

Inside the house, Stevens was hit with a tirade of abuse from Walker, who had noticed the pair drive up. He greeted Stevens at the kitchen door.

"Why the fuck did you bring some sheila back here with you? You better get rid of her. Goddamn it… Stevens, lord man, don't you even know who the fuck she is!"

"She's just some high-class hooker. Car ran out of gas. You can bet on the fact that she doesn't know what's going on at all. I just wanna spend some time with her, give her a drink and then let me be the one to take her back."

"Are you crazy? She can't go back. You want every cop around to find us? If you weren't such a damn good pilot, I'd kill you. You better be glad that I still need ya."

Reese listened from outside the kitchen door. She leaned slightly around from the doorframe and saw the group of men sitting round the table. Her eyes widened as she watched Branson enter the room. Behind him, hovered the girl from the airport. Reese watched intently. Kelly didn't take her eyes off Branson, who managed to never even look her way. Yet, still there was a connection between them; and one, that at this time would go unnoticed.

Branson looked different. He was a man on a mission for the department. Yet, she sensed something just didn't seem right. There was an intense look of subdued anger about him. The girl nervously handed him some coffee. Her hands shook. Branson took the cup from her and their hands touched. Reese blinked and looked again. Branson let his fingers stay very intentionally on the girl's. He sat down and listened to the banter. Kelly stood behind him, her hand resting on the back of his wooden chair.

Reese stifled her surprise.

"If you people want to stay here fighting over some girl, that's your thing. I have something better right here. Don't think you need my input. I'm going to bed," and he inclined his head towards Kelly. "You don't want to discuss things tonight, do you, Mr. Walker?"

"Guess it can wait. Just make sure that we do talk in the morning instead of you wasting time with my daughter. That ain't part of any damn bargain!"

Branson pushed his wooden chair back from the table and turned to walk away. He always loved leaving Walker holding the bag... the last part of the conversation anyway.

"No, but it sure helps pass the time in this hovel. Be glad when I'm done what I came to do and can get the hell out of here."

"Well, you aren't taking Kelly with you, so make the most of her now. While you got her," boomed Walker.

Branson never answered. Instead, he turned his back on them and left the room with his prideful gait changing to an almost saunter. Stevens couldn't wait any longer for his prize to be exhibited.

"Hey, you. Reese, come in here and meet my boss. He wants to say hi to you."

She did as she was told because to not do so, was never worth it. As she passed through the open door, Walker let out a slow soft whistle, almost choking on his coffee.

Years of experience had taught Reese how to not look shocked when seeing someone's face. This time was no different. Still, her thoughts were, "*So this is Walker.*" Drug dealer second to none except for the Californian Drug Baron he had dealt with before. He pushed Stevens out of the way.

"Some kind of woman. Too good for the likes of you, eh? Sit down. You want a drink, lady?"

He used some envelopes that were laying on the table to dust one of the chairs for Reese. The sight of her made him forget about his suspicions. Reese was about to answer his rambling question, when Kelly appeared back in the room.

"Where'd she come from?" scoffed Kelly. "Haven't you got enough whores in this place?" She picked up a bottle from the table. "Bit old for this place."

Walker caught his daughter's arm bruising it as he held it tightly. "Where you taking that? Let me guess? To Kane, right? What the hell, though you're old enough to do what you want. Just like your mother was. She also liked older men. Guess you're no different. Slut, just like she was. Go on back to him; but, remember I told you he'll break your heart. Or, maybe he'll even be the death of you, just as I was to your mother. You know, I caught her with some guy and beat them both, only she didn't survive." He laughed cruelly. "At least I know where you both are. Keep him company, darlin'. Make him happy while he's here. According to him, and the check we ran, that man has good contacts. So you go, do what you do best, girl."

Reese's expression went blank, as it had been quite a while since words such as these were spoken around her. Nevertheless, she knew what she'd heard. And so did Kelly.

Walker's daughter carried the bottle to Branson's room. She closed the door behind her, and the wings of the butterfly folded. Kelly cried.

"What the hell's the matter? Kelly? Did your father do something? What's that on your arm?" He pulled it towards him so that he could inspect the already bruising area. "That son-of-a-bitch. He do that?"

Branson cradled her in his arms. This should be his daughter. He thought of her again, but in a confused way. The misery one man and drugs could do. She snuggled into him, her tears running down his naked chest.

"Don't cry. Come on, baby. Justice will prevail." Branson was angry, for her and for his daughter. "Fuck, he deserves more than justice and I'm gonna make sure he gets his and soon."

She wiped her face on her sleeve. Mascara ran down her checks and her eye shadow smudged.

"No, Kane," and she pulled on his arm. "It won't help us, or your daughter." She paused. "He killed my ma, Kane. I always wondered and now I know. He just told me. Just in the kitchen. Why? Just because there's some broad in there that he wants to screw? That a good reason?"

She looked up at him. Branson could see the pain in her eyes. Now he had three reasons to even the score.

"Stay here. Go ahead and get yourself undressed and crawl into bed. You bound to be tired by now. I'll be back. I got some business to take care of before I can spend any more time with you."

Branson closed the door and hoped Kelly would get a little shut-eye. This was not in his plans. Too soon for confrontation. But if Walker were in this kind of mood, he would go back for his daughter. Walking further down the hall, he soon ran into Walker.

"Walker, need to talk to you."

"*Mr. Walker* to you."

"Mr. Walker. What the hell did you do to your daughter? Why did you rattle on about all that stuff about her mother? And why, now? You knew she would tell me. Or was that the plan? Admit it, you don't like me. You always like this with your daughter's boyfriends? Where do you get off treating her that way?"

It was at this point he caught sight of Reese. Branson hid his surprise well enough.

"I repeat. Why did you hurt your own kid like that?" His fists hung by his side.

"Just cause you're screwing her doesn't mean you own her. I told you that. She's a hooker, same as any other girl I got. But if you want her, she's yours, for now. Just trying to keep you happy, is all she's a doing. I have one waiting in the bedroom and a much better deal here." He inclined his head to Reese.

Years of attempting to raise his daughter without a mother had increased Walker's indifference toward her. Bitterness and hate constantly welled inside of him and he no longer gave a damn about anyone or anything except power and money. He only cared about the money because it increased his feeling of ever growing power.

Walker did not remember exactly what year it had been when he began to look at his daughter as just another one of his girls… his possessions. But, now… this mattered to neither of them. Their relationship was something that they were both accustomed to and it probably was not going to change ever. How could a man such as he become a good loving father now? Absurd… it just wasn't in the cards.

Branson looked at her, his eyes piercing. She smiled coyly.

"Car ran out of gas. Just came for some fuel and maybe a drink. Then I'll be on my way back to town. Mr. Stevens promised he'd take me back. Isn't that right, Mr. Stevens?"

She crossed her legs. They all noticed.

"Sure, I'll take you, but not just yet. Mr. Walker and I would like to get a 'lil better acquainted with you first."

"Both of you? That will cost you plenty. Women like me don't come cheap."

She undid her raincoat and let it slide down onto the chair. When the raincoat came away from her, the smell of her perfume made them all smile. Underneath the raincoat, was a tight fitting t-shirt showing a figure to perfection. Walker ran his tongue across his lips.

"This, Mr. Kane… this lady right here… this is what I want in a woman, not the kids we normally have around here."

Stevens looked at Walker. He hadn't brought Reese here for his boss and the goons to ogle. Resentment was creeping in and causing his blood to rush. Branson was good enough to play on it. Just what did the marshal think she was doing?

"Yeah, she's not bad… maybe a little old though, for me anyway."

'Old? He thinks I'm old?' She stared at Branson. "Excuse me, and you would be?"

"Don't mind him. He's here with my kid. It's just me you have to worry about," butted in Walker.

"Mr. Walker. I brought her here. You may be my boss, but you ain't my…"

They were interrupted.

"Kane, what's going on?" Kelly asked.

She was wrapped in a blanket. Threadbare, it hung on her body. Kelly moved in behind him and he put his arm back around her. She nestled into him.

"Got her where you want her. Or so you think. Unusual for Kelly." He pondered a moment.

"Maybe I underestimated you. I can be generous. You want to take them both on?" Now he was baiting his own daughter.

There was no way out for Branson. Walker was pushing; he was egging him on to see what he'd do next. For once, Branson was unsure of what to do next. Reese came to his rescue.

"I'm game, if the gentleman is." She eyed him up and down. She had to talk to him in private, and this looked the most private it was going to get. Stevens was in the background and was becoming more agitated by the minute.

"Boss, that ain't fair! I found her." He turned on Branson. "You want to fight for her?"

This was getting out of hand.

"Fight you?" He gave him a disparaging look. "If that's what you want? Don't think she's worth it. But maybe if it's a fight you want… then a fight is what you'll get…"

He brought his fist up and hit Stevens in the stomach. The man doubled over. As he rose, Branson hit him again, this time in the face. Breaking two teeth, the blood spurted from Stevens' mouth. The blow-back of the blood made splatter everywhere and caused him to reel back and fall onto a chair. Branson's ferocity surprised even Wade. He had gone after Stevens with venom.

"Okay, Kane. That's enough of that crap." He pulled Branson from his man. "You made your point. You get the girl. And after you, me," Walker called. "Take her."

Branson looked at Kelly. "Go back to my room; get into bed, and this time stay put."

"But I thought that you and I…"

"Just do as I say. I'll be back very shortly." He grabbed the blanket, pulled her to him, and kissed her hard on the mouth. "Go, and Kelly, be ready, there may not be much time." There was a double meaning; and although she had no clue what was going on, she knew what he was trying to tell her was for her to leave.

Walker laughed. "Don't waste no time, do you, Kane? Quite a show!"

"Mr. Kane, to you. I don't want her, but I will escort this lady back to wherever she belongs. She deserves better than this. *Miss?*"

"Quite the gentlemen, aren't you? In fact, almost too good to be true. Okay, you win. Get her out of here; but you stay. One of the guys will get fuel and take her back to her vehicle. Escort her to Stevens' car and ask one of them to drive. He isn't going to be around for a while. I have my own little whore to go do a little visiting with, and so do you."

Branson took her by the arm. "Let's go, *Miss*."

He dragged her through the door and out into the night air. Outside he pitched into her.

"What the hell are you doing? Did I call for you, or come get you? For God's sake, woman, you want to get raped?"

"How dare you yell at me that way. What kind of nerve is that? You're screwing Kelly. Does that make you any better than them? You bastard! She's a kid and you're doing what they all do to her."

She raised her hand and hit him. He could have stopped her, but he didn't. The blow stung in more ways than one. He grabbed her by the arms.

"Do you know who else is in this place? Did you ever think there might be a good reason I took her to bed? Did you? Does anything ever cross that pretty brain? My daughter's here. That's the hooker Walker was going back to visit. Would you have rather me let him take you instead?" He let go of her.

He walked fast and reached the car before her. It stopped raining and a million stars twinkled in the sky. She moved in beside him with more emotions going on than even she was able to handle. Maybe Kane could help her.

"Kane, I'm sorry. God, I'm sorry. What do you want me to do?"

"Get the hell out of here. Get backup. I really am not sure I should try to take the place on my own, or even with just your help. And, now he knows you. If only you'd waited, damn it! Too many guns in here. Every man in this damn place is carrying. Call Buchanan in Sydney. Ask him to send more men. I was going to take Walker out tonight, but *you* screwed that up."

"Out of here, you mean? They would have killed you," Reese argued.

"Yeah, they would. What's that to you? You nearly blew this." That's not what he meant at all.

She climbed in the car and looked back through the glass at him. Branson let go of the handle and watched her speed to freedom. From the porch, a lone figure watched.

"Thought you may need some help."

Had Walker heard? Probably not.

"I can manage." Branson rubbed his jaw in mock gesture.

"I'm sure of that. Seems like you do have a way with women. Can you fly a chopper as well?"

"Sure, why you asking me that?" Branson's eyes narrowed.

"Ain't got a pilot now. Need someone to fly me around first light. Can you do that?"

"Sure. Where you needing to go?"

"Near Brisbane Airport."

"Fine. Whatever you want. How long we gonna be gone? Day trip?"

"Yeah. Be back by dinner. Got that buyer coming in soon. You know, the Californian. Do most of my business with this guy. I'd really prefer leaving at six… can you pull that off for me Kane?"

Branson nodded.

Walker was gone, back into the skulking shadows of his life.

Branson was getting in deeper. Just what he wanted, or needed maybe. A smile spread across his face. Aside from killing Walker, all Branson was concerned with was getting the girls out. He reflected on that. He had them both to worry about now. And he didn't know why.

Kelly dozed in the lamplight and he climbed in beside her. She groaned in her sleep.

"Kelly, wake up."

He kissed her full and longingly on her lips and pushed the strands of her long hair from her eyes. She awoke and looked in his eyes.

"You know you're different than the rest. They wouldn't bother to wake me. You said you came to kill my father. Did you mean that? What all else has my pa done? It must be some awful bad stuff if you want him that bad. Is there something I missed here?" She rose up on one arm and leaned across his chest. She shivered in the air. "Is there?"

Branson pulled the blanket around her.

"Kelly. I want you to answer me truthfully. It will help our case. Has he ever touched you in a bad way?

Has he hurt you in a way that you normally wouldn't explain to people?"

"No, course not." She was far too quick to reply.

"The truth, little butterfly." He touched the desirable looking tattoo on her breast and pulled her close down on him.

"Who are you? You keep changing and even I can't figure you."

"Who do you want me to be?" He pulled the blanket back and looked down at her nakedness. "Did he beat you often, or was it the nights when he screwed you that has hurt you the most?"

She buried her head in his chest and the memories came flooding to her. Especially the ones she thought would never be revealed to anyone. *Oh God, why now?*

"How did you guess?"

Branson had been a cop for too long not to know about the abuse he could sense. "Wasn't just his friends that took away your virginity was it?" He stroked her hair and pushed it behind her ears.

"No," Kelly sniffled.

"He'll pay, little butterfly. That bastard will pay for what he did to you, to Sage, and to my wife."

She looked up. "Your what? You said you weren't married?" She pulled his hand in front of her. There was no wedding band. "He left the city, cause police were after him. I'd already told the police I'd testify about the drugs. If there's anything else, I don't know anything more. Honest. He told me to come meet him here. Guess so he could keep an eye on me. Scared me a little, but the police said they'd send someone. Didn't know that someone would be you! I remember a ways back, he was bragging about a woman he had raped…"

She stopped.

"That woman you're thinking about happened to be my wife. I'm not *just* police, Kelly. It goes a little deeper than that. I'm with the Australian Federal Police drug squad. Your father is wanted for murder. The woman he murdered was my wife." He watched her to see her reaction. Now, Kelly knew it all now. Either she would stick with her decision to turn against her own father, or decide to turn him over to her father.

"Oh, God. Kane, I didn't know. Really, I didn't. No wonder they sent you." She stopped speaking and sat upright on the sheet next to him. She thought for a moment. She sniffed. "You and I make a good team. I want *him* out of my life for one reason, and you want him out for another."

She was caught in a net and the man right by her was a way out. This could actually be freedom and safety from the life she was living. Staring for quite awhile at Branson, she began to feel sweet desire, something inside her was stirring, feelings she didn't understand.

"Kelly, why did you offer to testify against your own father? You never really explained all that to me."

"I didn't tell you, did I? I think you know by now, Kane. He used me to…" Hesitating a moment, she said, "When you kill him, I think I'd get a bit of a pleasure just to be able to watch." Her eyes were round and full of hatred.

"Kelly?" He was shocked. "You're joking right?"

By the look on her face, he knew she wasn't.

"Promise?" she said running her fingers up his hairy chest. Even with his shirt on, the hairs made the shirt course on the outside.

"Kelly, I can't promise you that." He didn't believe he had heard her correctly.

"Why?" she rubbed her eyes.

"Because, I just can't, darling."

He'd called her darling, but in a soft and gentle way.

"Make love to me…please."

He kissed her very gently and his hands wandered down her body. She responded to his kisses in a way that meant so much to Branson. He could sense the change in her. For Kelly, it was the best she had ever known. This man had shown her things she'd only read about in romance novels - tenderness, concern, trust, and gentleness. And, most of all, he'd made her feel like a woman and not a whore. For Branson it meant letting go of the past. A bond was forged between them, one of freedom for both.

As the sun rose for a new day, Kelly awoke with a different outlook on life. She watched the man lying beside her, his chest rising and falling. Birds were actually singing outside the windowsill.

"Mr. Kane, I'll always love you for what you have given me. You've given me something no man in my life ever has. It feels something like what I only dreamed respect might feel like. Although we can never be together to stay, we will never be apart either," she said to him while sniffling.

Branson awoke with a start. "My God, what time is it? I'm late. Your dad is going to be livid! We are supposed to meet by the chopper at six. Walker doesn't need any provoking; or to start being pissed off at me even before we begin the damn trip."

"Relax, it's only five-thirty, you can just make it. Ten minutes is how long the drive will take you to get to the chopper. Will you be back tonight? Don't like being here on my own."

"Yeah, before dark. Save me a place at dinner. Can you do something for me while we're away? While we're out of this dump. Please see if you can find my daughter. If he sees me anywhere near Sage, he'll suspect there's more to this and quite possibly kill her just as he did my wife. Your father is many things and let me tell you; smart is one of them. So, please find her. Kelly, please make sure she's okay. When you find her and you start spending some time with her, if the subject of me comes up, please try to avoid talking about me too much. If she questions you, try to deny any knowledge of me. I'm pretty sure she recognized me. I hate that I cannot get to her right now. She's close to your age and so it will be easy for you two to come to have a friendship. Kelly, as far as you and I are concerned… well, what you and I have is more than just a business thing. We…"

She put her fingers against his lips to indicate to Branson to cease his ramblings. "I know what I am. You don't have to be so nice about it. Why don't you face who I am?"

He leaned forward and looked into her face. She turned her eyes away. He touched her face with his right hand while tracing a small line on her face. It was a small sweet sensitive moment in a stressful time.

"Can I finish? I was going to say that we are friend's…very good friends. I'll get you out and start you on a new life. You know, you're a good kid. One day, you will meet someone your own age, fall in love, and have a couple of kids. Won't always be some John and a fix. Okay, so I'm out of here." He kissed her gently. He tugged on his jeans and pulled the dark brown sweater over his head. By the time he'd finished dressing, Branson was geared up to go play pilot for a man he considered to be the scum of the earth. "You'll see, I'm right."

As he walked to the chopper, he wondered just whom he was kidding. He knew she was watching from the window.

Kelly held Branson's fantasy of what her future might be close to her heart and her fingers on her lips. "I already did. Keep safe."

She watched from the window as he climbed into the chopper. Within a minute, her father and another man stepped in with him. The chopper took off, causing the wind to pick up and the leaves on the ground to swirl. Standing there until it was just a dot on the horizon, thoughts bombarded her mind.

Quickly, she dressed in a bright yellow shirt and pants. The shoes chosen were sneakers so she could run easily if she had to do so. She then went in search of Branson's daughter. Pushing open the door of her father's room, she stared in horror at the young girl lying on the bed. Quietly, she closed the creaking door. Moving across the room was like walking on a boardwalk of beer cans. So noisy that it made her feel like everyone could hear her.

Kelly sat on the side of the king-sized bed and pulled the girl's hand towards her. Instinctively, Sage withdrew her hand from Kelly's hand as if she were a scalded cat and clung to the bed rail.

Hearing the screams as the walk took her down the hall, Sage could be heard, "No, please. No more," she begged for mercy and for her life. "Don't hit me anymore. I'll do anything you want," and she cowered atop the bed covering her bloody face with her hands. One eye was swollen twice its size.

"Sage, don't cry. Crying will make your wounds worse, all of them. Now stop please. It's going to be okay. I'm here to help you. Shush and let's dry your tears sweetie."

Kelly put her hand over the girl's mouth. Hollow rounds peered back from the gaunt face. The hair was matted with blood. God only knew how long Walker had been hitting her or what all her pa had done. Kelly pulled back the sheets that semi-covered the bed and noticed that the girl was almost naked. What also was very evident was that her body was badly bruised.

"Come on, help me here. We have to get you cleaned up before…before those goons get back. If you'll just relax a second and let me take care of you."

Sage looked up at Kelly whom she thought had been outside. The clouds dispersed in her brain. That's where she had seen her before. Wasn't she the girl with her father? She tried to sit upright. Kelly helped her.

"My father, he's here. I saw him, didn't I? Please tell me he's my father. I've needed a daddy for so damn long now. That to think he's so close to being him… and might not be… well, this is just more than I can bear." Sage finally clung to the other woman.

"Who?"

"Kane Branson." She muttered. "He was in the yard, wasn't he? Tall, long blonde hair. In fact, quite a nice looking man he is. I saw you there also. You were by him. Anyway, I thought it was you." She was trying to focus so it would all come clear and she could feel some real hope for herself.

Kelly was beginning to show in her facial expression that Sage might be right in her discovering her father. "Jeez, lady. Good job. You'd have blown his cover for sure. Branson's his last name? Kane Branson, AFP. Your dad and my pa took off out of here in the helicopter. If Kane sees you like this, none of us will get out alive. He'll finish the job right here."

Sage looked at her in a strange way. "Walker?" The thought registered in her brain. "My God, you aren't' going to be able to help me, are you?" through her pain, Sage asked while pushing Kelly away instead of open- ing up more.

"I will help you, just shut the hell up! Actually, the truth is that Kane sent me to find you. He wants us all to get out of here and then…well, you don't need to know that part yet. Kane says…"

"Kane…what's he to you? Oh, God, you do know him. That's who your pa was talking about at the time. You and my father! You're the hooker…"

"So what if I am? It's all part of the big picture. You don't have a right to judge me for what I might or might not be, little lady. No one forced you here, now did they? You don't look like one of the whores Pa usually keeps around. Maybe you're one of them that he plans to sell. And, why was my Pa talking about Kane?"

"Well, I'm really not one of them. That's not how it happened. I came down here from Rockhampton because I heard there was a job on a ranch and that it would be a little bit of work and a whole lot of fun. Really, I didn't know it was *this* kind of ranch. Thought it was a horse ranch. Once I got here, I couldn't get out of here. My money, of course, soon ran out and my dependence began to run high," she finally took a breath and stopped talking a second.

"Last night, your pa talked about a man who had beaten up his pilot. Said he was doing some business with a new guy. Said this guy, whoever he is, handled himself well."

Her lip suddenly split open. Blood trickled down her chin. She grabbed some Kleenex, applied them to her injury, and then pulled the sheets around her torn body.

"Sage, you can't hide much now. Just look at yourself! Some dude ranch, eh? Let's get you cleaned up a bit. Sounds like he's wondering about the whole situation, if he's talking out loud."

Sage Branson slowly got herself out of the bed and looked around for some water. "*Was this flight a setup? Was her father bright enough for that?*" Sage Branson stepped out of bed. She almost slipped and fell when her hair fell away from her face blocking her vision, which was already prohibited.

Even underneath the blood and tears, Sage Branson had now become a stunning girl with a killer body and long blonde hair, just like… She pushed her father from her mind.

"Best get you dressed. Have a feeling we may be leaving quicker than was intended. You got clothes anywhere around here?"

Kelly looked around the room to see if there might be something decent for Sage to wear. The room looked fit for a princess… some fairy princess… a nightmare is what it had turned out to be.

"Your father took all my stuff with him so that I wouldn't be able to get out of here."

"I have some extra togs in my bag. Let's go."

Kelly wrapped her in the blanket. Sage looked at her suspiciously. They slipped from room to room slowly but with determination. It was still early, and Kelly had done all this before… it was familiar and she was now on her way to fast becoming a getaway pro.

Sage stumbled as they entered the bedroom. Kelly pulled her bag from under Branson's bed where she had stuffed it last night, before Branson had come back to her. Kelly wasn't stupid. Sage watched.

"This my dad's room, then? This where he's been staying?" she asked while eyeing her dad's clothes leaning against a chair by the window over-looking the compound. Sage stared at the bed where she sat, looking back again at the girl with her. The girl's T-shirt was low-cut, and she could just see her butterfly wing.

"Something bothering you, *Miss* Branson?"

"How could my father…"

"Sleep with me? That what's goin' through that pretty head of yours? Well, since you really don't know him, I'll tell you a thing or two to give you a better picture. You may be his daughter, but you have no clue about the man."

"And I suppose you do?" Sage asked raising her voice an octave or two.

"Keep your damn voice down. You want to alert everyone? They'll kill him and us too; if they find out you two are connected. Pa doesn't care what I do. I'm just a whore to him… a nothing. Kane's gonna come back and look after me. So much as told me so…"

"And, you believe him?" She laughed in Kelly's face, which was now, distorted with anger. "He was never there for me or my mother. Why would he be there for you now? He was always working undercover and never home. We never knew where he was or who was with him; but then, I wasn't sleeping with my father like you are. Maybe that's the dif-ference between us."

Kelly flinched. "Oh my lord, you don't know, do you? About your own mother… where the hell you been Sage? You've been messing up so bad that you're in the dark about your own family. Oh, God, you really don't know do you?"

"What about her? What do you know 'bout my mom? She's okay, right?"

"Kane should tell you. It ain't exactly my place to tell you." After seeing the reaction on Sage's face, a different decision was made. "Your mom's dead, Sage. Don't know all the details. Just that my pa was involved and that's why your father is here. Well, that's sort of most of it. He'll tell you the rest. Especially if he finds out I already started spilling the beans about it and all."

Sage couldn't cry or anything else except stare ahead. Her mother was dead and it had been so long since they had last talked.

"You okay?" Kelly put her hand on the girl's shoulder.

Sage pulled away. She stood up. The fact that this girl and her father had just slept here in this bed was more than she wanted to think about for the moment. Trying to change the subject, she began walking again.

"Is he coming back soon?" Sage asked abruptly.

"By dinner. We should be ready just in case his plans have changed."

"Plans?" Sage was curt.

"Kane has plans. I'm gonna be under…" She stopped.

"I bet you are!"

"That's it! I said I'd help you because you're his kid. He never said you had a smart mouth. I'll stay with you till he comes back. Then he can look after you. I felt sorry for you 'cause of what my pa might have done to your mom. Sage Branson, you may be your father's daughter, but you sure are one pain in the butt, which is nothing like Kane."

By the time they reached the living room, they were tensed and tired. Looking at each other, and letting out a sigh of exhaustion, Kelly sat on the chair opposite Sage. She reached over and picked up her slut jeans and a green T-shirt that had been lying on the bed. She took hold of Sage's shoulders.

"Put these on, and then you can look like a real whore just like me." The jeans were the most provocative types that Sage had ever seen.

"Now you listen to me. You give your pa away, and I'll kill you. You understand what I am saying to you? You give him away, even accidentally, and I will follow through with my threat. I've been taught how. On that you have my word. Now let's go, we've got no more time to sit around pining about our crappy past."

Kelly shook as she spoke. It was very clear to both girls that Kelly had feelings. And to Kelly, it was a new and the most frightening thing she had ever encountered.

CHAPTER 7

As shades of pink filled the dark sky, Walker's chopper landed at a private strip just outside of Brisbane. Branson had been as good a pilot as he had claimed he would be. But then… Branson was good at everything he turned his hand to do. So far, all the things he had learned had paid off in one way or another. Looking across the strip, he noticed that parked on the private airstrip was a black stretch limo. Its engines were purring in the quiet of the morning air.

Walker looked around at their surroundings for what might be lurching to end up as a surprise. He wanted to make damn sure all was the way it was supposed to be.

"You stay in the chopper. May need to make a quick exit. Not too sure of this guy anymore. Not since…"

Walker motioned his other muscle to walk a step or two behind him to cover his back.

Branson sat back at the controls, leaving the engine on, with feet propped up on the ledge and he waited. He thought, "*This craft may come in handy later.*" He slid his hand along the cold black metal of the inside of the chopper. He had especially liked flying this thing. His mind drifted for a second, and he hoped that by now that Kelly had found his daughter. Thinking of these things shifted his focus.

Walker walked toward the limo. One man stepped out of the car and held open the back door. Another man… tall, graying dressed all in black, also stepped out, looking like a kingpin. Branson sat upright. He'd seen the AFP files on Miles Stratton. Standing on the tarmac was the Californian Drug Baron himself, as though he'd come back to the scene of his crimes. Interestingly enough, the men appeared to be arguing, which distracted Walker, causing him to glance back at the chopper more than once. Branson's hands began sweating. He could step out of the chopper and take these two out in one go; but that wouldn't solve a damn thing. Making sure he got the girls was more important to him now.

"We agreed you'd buy the whole damn lot," Walker said. "I want out of this. Already had people snooping around. We lost Pierce. Guess you saw that on the news. Too much activity going on at this time. The guy back in the chopper is after some of the stuff. He's got some good contacts. My kid picked him up on a damn plane."

Miles Stratton's voice was slow and deliberate. "Need to keep the broad under control. How old is she now? Twenty-one? Wouldn't mind meeting that one again someday. Good lay, if I remember right. Anyway, couple more days and I'll be out of the country. Made enough over here. You worry too much. If it makes you happy, I'll buy most of the stuff. Can you send it over to the States? Can hardly take it with me on a damn commercial flight, now can I…especially now that they wanna serve some stupid papers on me. Two or three large suitcases should do it. Make sure you cover it so there won't be any heat. Prison isn't where I want to end up because of your ass. You have someone you can trust to get his deal done right?"

"Yeah. Stevens can bring it once he gets himself straightened out. Guy in the chopper took him apart over some woman."

Stratton pulled off his shades and chewed on the stem of them. He looked across at the chopper. "Like to meet this guy. King, you get your ass in gear and go get the dude!" he yelled out some orders.

Branson watched the guy walk toward him. Feeling a problem approaching, his hand slid onto his gun. The man reached the helicopter.

"You! Out! Boss wants to see you."

"Whose?"

"Mine."

"I don't take orders from your boss. In fact, I don't take orders from anyone." He leaned back in the seat.

"Better get the hell over there. Mr. Stratton doesn't like to be kept waiting."

"Too bad."

"Boss, this guy doesn't want to get out of the chopper," yelled King.

Stratton looked at Walker. "He got a problem taking orders?"

"He doesn't work for me - only with me. I could ask him." Turning toward Branson, he said rudely but at least directly, "Mr. Kane, care to join us?" Walker yelled.

"Now I'll go," stated Branson. "Just needed you to ask politely," he said with sarcasm.

With an air of arrogance, Branson climbed out of the chopper and crossed the shimmering tarmac. Stratton watched him with an immediate dislike. The man was too arrogant for him.

"Stratton, this is Kane. He's my new associate."

Branson acknowledged the title with a sideways glance. Stratton looked Branson up and down. Not his usual kind of associate. But Walker never did things by the book.

"*Mr.* Kane. Walker tells me Kelly picked you up on the plane. And you'd be from where?"

"Around… and for the record, it was I who picked her." He didn't take his eyes off Stratton.

"Not much of a talker, are you?"

"Nope."

"You cost a lot, *Mr.* Kane?" Stratton viewed him with caution.

"Not for sale."

Branson pushed his blonde hair from his forehead. He pulled cigarettes from his pocket and lit one. Smoke twirled up in into the air.

"You always this arrogant?" asked Stratton.

"Depends." Branson removed his shades.

Stratton raised his eyebrows. Branson was out-bidding him in looks. "If you ever want a change of scenery, and are looking for work, give me a call. Ever been to the States?"

"Yeah. I've been there. Got good bonuses where I'm from," he replied.

"You *know* Kelly then?"

"Butterfly Kelly? Yeah, I know her, and I intend to keep on knowing her. Any objections?"

"She's not my daughter. Makes no matter to me, suit yourself," Stratton replied.

Branson flinched. "Now you've met me, I'm going back to the chopper. I'll wait for you there, Mr. Walker."

"Mr. Stratton just wanted to meet you. You fancy another trip to the States at some point? I know your contacts are at the other end of the globe, but it might be good for your interests."

"Maybe not so good for my health." Branson squashed the cigarette into the ground.

Walker chuckled. "Right. Whatever." He turned to Stratton. "Will have the white ready in the next couple of days. Someone will follow you over. Have a good flight back to the States. Mind you don't get extradited." He laughed.

Stratton leaned across to Walker and put his arm around his shoulder. Walker appeared nervous.

"Cute, *Mr.* Walker, if I go down, you do, too. I don't trust this guy much. King, get the door."

As Stratton climbed into the car, a chill ran through him. He glanced back at Branson.

Walker turned away.

"Okay, Kane, it is time for us to go."

Branson took a last look at the Americans he was going to kill and headed back to the chopper. He walked with deliberate steps alongside Walker. They climbed inside.

"Take her up and make sure everything's right."

The chopper burst into life. The early morning sky had turned to an early afternoon sun. They headed back to the ranch. It was quiet onboard. Walker dozed. Looking down over the terrain, Branson could see only one quick way out. That was by chopper. By road, they could easily be followed. He wondered how Reese had made out with Buchanan. When they returned to base he would contact her.

Dropping slowly and methodically down in the dirt, the chopper landed blowing dirt everywhere. Walker hurried into the house, but Branson lingered a minute scanning the grounds, counting a couple dozen men. He would take care of Stevens tonight. Didn't want to leave even one of them behind. Branson had a plan and was going to do everything he could to make it right.

Walker sat in the kitchen. "Where the hell is dinner? What does it take to get food around here?" He turned his attentions to his daughter. "Hey, Kelly, get some of these bums to do something. Don't want your pa to go hungry, do you? Or your man?"

On cue, Branson came through the door. "Did I miss something?"

"Pa was asking for food, as usual. You?"

"Not hungry...for food anyway."

"You have one huge appetite," he laughed. "You might want to consider going to the States for me." Walker took the huge bowl of soup Kelly offered him and slurped it down like a pig at a trough.

Kelly looked surprised. "You going somewhere, Kane?"

"Maybe, maybe not." He propped his feet up on the chair opposite him.

Kelly sat down on his lap. "What you want then, if not food?" She nuzzled into his hair.

"I'm trying the hell to eat. Take your sex appetite someplace else, would you?"

"With pleasure. Kane, why don't you go ahead and I'll fix Pa some more food?" She nodded her head towards the door.

"Sure. Don't keep me waiting too long; or, I may find someone else for the night."

He cut his eyes at Kelly and left the room. He wasn't sure how Sage would react to him again. Not knowing how much she had been told, Branson hesitated a second, and then turned the handle to the girl's door. Sitting on the bed was his daughter. She had become a beautiful grown woman. Dressed in slut jeans and T-shirt, hair slicked back; she had grown into what appeared to be a tart. Father and daughter stared at each other. He cleared his throat, and approached her on the bed.

"Sage, it's me. I don't know how to quite tell you everything I need to explain to you… but, I'm your Dad."

He felt stupid, a feeling that he was not accustomed to having. Looking at her bruised and battered face, Branson then eyed her split lip. Anger rose inside him. He couldn't wait to get Walker back for doing what he had.

"I know who you are, even under all that hair. Kelly told me all about you."

"There's a reason why…" He stood in front of Sage.

"You don't have to explain. She told me about Mom.

I would rather of heard it from you. Why didn't you try to find me? Anything would have been better than finding out from that…"

"Watch your mouth!" He checked his temper.

"You haven't changed a bit. Now I remember why I ran away. Mother always wondered what you were doing when you were away. I could hear her crying some nights when you didn't come back. Now we know…"

"No, you don't. I was never unfaithful to your mother. Never. Not from the day I married her." He sat beside her. "You mind?" Branson asked his daughter politely trying to calm her down.

"Do I get a choice?" she asked sarcastically.

"Let me look at your face. Son-of-a-bitch. Walker? I'll kill him!"

She pushed her hair from her cheeks. "And a man named Stevens hit me because I wouldn't sleep with him. Know what I mean?" Her eyes were cold toward him.

Quietly, inching toward the door opening, Kelly slipped into the room. She stood in front of the two of them motionless. Sage's eyes darted upwards. Branson looked up also. Bad timing.

"I didn't mean to interrupt, I'll just leave."

Kelly's outfit today was just as bizarre as the other days. Her jeans were as tight as she could get them and a purple, copped off T-shirt covered only some of her upper torso and that was it. One butterfly wing could be seen.

"Darling, Kelly, I have a favor to ask. I need you to go find Stevens. Then do something to keep him occupied," Branson said.

Kelly flinched and a tear fell slightly to her cheek. Something inside of her was changing with the way Branson was treating her.

"I don't want him to…"

"He won't touch you. You have my word. Just keep him there. Try talking to him about himself. That man there is a bragger and you'll be able to get him to talking forever. I'll be waiting. As for your pa, put this in his drink," he said handing her a tiny white clinical tablet. He'll sleep right through 'til Sunday. Will you do this…for me?" he creased his eyes at her.

"You trust her? Her own father? His own daughter? She'll turn you in and you'll end up sorry you trusted her," snapped Sage.

"I thought we talked about that. Kane is helping me. I could have turned him in the other night. I didn't and I won't because…" Kelly stopped, mainly because Branson was shaking his head at her. "He promised he'd get me out of here. And even if you don't believe him…I do. You don't know your pa. Perhaps you should take time to know him," taking in a breath; she turned to Branson and blurted, "He's good. For you, Kane, I'll do it. But you better be there."

Branson rose from the bed and moved swiftly towards the door. Gently, turning around, he grabbed Kelly and he kissed her full on the lips. He handed her a tab Ecstasy and she disappeared back though the door.

"That wasn't necessary," pouted Sage. "Kissing her like that."

"Yes, it was. Kelly's coming with us, whether you like it or not. Before we leave, everyone in this compound will be dead. Everyone. And I gave her my word. She's…"

"Like me? Is that what you were going to say? Both of us are whores? Say it. It's what you think, except her father had me and you had his daughter."

"You're both special to me. Then, you're nothing alike. You want me to spell it out for you? Walker's hurt her before in a really bad way."

"Oh, God! I didn't think he'd touch his own daughter…"

"No. You might not. That was most of the problem back then. However, this is now, and she goes with us. I need to protect her. You stay put here. I have some business to attend to that needs my undivided attention. We'll come back for you. Don't leave this room until we come for you. You understand me?"

She sat on the edge of the bed and bit her lip. The words didn't come easily. "Dad, I'm sorry for being…" she was finally warming up to the idea of him being a good father.

He came to her side. "It's okay. We'll be out of here soon. It's okay, really. You can cry. Cry it out for now."

She buried her head in his soft brown sweater and then let go.

Kelly had no problem putting the drug in Walker's drink. She felt no guilt, just a strange sense of satisfaction. Since she was going to wait a few minutes, she took the time to pour herself some coffee. She sipped a few sips.

"What you staring at, Kelly?"

"Nothin, Pa. You want anything else before I go?"

"No. Go keep that damn guy amused. Kane took Stratton off guard today. Found it somewhat funny. Nothing ever seems to faze Miles Stratton. Kane did though."

Kelly muttered under her breath.

"Say something, Kel?"

"No, Pa."

Finding Stevens was easy. Getting into his room was a little more difficult. He didn't want company. Not even female company. His face still hurt and his teeth had taken the brunt of Branson's fist.

"Thought you were Kane's little pet. But guess as you're here, you need something?" He asked while peering around the door. Then he turned his back to her and walked towards the bed.

"She is!" came an angry voice from behind.

Stevens spun around. Branson slammed the door shut and backed Steven's towards the bed. "Where the hell did you come from anyway?" Fear showed in his eyes. "Mr. Walker will get you for this."

"Don't think that's going to happen. It's just you and me…and Kelly. Sit down Mr. Stevens. We have something to talk about and we need to do it right now. We got someone in common, you might say."

"Shit we do. I'm gonna go…"

"You aren't going anywhere. Sit!"

Branson pushed him into a chair. From his boot he produced a blade. He picked at one of his nails for a second with it and then held the knife near Stevens' face.

"Kelly. Stop staring and go get the bag that's under my bed. Kelly."

She peered at Branson not sure what he was going to do.

"Go, Kelly."

She opened the door and left, not looking back.

"Now it's just you and I. You took something from me that's very precious. You said you liked older women, right? I remember you saying that."

"So what?" Steven's voice was shaky.

"Just something to think about while we wait. Here's something else to think about while you're busy reminiscing. Remember some time back at an airport? You, Walker, Pierce, King, and Miles Stratton. Coming back to you now? Probably all fucked up… there was a woman there. Seems as though Pierce picked her up in a cab."

Big blobs of sweat began to drip from Steven's face.

"Something wrong? You wondering how I know all this?"

"Yeah." The look in his eyes was one of sheer terror. His eyes popped and he swallowed hard.

The door reopened.

"Kelly, you're back. Hand me the bag."

She did as she was asked and waited with determination to help Branson in anyway she could.

Branson laid the knife on the floor by his feet. He pulled a picture from the lining of the suitcase. He stuck it in Stevens' face.

"This face look familiar to you? You beginning to understand?"

Stevens stared at the picture and let out a groan, "What's she to you?"

"You mean *who was* she to me? Yeah well, she was my wife, you bastard. You all raped her and then filled her with drugs. Afterwards, you all walked away from her and let her die."

Kelly could tell she was about to witness justice. "What you gonna do? They'll hear him. Use your head."

"No, they won't." He fetched out a pair of black leather gloves and slowly pulled them onto his hands.

Still the knife lay on the floor. Stevens made a play for it. Kelly still stared.

"Turn away, Kel!"

Branson grabbed him by the throat and slowly wrung the life from him. Stevens kicked and fought with his face first turning bright red then it turned to an almost gray. Thrashing in Branson's grasp, Stevens' eyes bulged from his skull.

"You bastard! You won't be hurting any more women, older or younger ones," he hissed.

Kelly turned away as Stevens died while choking on his own tongue. He slumped in Branson's grasp and his lifeless body dangled there.

"Get over here and help me. Kelly, you hear me?"

She moved in slow motion fear finally gripping her.

"I need your help, baby. Open that door into the side room. Let's get out of here before someone finds us. Maybe they'll think Walker killed him. Take my bag and go back to Sage and wait for me there."

Branson covered his tracks well and they moved fast to make a good getaway.

Meanwhile, Kelly burst into Sage's room and promptly threw up in the washbasin. She vomited until she could wretch no more.

Sage walked over to Kelly and shook her, "Where's my father? Where is he? What did you do to him?" Kelly slumped down over the bowl.

"Nothing," she spluttered through the vomit. "It was something else he had to do."

Branson came in behind her, closed the door and locked it.

"Leave her alone. I'm right here." He hurried over to Kelly and cradled her in his arms. "Everything's going to be okay, baby. First light, we're out of here. Sage, hold her."

Sage looked at him like he was crazy.

"Just do it. She's sick from too much junk in her body," he lied, not wanting to explain the fact that he had just murdered a man.

He handed her over to his daughter. Branson pulled the mobile phone from his boot. It was tiny and slid in there comfortably. After a couple of seconds, the connection was made.

"Wade, where are you? One man down. We need to get out of here and there's not much time. Only three of us. You got my message okay, then? Was afraid you wouldn't pick it up on time. Things somewhat changed around here very quickly. What time you coming in to help? Four's good. I can get my own guns. There's an arsenal here. Guards everywhere. Then you saw that for yourself. We'll take the chopper. Don't worry about us. Just show up and help me take this place down. Buchanan sent extra men, right? Good."

He replaced the phone. Pulling out his Glock, he checked it. It was fully loaded.

"Let's try and get some sleep. Kelly, anything you want to take from here? Some things you need to collect?"

"Got to get my purse. That's all I need and it's underneath Sage's bed. These are all of the clothes that I have here. You'll buy me nice new stuff, right? Some nice pants where I won't have to wear these slut jeans and some better shoes…"

"Anything you want."

He pushed his wife's picture inside his pocket. He had his gun, and his credentials were tucked neatly inside the inner pocket. The rest could stay there. It wasn't safe to walk back out of the room. He pulled the blankets back on the bed.

"You two lie next to me. Both of you try to sleep. We'll need our rest."

The girls climbed onto the bed. Kelly positioned herself in the middle. Sage turned away from them and stared at the filthy wall. Branson didn't close his eyes. He propped himself up on the bedrail, his gun next to the pillow. Kelly moaned and turned toward him. He put his arm around her and she quieted down. This evening's events had been too much, even for a tough girl like her. The hour ticked by too slowly. Branson couldn't sleep because he was busy listening for intruding sounds. He so far had heard nothing unusual. If they had found Stevens, all hell would have broken loose by now. He looked across at his daughter and thought about her mom.

"Are you awake?" he whispered to Sage trying not to move.

"Yes. Is she?" Sage turned her head to look at the other girl.

"No. Just you and I." Branson pulled Kelly tightly to him.

Sage, being still awake, looked at Kelly curled into her father, his arm wrapped around her. Hatred began to burn in Sage's heart.

"Don't hate her. It isn't her fault. There's a lot you don't understand.

Someday you will. She may be young, but she's lived more in her life than you ever will. It's almost time to go. Get your things together and I'll wake her."

Sage slipped off the bed and pulled their few belongings together.

"Kelly, Kel, wake up. Time to fly, baby."

"What you want? What time is it?" She rubbed her eyes. "You want me to…?"

"We aren't alone, remember?"

She glanced around the half-lit room. "Um, forgot. When we get out of here, will you still want me?" she whispered, pondering her own thoughts and ignoring Sage to a point.

"Of course. You're stuck with me. Come on, let's get going." He kissed her very gently. "You both ready to get the hell out of here?"

They nodded. He looked at his watch: Three-thirty. Time to get within striking distance of the chopper. Branson led the way. It was still dark as they made their way past the guards. Silently, they slid from shed to shed, until they reached the arsenal. Stevens had been stupid enough to show him where it was. It was a cold and dank place, but still it had served its purpose. With a flashlight, Branson picked out a couple of AK 47's and ammunition. He slung the rounds over his shoulders and handed Kelly a gun. He figured she would know how to use it.

"Don't I get one?" whispered Sage. "Guess not. He probably doesn't think I know how to use the damn thing."

"Follow behind, real careful. Kelly, help Sage. Watch her back."

She mumbled a reply that Branson thought he heard.

He stopped.

"Kelly, do it."

"All right!"

In front of him stood a guard. He handed Kelly the weapons and moved in behind the man. Quietly Branson slipped up behind him and with a sickening crack snapped the man's neck. The body dropped limp in his arms and he dragged him into the bushes.

Sage stared in horror. "Oh, my God. He killed…"

"Shut the hell up! You're bound and determined to give us away! How stupid are you? Kane, you better talk to her. If pa wakes up before this goes down, we'll all be dead." She hoisted the guns up onto her back.

"What's the problem? You want to get out of here or not? If we blow this deal before backup arrives, we're dead meat. Those goons might even use us for a bartering tool. You want to be Walker's little punching bag forever? Without me around, that's what you'll be," whispered Branson.

It was obvious even to Branson that there was no love lost between the two women that were now in his life.

He looked at his watch. In the flashlight, he could see the time. Three-forty-five. Just enough time to get into position. The chopper stood in the middle of the grounds, its blades still like a giant grounded bird.

"You two wait here. Whatever happens, get on that chopper and wait for me."

"Where you going? You aren't gonna leave us now are you?"

"To get your pa. This way's too easy for him. Dying here."

"Come on, Miss Branson. You should do what your daddy says. You can manage that, can't you?"

Branson went carefully back through the yard. He entered through the kitchen and found Walker's room. Big and bloated, he lay passed out on the bed. The drug was just beginning to wear off a little. Walker moaned.

"You bastard! Wake up!" With some difficulty, he pulled Walker into a sitting position.

"What the hell's goin' on here? Feels like someone's damn-well drugged me." He rubbed his fat fingers across his face. "What's happening here?"

"You, my friend, are coming with me…whether you can stand up or not." Branson helped Walker to his feet.

Jerking Walker around and grabbing his shirt, he threw it at Walker, saying, "Put on your shirt now."

"Who the hell are you to be givin' me orders, mate?"

"From now on, you do what I tell you." He smacked Walker hard two or three times across the cheek with his gun.

He peered at Branson in the light of the flash lamp. "I've been think-ing that there was something about you that didn't fit."

Branson pushed Walker through the door and they made their way back through the route Branson had come. "From now on, you do what I tell you."

He smacked Walker two or three times across the face. No one saw them. Blood spurted from his face and he staggered. When he faltered, Branson helped him move with the assistance of his Glock pointing it at his back.

"Make a sound, and you're dead."

Walking down the hall, they passed the girls. Through the haze, Walker focused on his daughter. "You set me up. You bitch!"

He raised his hand. The blow caught Kelly across the face. With the power of the reach, Branson spun him around and hit him with a clenched fist. More blood shot out but this time, from his nose.

"Don't you ever lay a hand on her again!"

Walker wiped the blood from his nose and laughed. "Little slut. She's only good for one thing." Blood dripped down his shirt front.

Branson punched him in the stomach. "Your time's coming. You won't be hurting any more women."

Walker hugged his stomach. "Just who are you anyway?"

"You really want to know?" He grabbed Walker by his shirt. "Think I'll make you sweat just a little bit longer. Maybe I'll tell you before I kill you."

Walker managed a grin. "You can't kill me. Look around. You'll never make it out of here. Specially with those two in tow." He looked at Sage. "Why's she with you? Know her, do you?" Branson was puzzled.

"Yeah, and I know what you did to her…to both of them. All I want from you is the heroin. I'm still making that trip to the States. You and I are going to take a little trip to one of the sheds and pick out enough to keep Stratton happy. Get going, you fat bastard."

Walker stared at Kelly. "Why did you do it? I gave all of you what you wanted in life. Ain't you had what you always needed?"

"Yeah. That and a lot more."

Sage looked from one person to another as if she was in the middle of some nightmare. "Dad…"

"Sage!"

"What the fuck? You mean that she's your daughter?" He looked at Kelly. "You knew that before? Or, did you just find out after you slept with him?"

"After. But you murdered his wife. And there's more to this than…"

"Kelly, no!" yelled Branson.

Nevertheless, slowly Walker was putting all of the facts and pieces together.

"You're a goddamn cop. She was your wife in that hangar. Wasn't she? My God, that's why you're here. We killed a cop's wife. However, mate; before she died she gave us a damn good time. You'd been proud of her."

Branson pulled his knife out and lunged at Walker. He fell back against the shed. Kelly grabbed his arm and tried to stop the knife from reaching its target.

"Kane, no! Now is not the time, Kane! Sage, help me."

"She's right." She pleaded. "You need him. Dad, don't." Kelly pulled on his other arm.

Their voices were loud enough to attract attention.

"Stop it! We'll all be killed."This time Kelly's voice got through to him. "I'll go back for the stuff."

"The hell you will, baby. We'll all go without it now.

I'll find another way of getting to Stratton."

Branson was breathing hard. He never lost his cool, but Walker had pushed him over the top. The time was almost four. He had to get the girls out, and with his prize. The AFP would come in and wouldn't stop to find out if they were clear. His job was over and Branson had proven what the place really was. Reese would have told them all the details. He'd got his daughter back and someone else's, too. Now it seemed it was time to go.

"Your daughter saved you, for now. But what you did to my wife, to my daughter, and to your own…by God, you will pay."

"You ever heard of the legal system, cop?" Walker taunted.

"You heard of Branson's Country?"

Walker flinched. "Branson? My God!"

"Don't need any damn court for my kind of justice. Get going. Anyone gets near you; tell them we're taking a trip. You understand me?"

Walker nodded.

Branson stuck the knife deeper in Walker's back, just jabbing him to guide him into the spotlight. When the guards stepped forward, Walker waved them back. They made it inside the chopper. Branson glanced toward the gate. It needed to be open.

"Kelly, keep a gun on your father until I get back. I'll just be a second. Can you do that for me, little butterfly?"

"You said we'd go without the stuff."

"Going to open the gate. I'll be right back. Do this like a good little girl," Branson said hurrying as fast as he could.

"Don't leave us…"

"I'll be back, Kel. Just keep the gun on him. If he tries to warn anyone, shoot him."

Tears rolled down the girl's face but she by now only wanted to please Branson.

"Dad, she can't kill her own father."

"Yes, I can," Kelly said with determination.

Branson reached for his daughter and hugged her. Turning to Kelly, he held her in his arms for a brief second, whispered in her ear, kissed her on the lips, and was gone.

"What the son-of-a-bitch say to you? Something cute and pretty to hold you?"

"No, Pa. He told me if I had to, to shoot you in the back. You know what? I will, too."

Sage watched her father run across the compound. She heard the guards. Their suspicion had been aroused. They began scurrying like ants up a hill. She watched Branson reach the gate. Then she saw the head-lights of the cars outside. Branson grabbed for the nearest man and slit his throat. Another one attacked him and one from behind.

Helping her father had been very important.

"You stay put," Kelly yelled at her.

"But there's too many. They'll kill him!"

"I'm touched by your concern. Bit late, don't you think? You stay here with me. Kane don't need your help. He's a big boy. He knows what he's doin'. You'd only be in the way."

"Yeah, and you'd know about that wouldn't you?"

"Sure would, little girl. Know more about your father than you do."

"And I know more about that man you call 'Pa'," Sage said.

"I doubt that."

Walker edged to the door and swung his legs out.

"No, Pa. You aren't goin' anywhere," she said staring at her father's eyes with even more hatred than ever before.

"You gonna shoot your own pa on another man's say-so? Don't think so. What else did that bastard promise you?" Walker grabbed for Branson's Glock.

Branson freed himself. He could take on two men without hesitation. Leaning over, he reached down and picked up the rifle that had dropped to the ground. All around was panic. The men in the compound had seen the lights and heard the choppers overhead. He turned for the entrance gate and then shot off the lock. Pulling back the steel doors, he flung them wide open. Looking through the door, he ripped his hands on the barbed wire. Inside the compound, Walker's men opened fire.

Branson crouched down, firing back at the men, as many as he could see.

"For God's sake people, get in here!" yelled Branson.

It seemed like ages before the AFP found them. One car stopped. Wade jumped out and moved in alongside him.

"What the hell are you doing here?"

"I know the layout. They don't. Now we can get you out."

"I'm headed back to the chopper. The girls and Walker are in there."

"Girls?"

"My daughter and Walker's daughter, Kelly. You coming with us?"

She pulled the gun from her waistband. "Let's go!"

Her voice was drowned out by gunfire as the whole place lit up like Christmas. They ran back along the sidewall. Reese didn't need anyone to cover her back and never had. The compound had turned into a war zone. Branson did his share of killing on the way. He fired until the rifle he had picked up was empty. They made it to the chopper doors. Sage was hysterical and her hands were covered in bright red blood.

"She tried to stop him. Really she did. He shot her with your Glock but then he escaped. I tried to stop the bleeding. Is she dead?"

Drooped across her lap, lay his little butterfly. He put his fingers on her neck.

"She's still breathing. We have to get some help fast. Oh my God!"

Branson knew Kelly wouldn't breath very long if they didn't get away from this sheer madness. He ripped away her T-shirt. The bullet was lodged in her chest very close to her heart and the butterfly wings seemed to be fluttering. He touched them gently and lightly. As the blood became apparent on his hands, his body began to shake with rage. He had a choice now…to fly her out, or go back for Walker.

Reese watched him and could tell; by the way, he touched Kelly, that there had been more than just sex between them. Maybe there had been a bond as well. He laid her on the seat next to Sage, her face pale. Branson whispered in her ear.

"You will see him die. I promise you."

He should never have left them. If she dies…

"I can fly this thing, Branson, if you want to go after him."

He looked at Reese like she was crazy. He could see her in the lights - attractive even dressed in combat fatigues.

"I'll fly it. You take care of my girls. I'll get Walker at a later date."

"But your cover, Dad, he knows you," Sage argued.

"And I know him, and in the first place, he will run especially if he believes that Kelly is dead."

He lifted the chopper into the air. It circled once around. Branson made sure that his comrades had it under control as he watched the sheds go up in flames, the China white destroyed. That was his job. That's what Buchanan had sent him to do. To take it down, and to get Walker and the girls out... Dead or alive. That was still his mission. The one thing he was glad about was that he had found his daughter. The other thing he had not counted on or wanted was that he got a woman that he cared about shot. For the first time in his life, he had failed. And failure was not part of Branson's resume.

CHAPTER 8

The chopper clipped the trees as it landed on the hospital teleport near Brisbane. As paramedics stood by, Branson climbed out of the chopper. Hurriedly, they carried Kelly to the waiting ER. She was unconscious, rapidly losing blood, but still breathing. Sage tried to chase after him. However, Reese grabbed her by the arm and held her back.

"Come on, let's get some coffee and wait for him outside." She tried to usher Branson's daughter down the hall.

"But, Dad…" and Sage pulled away from Reese.

"He needs to be alone with her. Kelly's fighting to stay alive. She might not make it and your dad does care about her." Reese then became quiet.

"Oh dear God, she was so nice to me, Kelly just has to live… she just has to stay alive. I have to tell her she was right about me. I almost blew my dad's cover. She really does understand him, and I don't. I watched him in that place. He was someone I didn't know; but she did. Kelly had even been able to anticipate his moves," she spoke through her cries.

Reese placed her arm around Sage. "Don't cry. Your father was doing his job. Sometimes that job takes him beyond the normality of police work. After all, he brought Kelly out for a reason, and he cares about her…"

"He's sleeping with her. You don't have to hide that fact. They sure didn't. Marshal Wade, I might not like her, but I don't want her to die. It's not her fault she has a bastard for a father."

Sage pulled the bright green T-shirt, tightly around her. She sat down on a bench outside ER. Reese sat alongside her. They both commenced to worry about Branson. The compound was destroyed. He had let Walker escape in order to save the girl, but somehow, this seemed like a good thing.

Branson held Kelly's hand as the orderly wheeled her into ER-10.

"You have to leave, sir. We need…"

"I'm not leaving, so don't even think about asking me to do that," Branson stood his ground.

"Well, we…" The doctor tried to present a case.

"I can get the authority, if that's what you want. But for God's sake, get to the girl. If she dies, I'm not gonna be responsible for my actions in this damn place."

"Okay, just stay out of our way," one of them replied.

The doctor made him don a mask and gown. For once, as he was allowed into ER-10, he did what he was told. Branson stood at the back of the room while they removed her clothing and watched the nurses insert tubes everywhere. Blood dripped from a bag, pumping life through her veins. Her eyes were closed tight. Branson's were wide open as anger surged through him. He watched as the doctor removed the bullet and dropped it with a metallic sound into the dish beside the bed. A bullet from his own gun. He looked around. The clinical white tiles were sterile clean and in contrast a ton of red blood. How would she survive? He heard the doctor's voice.

"Okay, let's get her onto the gurney. Careful. She's nowhere near out of danger yet."

They wheeled her through the door back to her private room. Branson followed, and turned to the doctor.

"Doc, what's the chance of living? She will make it, won't she?"

"Too early to say. She your daughter?"

"No."

"Oh, I see," replied the doctor.

Branson gave him a look. "I doubt that you really could."

Branson left the doctor standing in the doorway and sat down next to the bed. The room was warm, the faded tan curtains pulled tight. Smoothing the stained sheets across her stomach, he watched a monitor connected to her heart. The trappings of life clung to her. He took her hand, unaware that his daughter and Reese were slipping through the door very slowly and silently.

"Don't die on me, little butterfly. We'll see this through together. I'll find your pa and take him down for you. I give you my word. Just hang in there, Kelly."

He leaned close to her face. He could feel her breath on his cheek. Gently, he stroked her hair, kissed her forehead, and then inched downward to her lips. The strands of her hair lingered on his fingers. He stood up and caught sight of his onlookers. Turning to look again at the girl, he left the room. Branson wasn't happy about the people watching him. The last thing he wanted was to have to talk to an agent right now.

"We weren't spying on you. We just got some news from the branch. They have Walker."

Branson stared at Reese, his face contorted with hate. "They have him? How the hell did they get him?"

"He was taking a Jeep out the back way and a couple of the agents caught him. Weren't sure who he was at first, but they ID'd him about a half-hour ago. He's on his way to jail at last."

"Which jail?"

"Let's just say, well anyway you can't go after him. Let justice take its course. You got the girls out of there. Isn't that what counts now?"

"Listen to her," Sage said. "It won't help Kelly, or my mother, if you get arrested now."

He ignored her. "Where did they take Walker?"

"About two miles from here. I know where, but Kane…"

"Take me to the place, damn it. Sage, you stay here. Here's my mobile phone number." Branson scribbled the number down on a tiny piece of paper. "If anything changes, you call me. Anything! Let's go." He grabbed Reese by the arm.

"I won't be a party to murder!" retorted Reese.

"Didn't ask you to; just take me there and leave. Go the hell where you want. I have a job to finish. That girl in there has more guts than any of us, including me." On his sweater and jeans Branson wore splotches and smears of Kelly's blood, like a knight about to do battle. "Give me your piece."

"Where's your Glock?" Reese asked.

"He used that gun to shoot her. In fact, he still has the damn gun; or, the AFP does. Doesn't matter anymore. I don't need a gun to do what I have to do."

"What are you thinking about doing? You're just thinking about walking in there to get rid of him? Can't be done."

He looked at Reese. "What are you gonna do, arrest me? Don't think so. So you going to drive me or not?"

"Dad, don't go, please. I don't want to lose you," Sage pleaded. "I only just found you again." She pulled on his sweater and tried to make him see sense.

"You do as you're told and stay outside of Kelly's hospital door. I should have told you years ago what to do. Perhaps you wouldn't have gotten into the mess you did if I had. Reese, let's go."

He took off down the hall. Reese caught up with him at the door.

"Did you have to be so hard on her?"

"She deserved that. Sage has picked on Kelly from the start," he answered.

"And you. What do you need? Revenge?" she argued. "Now you're resentful and feel like placing blame on her. Why are you revengeful to your own daughter? God, Branson, she just recently came back into your life. If you're not careful, you'll push her away again; but this time, to stay gone."

Branson stepped out into the cold, gray evening. One of the AFP agent's cars was parked out front.

"Need to borrow your keys," he told the agent.

"Sir? I can't let just anyone take a car…"

"I'm Kane Branson. This is Marshal Reese Wade. We need that car now." Branson was becoming irritated.

"You have ID, sir?"

Reese stepped forward knowing full well he didn't right now.

"Agent Branson is undercover. I'm a United States Marshal," and she showed him her badge. It was enough to obtain a car.

Branson climbed into the car. "Thanks. You drive. I fly choppers and ride bikes. Don't drive damn sedans."

He lay back on the seat. Reese tried to think of a way to stop him from going after Walker aside from alerting the force.

Feeling as if there were no other choice, and because no other solution came to her, she half-turned to him.

In the warmth of the car, Branson dozed. The next thing he knew, they were at the jail and two burly cops were wrestling his wrists into handcuffs. They pulled him bodily from the car.

"What the hell? You bitch! You caused this shit!" He looked at Reese. "This the way you repay me?"

Branson struggled violently as the agents led him into the jail. They pulled him down the stairs and his back hit the walls as he went. This made him more irritated. The jingling of keys echoed throughout the cells. The door swung open. It took both cops to get Branson inside his assigned cell. For a moment, he stood in the middle of the four by six block. Then he sat down on the hard gray and dingy tan cot. Reese made an appearance.

"Which seedy part of Brisbane are we in now?" he demanded.

"By the airport. You're supposed to only stay here overnight. Buchanan's orders. He's on his way up."

The bars were cold when she touched them causing her to let go quickly. Branson saw her reaction and wondered if there wasn't something more to her reaction than met his eye at the moment.

"Just like you. Cold." He turned away from her.

"I did it for your own good. Your daughter needs you, and so does Kelly," Reese said to him.

"Kelly? You don't like her and neither does Sage," said Branson. "I had to get your attention and it felt like the only way at the time to get you to see."

"See what?" he asked Reese. "That you're jealous? Did you fancy a shot at me? Is that why you wanted me stopped? If that girl dies, there won't be any bars strong enough to hold me. You understand?"

Tears filled Reese's eyes. "They promised to call if there was any change in Kelly's condition. If there is any, I'll make sure they take you back to the hospital so you can visit her. Buchanan said…"

"Fuck Buchanan!"

"It was all I could think of to stop you from going after Walker. You'd kill him… or worse yet, he'd kill you. Damn that's what I was afraid would happen," she argued.

"That's the first smart thing you've said all night. That was my intention, maybe not the departments, but it was mine. That's my job to stop the damn criminals." He paced up and down in his cell like a caged animal, which with his anger rising, is what he felt like.

"I know that, still not in cold blood. That's not your job. Or is that what you've become?"

"Think you're so smart, don't you Marshal Wade? Think you know me from a few brief meetings and a file? You know nothing about me at all." His voice was full of animosity.

At that moment, the guards caused the cell block doors to fly open in order to admit another prisoner. Two burly uniformed cops emerged in front. Reese caught a brief look at the guy and then she stared straight at Branson. The look on his face made her blood run cold. Two federal agents appeared walking behind the group and between them, they had a badly beaten and chained man. The prisoner with apparent bruises and swollen eyes looked at the badge hanging round her neck and spat at Reese.

Looking up at the noise, the chained criminal was making, Branson saw that the cuffed man was Walker. His gaze stayed on the man who was showing up on the same block. Through his pain and anger, he laughed maniacally.

Walker spoke first. "Well, well. If it's not the famous Kane Branson," Walker announced through split lips. "What they got you in here for? Trying to kill innocent citizens? What's it like, you being locked up for a change? Feel good, huh? With you there, now you can't get me, and you sure as hell can't get to Kelly. In fact, I kind of like you being there. Just so you'll know, I shot her with your own gun. Stupid little bitch tried to betray me. Her own pa, in favor of you! Can't tolerate no traitor, now can I?"

Red-faced, Branson lunged at the bars his handcuffs clanging on the bars.

"That's enough, Walker." She turned to the APF agents. "Get him away from me, or I may just turn Agent Branson loose on him," yelled Reese.

They pushed the gross little man though the cell door, his stomach catching on the bars. "Watch it, you sons-of-a-bitches! Your department want a lawsuit?"

Branson moved around to the left side of the cell and focused on Walker. The rest of the world disappeared. It was just Walker and Branson. Kane turned his attentions to Reese. His brow furrowed in anger. Turning his back on her, he walked slowly and deliberately over to the cot. Lying down on the dirty mattress, he stared at the piss stained wall by the urinal.

"You want me to check in about Kelly?" Reese asked, timidly. Branson didn't reply. "I'll go back to the hospital and stay with her as soon as I leave here," Reese said when she didn't get a quick reply.

Slowly he turned over on the uncomfortable cot, and said, "A woman as dangerous as you… one that will turn on a friend, well I'll tell you, Reese… just you keep the hell away from her." Then he closed his eyes until she left him to brood.

As she hollered for the guard to let her out, she glanced back for what felt like one last look. Her eyes filled with tears. The cell doors clanged behind her.

Branson lay there awhile. He had to get out of this hellhole, one way or another. Yelling for the guard, he watched until one arrived.

"Can you take these cuffs off me? I need to take a piss. That's my right, and with my hands like this, that proves just a little difficult."

"Stand over by the bars and put your wrists up high. We are not supposed to enter a con's cell. I was told not to come in there with you."

Branson did as he was told to do. The key turned in the lock of the cuffs and then they came undone. He massaged his red sore wrists. Then he used the urinal in the corner and unlike most of the other occupants, he didn't miss. Afterwards, he sat down on the bed, reached down, released the top of his snakeskin leather boots, and pulled out his mobile phone. Branson found the hospital number and dialed.

"You a relative?" asked the crisp formal voice on the other end of the line.

"Well, actually, I was wondering if there was any change in Kelly's condition. I'm her boyfriend," he replied.

"No change. Is there a number where we can reach you?"

As soon as he gave his number to them, the phone snapped shut. He held it in his hand and made a good show of making loud conversation down towards the phone as if he were still in conversation. He shouted through the door. "Guard! Something's wrong at the hospital. I need to get out of here. Guard, where the hell are you?" he yelled.

Walker was watching him from the safety of his cell. "We'll get you, Branson. I still have friends. It was you who took out Pierce, and I'm sure you made Stevens disappear, too."

"Yeah, well don't get too comfortable, 'cause you'll soon be joining them. You sure as hell don't scare me none."

"No? I have some powerful friends. It might be your turf, but seems you're on the wrong side of that right now." Walker was enjoying baiting the hook.

"That's where you are wrong, you son-of-a-bitch. It is you who doesn't need to plan on living much longer. I'm getting out of here, and then I'll make some phone calls and I'll go for Kelly."

"She really took to you. Made me wonder why. Why, Branson? Wasn't just her body you were after, was it?" Walker wiped his sweaty face on his sleeve. He had begun to put the pieces of the jigsaw together. "You're a damn cop. She knew that all along, didn't she?" He paused.

"Guard…get me out of here. There's an emergency! I was told I'd be able to leave if there was one. Where the hell is my release guard?" screamed Branson.

"That little bitch was gonna turn on me, betray me. That's it; isn't it? You were there to protect her. My God, I should have finished her off when I had the chance." Walker's face was red with anger. "But I'll get her yet. You can't protect her day and night!"

"The hell I can't," Branson snarled. "Guard, get me out of here, now!"

"Agent Reese said not to let you out unless…"

"Look, sonny, you let me out of here now or I'll have your badge. You do know who I am, don't you?"

"Yes, sir," replied the guard timidly.

"Then open the goddamn door. I have to get to the hospital. One important lady is close to dying. You want a death on your hands, boy?" Branson was yelling.

"No, sir." He turned the key in the lock.

"Hey you, guard. If he gets out he'll see to it that I'm dead! Don't unlock that door. Your boss told you not to do that. Don't you obey orders?" Walker licked his lips nervously.

Branson pushed the door open and then leaned toward Walker and hissed through the bars. "I'll be back for you or send for you, one or the other!"

"You heard that, guard. You heard him threaten me!"

"No, sir," said the guard. "Never heard a thing." His tone reflected nervousness in the face of Branson. Most of the seasoned guards had heard about Branson by way of the inmates talking about the bad ass cop who got them finally put under lock and key. "Your belongings are waiting upstairs for you."

Branson was only gone ten minutes when he commandeered a motorbike, parked in the back of the jailhouse. Easy enough to hot-wire and in a flash. Similar to the one he rode back home, so with not much thinking at all, off he went. Taking to the streets, he followed the necessary signs to the hospital. He pulled over and left the bike running. He turned his mobile phone on and immediately it rang.

"Dad, where are you? Your phone was turned off," she cried down the line.

"Is it Kelly?" He tried to keep calm.

"She's the same. Reese is furious with you. Said you left jail without telling her. What were you doing in jail? You didn't do anything, did you?"

"No. That damn Reese had the nerve to lock me up *for my own pro-tection*," he sneered. "Then once I'm locked in there, in walks Walker. Son-of-a-bitch had an adjoining cell. She thought I'd kill Walker. I didn't touch him, yet. I'm on my way to see you two. Chances are they won't let me near Kelly because I'd run off with their witness. Last time I almost got her killed." Branson paused. "Fuck. Did she wake at all yet? Has she said anything? Has she asked for me?" He struggled with the line.

"Dad I'm losing you, you're coming in very faint. Is there traffic by you or something? Dad, if you can hear me, don't come here. I'll call you again later to let you know when it's safe. I'll tell Kelly if I can later on that you are safe and asking about her."

Branson powered up the bike and headed for the nearest motel instead to make plans. On Seventh Street, he found what he needed. A seedy joint where he could hang out until things settled down. He parked the bike around the back of the motel. At the front desk, Branson asked for a single room where he handed over a wad of cash. The desk clerk looked like he had stepped off Walker's compound. He asked no questions and handed Branson the keys to room 3D.

"Top of the stairs, first right, mate. Number 3," the clerk said, looking down at the register, "Mr. Brown. Right. Store on the corner there if you need anything." The clerk sniffed and wiped his arm on his sleeve.

"Just some privacy," answered Branson, handing him some more cash.

"Good as done, governor." He stuffed the money in his back pocket without counting it.

Branson climbed the stairs, unlocked the door, and switched on the light. It flickered twice, then died. From the hall light, he could see another lamp. He tried that and it worked. Not a brilliant light, but better than nothing. Then he closed the door to his room, wiped his hands hard across his face and let out a "fucking hell."

Branson pulled his jacket and boots off. Laying the mobile phone and his knife by his pillow, he sat on the bed covered with a Chenille bedspread. He stared at the now fading, flowery-flocked pink wallpaper. Branson leaned back and pulled the pillows under him. With his arms folded back under his head, the pillows cushioned his neck. He looked up at the ceiling and listened to the truckers running by the hotel. The ceiling matched the room, it was filthy dirty, but the radio worked and he just zoned out on some music and rested.

So much had happened in one day, now he was tired and a victim of his own justice. He could go back and hand in his badge. Maybe he should. Maybe that was best. All he had done was do his job until self-satisfaction and Kelly got in the way. Reese had only done what she thought was right. He couldn't really blame her. But he did blame the system. It would sentence Walker and at least keep him locked away. That wasn't good enough. Walker needed to pay big time for what he'd done, Branson just didn't know how best to do that yet.

Branson awoke with sunlight streaming through the windows and shivered from the cold. There was no heat, and the cool of the night had brought a chill to his half-clothed body. He pulled a blanket around him and sat in a chair by the window. Shadows of death had flickered in the half-light during the night and run into Branson's dreams. Branson was glad to be awake. He should go see Kelly. Wasn't like he was on the run. Or was he? Did Walker have some of his goons after him?

He flipped open his mobile phone and checked his voice mail. There were three messages.

"Mr. Branson. Kelly is asking for you. Please return the call." They left a number. He returned the call.

"This is Kelly's boyfriend, Mr. Branson, returning the call you left for me." He used the term loosely. "How is she?"

"She needs to see you. Been asking for you half the night. We tried to reach you several times. What do you want us to tell her, sir?"

"Is she out of danger?" Branson asked.

"Not yet. But she's young and strong. Your daughter's here. She said she tried to call you once or twice in the last hour."

"Put my daughter on the phone," Branson replied.

He waited on the line.

"Dad, where are you? I tried to reach you. I shouldn't have told you not to come here. Reese explained why she had you placed in jail. Kelly needs you desperately. No one else will do. Will you come? Dad, I…"

"And what about you, Sage? You need a father yet? I'll be there. But first I have something I got to do. Can't do this on the right side of the law though. Is Reese there? Put her on the line if she is."

He looked around the room and waited for Reese to respond.

"Reese speaking."

"Do you know where Buchanan is yet?"

"Branson? Oh, it's you. Yes, he's at the hospital. Why?" Reese asked.

"I have a present for him," came a quick reply.

"You didn't do anything…"

"No. I want to hand him my badge."

"You want to do what? Look, I'm sorry about last night. It was all I could think of to stop you. But to go and turn in your job… your badge, well that's just insane, in fact, that's lunacy."

"Then call me a lunatic. Just make sure he stays there. And tell Kelly I'm on my way. I'll be there in just awhile."

"I'll tell her…Kane?"

No answer, just a dial tone.

He walked into the bathroom. When he turned on the light, two large cockroaches skittered underneath the sink. After showering, he put back on the same jeans. He'd scrubbed them with a tiny bar of soap but it hadn't made a lot of difference. The stains and some of the odor had still lingered. His sweater was a complete mess. Maybe his bag was still at the hospital. A store. The man said there was a store nearby.

He bought a black sweatshirt that did not help a lot. He was still cold. By ten, he was on his way. The bike was still behind the motel. No one seemed to have messed with it, or found it either. Tracing his way back, Branson located the hospital and enjoyed riding a motorbike again. Speed gave him the ultimate freedom he needed and loved so much. Branson turned into the parking lot. Sitting astride the bike, he thought about what all was happening. If he gave up his badge, he could go after them his way. There would be no law to abide by or department to get in his way. There would also not be a job when it got back… nothing…except his daughter and Kelly. Kelly. Finally, the hospital was in his sight.

"I'm here to see Kelly Walker."

"She has been moved to a side ward. Down there, first door on the right. Can't miss it. There's police everywhere. You a relative? Maybe, I should call down there?"

"You could say that I am. No need to call. They know me."

Branson walked down the hospital corridor. It seemed different from last night. He remembered it all being different. The events from last night had clouded his mind, and he hadn't remembered Kelly being rushed down that lobby very well. He saw Buchanan by the door talking to Reese. Behind them, stood his daughter who was talking to a cop. They saw him and their conversation stopped. Sage approached him first.

"Dad." Sage threw her arms around his neck and cried.

"It's okay. I'm here." He looked at Buchanan. "I need to see you."

"Don't you want to see Kelly?" he asked.

Buchanan looked tired. Branson was his usual arrogant self.

"You first. Is there somewhere we can talk?"

He peered through the window at the girl. They had given her something to relax and it had helped her so well that she was sleeping. He couldn't help notice how someone had cleaned her. Gone was her makeup, no pink lips, and underneath was a pretty young woman. Her hair was pulled back from her face. She looked so innocent. He felt that feeling again. Each time he saw her now his feelings deepened.

Buchanan opened the door to a side room. Branson stepped past Reese and completely ignored her. If there was one thing he was an expert at, it was at holding a grudge. Buchanan sat down on the bed. Branson stood.

"So, you wanted to see me, Agent Branson?"

Branson paced back and forth in the room. He looked through the hospital window out on to the yard. It was a busy place. His thoughts returned to the previous night and the landing of the chopper on the emergency pad.

"You okay?" Buchanan asked.

"I'm giving you my badge, hypothetically speaking, since I don't have it on me. I am resigning. And also my gun, which I believe you already have. There's something I have to do that's not going to fit in with department rules. And I believe you already know about Kelly. I plan on taking care of her, witness or not. It's something that's not going to sit well with anyone."

This was not the man Buchanan knew. This Branson was arrogant to the point of total abandon. Something had changed, and he guessed it had more than its share of Kelly attached to it.

Branson continued. "I also have to get my daughter straightened out, among other things. It's going to take time." He paced like a caged tiger.

"Then take time. Take a month off. Don't just hand in your badge. Just take the damn time and do whatever you have to do to stay on the force. The AFP won't be going anywhere. Take Kelly. Talk it over with both her and Sage. Decide where you want to go back home, or if you want to stay in Brisbane. We'll fly you all back, and when Kelly is ready to testify, she can. You take the leave."

"What?"

"Take the leave. I don't want to lose you, Agent Branson."

"Why are you doing this? You don't owe me." Branson suddenly saw Buchanan in a different light. "I'll think about it, but I doubt I'll change my mind."

Branson left the room and closed the door behind him. Walking back down the hall, he approached Sage and smiled. Then he saw Reese Wade, and his expression changed. She was a fine-looking woman and her interest in him was obvious, but his loyalty lay with Kelly. And still he didn't understand why. He took Sage's hand.

"You still have my bag? I need a jacket or something."

"You're freezing. Are you okay? You don't look good." She rubbed his hands.

"I'm fine. Just tired. You want to come back home with me? We can sort things out before I leave for the States."

"You're leaving?" his daughter asked, peering up at him.

"Not just yet. I have something to take care of here. And I have to do right by Kelly."

"She's coming with us?" Sage asked.

"Is that a problem for you?"

"I don't know. I do know she would have given her life for you." Her voice was soft, and her hands lingered on her father's.

"Yeah, I know. And I'll do the same for her."

In his mind, he had already given his plan, a code name of Sage for his wife and for his daughter. All he had to do now was to continue the practice.

Quietly, he opened the door to Kelly's room. He stood and watched her for a moment. She was connected to a heart monitor. It would be a couple of days, at the very least, until they'd let her out. Walker wasn't going anywhere. The Brisbane branch of the AFP would make sure of that. Sitting next to the bed, Branson took her hand, stroked her hair, and whispered in her ear.

"I failed, little butterfly. Your father is stuck in jail and the other bastards have left for the States. It's not your fight and yet somehow I made it that way. If you're willing, we can go on together until it is finished. You're the only one I trust. I know you can't hear me. I'll tell you all this again when you can."

Suddenly she squeezed his fingers. "I hear you. And I believe in you." The words came out in a whisper, barely audible but he heard them.

"Kelly…I thought you were asleep. How much did you hear?"

He leaned closely to her.

"Most of it." Her voice was gaining strength with each word.

"Don't talk. There's time for that later." Stroking her hair, he said, "You rest, and I'll stay by you." He watched her grimace. "Bet it hurts like hell, huh?"

She nodded and tears streamed down her face. Branson tried to change the subject.

"We'll get you out of here, buy you new clothes, and then you can come back and live with me. I have something to do, Kel. Only you seem to understand. The people out there don't. I think I figured out what you see in me. I'm way older than you. I can't be a father figure. We both know that. Maybe it's a lover you want. I don't know why you picked me. If you want me, you have to make concessions. No drugs, no drinking, and you only sleep with me. Can you do that, little butterfly? Can you forget about your mother's life and what your own father did? He killed her in the same way he killed my wife."

Kelly turned her head away so he wouldn't see her tears. Gently he turned it back.

"In your mind you always knew, and in the kitchen he confirmed it. It's okay to cry. We'll make them pay, and Sage will help us. You want to come with me?"

"Yes," she whispered. "You know I do. It's what I dreamed about since I first talked with you and you made me feel so different than any other man has."

"Then it's settled. I admire you, Kelly. You have guts. You'll grow up to be a fine woman. And I will have the pleasure of watching you do that. I'm going outside a moment, but I will be back. Just rest."

Branson tried to let go, but she clung to him. Above the top of the gown, he could see the butterfly. He swore the wings were open. He had reached her.

"Kane," she whispered. "Kane, I…"

"It's okay, darling. I'll be back. You have my word. And you know you can live or die by Branson's word."

She smiled at her friend and lover and blew him a kiss.

"Later."

Branson gently closed the door behind him.

Branson met Buchanan out in the hall. "Hasn't changed, Buchanan. I'm leaving just like I said. If you want it in writing, you can have it. The

time is not enough. When she's ready, we'll go home. Change her name…
to Branson. Lord knows maybe even the legal way. It will give her the
protection and the reassurance she needs."

"Did I hear you right?" Sage looked astounded.

"You heard. I'm quitting the force," returned her father.

"Not that, Dad. The part about her name."

"You heard right, and you're coming with us back to the apartment and
to a real life. So I don't want to hear anything else said."

"Are you going to marry the girl?" Buchanan asked.

"Didn't say that. Said I was going to change her name. What girl that
age would want to marry me?"

Branson was tired and it showed; he leaned on the wall. Tired of killing and lonely. He realized he wanted to stop chasing shadows, maybe
settle down, and just possibly, he could do that again.

Reese, shocked at what she was hearing, stared at him. "What woman
wouldn't want to marry you? I mean…"

She turned away embarrassed. Sage tried to cover for her.

"Well, she's right. And I don't think I want someone my age as my step-
mother, especially someone like…" she stopped. Her face was red.

"Someone like Kelly? If it hadn't been for her, you and I might be dead.
Let me spell it out to you. I'm not marrying her, just looking out for her.
And, yes, she'll be living with me. Where I go, she goes. Do I make myself
clear? And Buchanan, if you give me two months, I may think about it.
Otherwise keep the badge."

Branson took the bag from Sage and pulled the jacket from it. Slipping it over the black sweatshirt, all zipped up he cut a menacing figure,
all in black with blond hair. He stood there quietly daring one of them to
break the silence. Buchanan cleared his throat. Branson had just regained
his turf.

"Two months, Branson, even three. The department can't afford to lose
you. And the girl's in your protection."

Branson nodded and turned on his heel. Closing the door to Kelly's
room, Sage let go.

"My God, when did he get so intense? I hardly know that man. He's
not the same Dad I knew."

She looked towards Kelly's door, and sat down again on a bench. Buchanan sat beside her.

"It happened after your mother was murdered. He became reclusive and made it his job to go after the five men. I tried to help him by sending him on this assignment, because he knows so much about the case. All I did was made it worse." Buchanan sighed heavily. "Branson seems, God forbid, to have found some sort of consolation in that girl in there. If she helps him, you have to accept it. We may think he's wrong, but Branson has to do what he thinks best. Go home with him. Let him be your father again."

Sage looked to Reese. She had watched the proceedings in a subdued manner.

"I'd rather you were going with us, Reese. At least you're nearer his age. I don't know if I can live with him and her as a team," she pondered.

"You can't live without him," Reese said.

Branson pushed the strands of hair from Kelly's face. She was awake and talking.

"I will make it out of here, won't I? You wouldn't lie to me, would you? I'm expecting you to hold to the promise you've made me." Her face was pinched with pain.

"What are they giving you, darling? Morphine or what? Doesn't mix that well with Cocaine, does it? I'll make sure you get out of here. We have a job to do." He took her hand. "I told that you would watch your father die and you will. But it's our secret. You won't see me again 'til I have things worked out for the best. I will make sure you know where I am." He pushed his mobile phone into her hand. "Keep this with you. I promise to return for you. Trust me."

"I do," she whispered, and clutched the mobile phone in her hand.

He leaned down and kissed her. She responded, her lips parting for his kiss. The bond deepened.

"You okay?" she murmured.

"Yeah, I'm fine. You sleep now. I'm gonna bail. You listen for my call. I won't be far away. Not ever."

He passed the group on the way out, not stopping to say goodbye. A man on a mission; one that would take all the energy he had. It was warm and yet he shuddered. He couldn't shake the feeling something was about to happen. Outside, in the fresh air, thinking came more clearly. He had promised himself that each man would die in a different way: one by an explosion, another by strangulation. Walker was next. There just had to be a way to get to him and that was just the first problem.

CHAPTER 9

Branson sat astride the bike with the bag stashed on the back. His suit was gone, but he had some other clothes left. He needed to get back to the motel. Riding carefully through the streets, he hoped not to attract attention. Parking at the back of the hotel, Branson unhooked the bag from the back of his bike and climbed the flight of stairs that led to the bedrooms. Inside his room, he pulled out the picture of his wife. He leaned it against the dresser mirror and moved to the window.

"What the hell am I doing, Sage Jay? I found our daughter, only to find a bigger mess. Got myself involved in this, and I cannot seem to stop killing. I don't know what's wrong. I'm tired of it all. When I look at Sage, I see you. She's a constant reminder. And then there's Kelly. She's a damn kid." He paused and sat down on the window ledge.

Although it was dark, he stared out the window and continued thinking. "I'm getting a feeling for her I don't understand. What is strange, too, is that I have no claim on her." His tone changed as a huge tidal wave of guilt washed over him. "And I have to find a way to get to Walker very soon, so this can all be over. I want some peace."

Branson always had a way, and this time was going to be no exception. He pondered a moment. Why not wait? Walker would be an easier target out of jail. This time, the AFP would make the charges stick and prison time was on the agenda. Branson turned away from the window, tired of staring at the darkness of the night. How hard would it be to get into jail? But first, he had something even more important to do.

It was becoming clear now that Kelly would heal, and when she did, he would take the girls back down to his apartment. Sage wouldn't be as happy as they would. Too bad, it was his life and he didn't feel like losing the chance at happiness. She'd led hers up to now without him and hopefully, she'd adjust. He sat down on the bed, leaning back on the black wrought-iron rail. Branson dozed.

A deeper darkness began to descend over Brisbane. He awoke startled at his surroundings. Solitude was not the answer. Company was what he really wanted. Getting a drink at a bar sounded good. Couldn't be too far to one. Pulling himself together, Branson turned off the lamp and then locked the door to Room 3D behind him.

"Hey, sport, where's the nearest bar?" he asked the desk clerk.

Branson had showered and changed clothes trying to look as clean as possible. He'd shaved his beard off, something he hadn't done for years. When he looked in the mirror, a man ten years younger looked back. Catalogue handsome he was… even with his unruly hair. The moustache stayed the color blonde enhancing his sun-kissed features.

The clerk stared at him with a puzzled look. "Fifth Street. You can walk it, if you've a mind. Look like you could handle any problems that might arise." The bucktooth clerk with jet-black hair pushed the day's take of cash into his back pocket.

Branson took the advice. A walk was just what he needed. The first two blocks went without an incident. By the time the third block came up, he found his safety going down hill rapidly. Seedy property, dirt filled streets and graffiti stained walls. Past a bus stop and on the right-hand corner was a guy with a tin cup pretending to be a Veteran, or blind, or both.

"Spare a dollar, mate? Could do with a cup of coffee." The pathetic creature didn't look that old, just down on his luck. The panhandler didn't look the type to drink coffee either. But, what the hell.

"Sure," he said pulling a five-dollar bill from his pocket. The bill dropped soundlessly in the cup.

"Thanks, governor." The guy, picking up the five, couldn't believe his luck and scurried away like a rat with a cat after it.

The transaction gave Branson an idea. If he played it right, it might just work. Having counted the blocks, he knew he only had a couple more. This one was a little different than the ones back home. The bar was more like a strip joint. Loud music, noisy patrons and young seductive girls in the brightest red underwear that Branson had ever seen. While listening to Fleetwood Mac's 'Red Hot Jam' blaring from the jukebox, he sat down at the bar to order a beer. The stool was high, and, turning his back, he leaned on the bar. Emptying half of the bottle in one go, he tilted his head back.

"You thirsty then, mate, or just had a rough day?" The bartender polished the smoky glasses.

"Both."

He watched the fancy girls dancing. Most of them had great bodies, and for the obvious reasons, he thought of Kelly. Would he always think of her in this light? Did their future hold something better for the both of them?

Everyone's head seemed strained upwards. A girl with a spectacular figure swirled her way to the stage area and introduced herself as 'Jazmin.' After the normal shrieks and yells had ceased coming from the audience, Branson did a double take. Jazmin wore a pale pink crop, trimmed in black lace, which exposed plenty of cleavage. Her black pants had gold sequins running the length of leg. Hot, nine-inch heels were wrapping themselves around a pole when Jazmin found Branson's eyes staring back at her. When they made eye contact, whammo! He cracked. Her gold choker and gold dangling earrings had reminded him of Kelly.

"You want a woman, mister? Can get you one for the night." He spat on a glass to bring up a shine. "Nah, guess a man like you already has one or two."

"Yeah, something like that, sport." He downed the rest of the beer and chuckled to himself. "Another."

"Sure, mate. Whatever you want." The bartender, who it appeared had seen better times, watched him looking at the stripper. 'It's Never Gonna Stop Me' by Rob Zombie began playing and another girl took the stage. "Remind you of someone? Not worked here long. Only twenty. She needed the money, so I gave her a job. Best I could do. So many of them come in here begging me to help 'em."

"Couldn't you have given her a job behind the bar?" The girl was beginning to remind him of Kelly.

"She's a whore. All she's fit for…"

Branson pulled him by his shirt halfway across the bar. "Don't ever say that. No one is just a whore. You hear me… mate?" he said speaking too loudly to be natural even for this bar and for the late hour.

"Whatever you say, boss. Course she isn't. Yeah, I guess she could get a better job."

Branson dropped him. "Now, down to some serious business. You know anywhere I can buy a gun? Quick, like tonight?"

"Excuse me? A gun?" He dropped the glass. It shattered. "Are you crazy man?" the surprised bartender asked Branson.

"You heard me. Don't look so surprised. This isn't exactly the Ritz."

He looked around. The place was packed full of drunks and deadbeats and some of them were beginning to watch him and the bartender banter. The women here would give you more than just a good time.

"What the hell you want a gun for…you gonna blow someone's head off?"

"None of your business. Can you get me one or not? A .44 Magnum would be good, anything will do. And don't tell me you don't know where you can get one, 'cause I'm pretty sure that would be a crock of shit. I'll be back this time tomorrow. Oh, and I wouldn't go running to the police, not if you want to stay alive."

"Cost you $200. Look here, mate, you ain't scaring me none, you ain't."

"No? Then why are you shaking? Give me another beer and I'll leave you in peace. Nice of you to give me this one on the house. Quite generous of you." When he finished his beer, he thumped the bottle down hard on the bar and glared at the trembling man. "See you tomorrow."

Branson left the bar with the strippers' music still ringing in his ears. The one girl that had most reminded him of Kelly was still in his mind's eye. Damn that girl, Kelly was really getting in his craw.

Sleep did not come easy and, when it did, his dreams were dark. He could see Kelly lying helplessly in her hospital bed. Someone seemed to be bending over her. There was blood on his jeans and he was frantically scrubbing them. Then Branson's vision moved to another memory where he could see his wife and her face merged into Sage's. Behind her, stood Reese and Buchanan, with frowns on their faces. Icy stares. Another scene; Kelly lying in the damn morgue. He jerked awake, sweat pouring from his body. Clothes soaking wet, he flung the blanket from the bed and looked in the mirror. He knew he had to hurry and get back to her.

"Nooooo!" he screamed.

Kelly was embedded in his mind. His palms were clammy and his mind had not stopped racing. Looking at his watch, he could see it was 6:00 a.m. He swung his legs out of bed tossing the spread to the floor. Lord he desperately needed to talk to Kelly. She had his mobile phone. After showering and dressing quickly, he ran down the stairs, skipping two steps at a time. In the street, the lamps were still lit, but their glow was fading. It sent a chill down his spine, as this was synonymous of the situation. Branson needed to hurry and find a pay phone. Finally, locating one in a better part of town placed his money in and dialed his own mobile number. It rang.

"Come on, come on. Answer it!"

"Kane, is that you?" Kelly sounded frantic. "I need you. Someone tried to kill me last night. Please, come get me. And hurry! I'm scared to be without you here. All I can do when I'm awake is to think about you, about us."

"Calm down, darling. What I need is for you to get some rest. Get some sleep Kelly. Someone tried to kill you? I'm already there."

Branson's chill was brought to full fruition. He ran back into the motel, sprinted back up the stairs, and unlocked the door.

"I knew I should have stayed there with her. Damn them natural instincts. I'm a stupid fuck." With intense anger, he pushed his soiled clothes and the picture of his wife, Sage, into the bag. Grabbing the handles, he left the room just as it was. The desk clerk watched the goings on, as Branson sped down the stairs.

The bike rack was the first thing he hit with his bags. Once the bike started roaring, he took off at a high speed. The gun. He needed a gun. Branson sped though the still sleepy streets, and parked the bike out front of the strip joint. The feeling of nervousness was becoming apparent again. Given he was not really wanting to see Jazmin, he didn't need to be set off again. Listening at the door, he could hear several voices that seemed to be speaking right above a whisper. Branson knocked once.

"We're closed, mate. Can't you tell that? Goddamn, men want drinks at all hours."

His boot hit it first, then the full force of his body. The door burst open under Branson's weight.

"What the fuck? Oh, it's you. Wouldn't you know it? I should have explained that to you earlier, not to bust up my club."

"I came for my gun." Branson stared him down.

The bartender backed into the corner. "Don't have it yet, it's ordered and on the way… tomorrow maybe."

"Then give me yours."

"Don't use one…"

"Cut the crap. You've got one. All bartenders have one behind here." Branson made a play toward the bar.

"The man said he doesn't have one," his strong-arm oversized friend interjected.

Branson swung once with his fist and laid the bartender's friend out cold. "Now, let's have the gun you keep behind the bar."

Branson shook his hand. It hurt. But if he had not taken him down first, the big guy would have jumped him another.

"Okay, take the bloody thing. Who are you anyway? If you were a cop, seems like you'd have your own damn gun," he said handing the gun over to him.

"This is a standard issue .38. Where the hell did you get this gun?" Branson asked, raising his eyebrows to the stranger.

"This one got left behind by a customer. You are a cop, right?"

"Was. Spare clip?" He checked the gun.

"Nope, that's it." He withered under Branson's steady stare. "Okay."

Branson weighed the gun. As he was checking to see how it handled, he pointed it at the bartender, and walking out said, "Thanks for returning it to the AFP. I'll make sure it gets back to them, on that you have my word."

The terrified man and shaking man was left behind the bar. Branson stepped over the broken door. Tucking the gun in the back of his jeans, he mounted the bike. Seventy was his usual pace. The hospital wasn't far.

Approaching the hospital, he could see it was surrounded with police. Branson dumped the bike, hired a cab, and told him to wait. He paid him well to wait and the cabbie pulled the 'for hire' sign down. Branson strode down the corridor with his usual air of arrogance. A cop stopped him. Reese, who was standing nearby, noticed them talking.

"Let him through," she yelled at the policeman. "Where the hell have you been? Sage tried to reach you. We found out Kelly had your mobile phone and that the calls were only going there. You okay? Something wrong?"

"Plenty, but none of it is your business. Who was on duty last night?" He moved over to Kelly's hospital door window and looked though the glass.

"I was on duty and so was Agent Dean. You know, don't you? You knew before you ever called Kelly?" Their closeness intimidated her because she could feel he was still infuriated with her.

"Like I said, Marshal Wade, none of your business. But whatever happens to that girl in there is my business. I can't believe that I got her into this. So what has happened while I've been away?"

"You got her into it?" She raised her hands up. "I think that's in reverse. We suspect it was one of Walker's men. He doesn't want her around to testify; although he claims it was self-defense."

"Yeah, sure it was self-defense! He shot her with the same damn gun I gave her. Sage saw the whole thing. What about Sage? He gonna kill her, too? Walker's still in jail, right?"

"Yes, and that's where he'll stay 'til you're on the plane back home."

"You think I'll go without Kelly and my daughter? If that is what you think, then you're crazy." He scanned the corridor.

"As soon as Kelly is well enough, they'll fly you all back home. You want to see her? She's been asking for you."

"I want an explanation as to how one of Walker's men got to her. He said he'd get me. Walker knows that he can't frighten me, but he can sure scare Kelly and Sage. Where did Sage stay last night?"

"With Buchanan. He took a suite at the hotel next door. She was worried about you. I stopped by there before coming here." She noted his restlessness. "A man came in dressed as an orderly. Looked like any other hospital worker. He tried to suffocate her with a pillow. I happened to walk in at that very moment to take her some water…" She tried to finish the sentence but was nervous and moved uneasily from foot to foot.

"What the fuck was she doing alone in the room? Where is this damn goon now?"

"He's dead. I was lucky enough to kill him as he tried to escape."

"God almighty! Can't you people do anything right? I needed the son-of-a-bitch alive. If this is the way U.S. Marshals operate, I'll be glad to go back home and just work with my people."

"It couldn't be helped. We knew it was Walker's man. Who could he have been?"

Branson knew he intimidated Wade. He knew she found him attractive. Now he could see that the more he harassed her, the more she liked him. She had told him that it was nice to see a man who was commanding and strong, not like the 'yes' men she knew from before. Taking a moment, he studied Wade. She was only doing her job and had helped in the compound. Yes, she was attractive, but, then what about Kelly?

Branson, calming down a little, said to Reese, "I'm sorry. You're just in the line of fire right now. Another time and another place, and things may have been very different between us. I would have asked you for a date. But this is now, and it's never going to happen. Kelly and I have a bond. Thank you for being in the right place. I'm sure Kelly's glad you were here for her and Sage. Whatever happens from here on, is not your fault. Okay?"

She looked confused. "What are you going to do?"

"You know the answer to that. I'm going to take Kelly out of this damn hospital before they find a way to finish the job they attempted once already. You can either help me or turn your back and say you saw nothing. Up to you."

"You want Sage, too? I'll get her and we'll meet you in Kelly's room. How the hell are you gonna get her out of here? She's still on the critical list. You can't just pick her up and go. Or can you? Oh, I guess you can. I forgot who you are," she replied sarcastically.

"I have a cab waiting out back. Kelly's tough, she can make it. You know as much as I do about the paramedic side. You game to help?"

"Yes." For him she was willing to take a risk, a big risk.

"Okay. You quietly go and get Sage. Reese…" He took her by the arm. "Understand something will you? I am developing real feelings for Kelly that…that I'm not exactly understanding. I have to do what's best for her. I let one woman in my life down…"

"On my way," Reese said pulling her arm from his grasp.

She walked down the corridor with tears welling up in her eyes. "I know that feeling, Kane…only too well."

Branson pushed the door open to Kelly's room. Kelly looked up at him.

"Kane," she cried, and held her arms out to him sobbing.

"Darling, it's okay. I'm here and I told you I'd be back. God, hopefully you believed me. I won't leave you." He cradled her to him. "I should have stayed with you. I didn't think for one moment that your dad would send someone after you first. I thought he would try for me first. Anyway, I thought you would be safe away from me. Lord God, why weren't you safe in this hospital with a ton of security around you? Seems I was wrong, yet again. Becoming a habit of mine. I would have been ready for him. One more day was all I needed. But now, they have left me no other choice. You're coming with me."

Kelly stopped crying and her pale and drawn face started to brighten. Still Branson began to see how pretty she was. She didn't need makeup. Kelly was a natural beauty.

"Kane, what about all these tubes and the equipment? I won't die if you move me, will I?" The saline bag pumped away.

"Of course not. You think I'd risk that?"

Pulling her hospital gown down around her trim body, he made sure the bandages were tight. The bullet from the Glock had missed Kelly's vital organs, but the stitches would leave a bodily scar as well as a few mental ones. She looked away. He gently turned her face with his hand.

"Hey, don't worry about the scars. From here on, I'm the only one going to see them."

Kelly fell asleep for a second with his hand on her face. She had blinked awake again, and began murmuring softly while snuggling into the warmth of his palm. His masculinity felt good to her. She felt safe and secure.

"Kelly, I…never mind. Let's get you out of here. We've got the future and we can talk then when it's safer for you. These damn fools can't protect you and your father will try again, if only to get back at me.

Can you sit up while I unplug some of this stuff?" he asked her. "As long as you can breathe on your own, we can take care of the rest."

"We?" she asked for the first time hearing him get closer to her heart.

"Wade and I are going to make damn sure you get out of this mess alive. She went to get Sage who was with Buchanan. They should be here any minute. Give me the phone, and where's your purse?"

"It's in that drawer. It has my passport and like personal stuff in it. That's all I have left."

"You have a passport with you? My God, that's going to come in handy. Okay, let's get these blankets wrapped around you. Let me lift you up onto the side of this bed. You ready?"

She smiled at him. "Ready as I'm ever gonna be," she said hugging his neck and shoulder to help brace her during the move.

Branson tried to be gentle as he smothered her in the hospital blankets, but she cried.

"God, Kelly, I'm sorry," he said carefully removing her from the bed. Switching off the apparatus was not as hard as removing the tubes from her arms. However, he got them both completed.

He checked the front of her gown as the blanket enveloped her. There was no fresh blood. The door opened and Reese and Sage came to the hospital bed.

"Sage, I've got her ready. We're gonna take Kelly out of here. Make it look like there's a 'body' in the bed with the pillows. Cover it up. Make the thing look real."

Once she had finished with her 'body' Sage looked at Kelly, and, for the first time, she felt sorry. "You guys go. I'll stay here. Be a cover."

"The hell you will. It's too damn risky. We all have to go together, or not at all. Buchanan has to think that Walker's people took us and Walker's people have to think we disappeared into hiding. Only Walker knows we are cops. Stratton and the others don't. For now."

Branson lifted Kelly in his arms, setting her on the chair by the door. She weighed nothing. Reese pulled the blankets around her.

"You two go up towards the main doors. Distract them. Reese, you're good at distracting men. When you get outside call me. I'll take Kelly out the back way."

Branson moved to the door. "Reese, get Kelly's purse. Take along any painkillers you can find and anything else you think she may need. There has to be a drug cart nearby. See what you can find. If you have to, break the damn lock on the drug cart. Let's do it, get something, anything. I don't want her suffering more than needs be."

Reese stepped out into the corridor. Two cops were down the hall. She muttered under her breath.

Branson looked down at Kelly. She was biting on her lip to stop the pain. Tears streamed down her face. But she didn't cry out again. He held her tighter to him and he could feel a lump forming in his throat. What was this damn feeling anyway?

"It's okay, baby. It'll be okay. I promise." It had to be.

Marshal Wade made it down the corridor to where the cops stood.

"Just taking Sage Branson outside for some air. We'll be fine." And, the two women stood chatting a moment to the uniform guys.

"I'll be back, darling. Be calm, and hold on. You can do that right, baby?" asked Branson looking down at her face.

"Yes," Kelly murmured fading.

"Just be ready." And Branson left her. "Hold tight, baby," he muttered to himself.

He slipped out of the room and into the room next to hers that he had noticed was vacant. Bundling the sheets in a heap on the floor, he pulled his cigarette lighter from his pocket. He waited at the door and then noticed Reese standing close. She and Sage were busy keeping the two guys occupied.

"Burn, you-son-of-a-bitch," he said as they caught light. Branson slipped back next door.

"Okay, Kel, this it. Time to go."

He picked her up and waited.

"Fire! There's a fire down the hallway!" The two cops rushed to the scene.

Reese and Sage made a fast exit out the front door and ran towards the cab that Branson had paid to wait. That seemed hours ago now. It had only been thirty minutes.

"Keep the engine running," ordered Reese.

"What's goin' on, lady?" asked the cabbie.

"Nothing you need to worry about right now. Just rescuing someone from a fire."

"Don't see no blooming fire?"

"Hang onto your cap, you will."

She looked at every angle outside the cab. Her gun was ready just in case. Reese saw Branson running from the back entrance with a bundle in his arms. Alarm bells sounded. She propped open the door and helped him with the bundle.

"Step on it, mate," Branson bellowed. "We need to get the hell out of here," he said to the cabby.

To Reese, he said "I had another plan, but that just went down the toilet. If Walker isn't blamed for this, you and I, Reese, are on the run with a witness in the protection program."

"That had crossed my mind. But they won't think it's you if you go back up there later on and ask to see Kelly…"

"And become totally insane when they have no explanation of her whereabouts…"

"Exactly." Leaning over the seat, Reese smiled at him, and he mouthed a 'thank you' to her.

The hotel was way past the city limits and difficult to find. Branson paid the cabbie a handsome tip to keep quiet. Wade checked them into two double rooms and carried Kelly upstairs. Sage unlocked the door for them. He set her down on the bed. Kelly started to cry. Her feelings at last were coming unleashed. The pain was too strong for her to hold back any longer. Branson held her close and slowly pulled the blankets from around her. She was shaking. But the wound was still closed. Sage fluffed the pillows on the bed and placed them with care behind Kelly's back.

"Deep breaths, darling. That's it, long deep breaths. Reese brought some painkillers for you."

Reese opened her purse and pulled out a bottle. Popping off the top, she handed Branson a couple of pills. It had been crazy breaking the lock on the medicine cart door, but she had to do it or Kelly would have suffered for too long. Hell, she probably would not have even been able to sleep and then she wouldn't be able to get well. Even with her inexperienced education in medicine, she had made out the bottle of Darvocet pills right away... after all, everyone knows those are red. She had grabbed the whole bottle and now she was glad she had. Kelly would feel better soon.

"Here, take these."

Sage fetched one of the waters they'd bought on the way. They'd stopped for ten minutes to pick up some junk food and fruit. The hamburgers smelled pretty bad, but they were food. However, the food had only made Kelly feel sick.

Kelly swallowed the pills and settled down on the pillows. "Kane?"

"Yeah, what do you need baby? Want something to eat? More water?" He sat on the bed with her.

"You," she whispered.

"Yeah, right."

"Tell me how I look. I look a sight, don't I? No makeup and my hair looks like shit. Why'd you do this? Why risk everything? You could have gone after Pa and the others first." Her voice was so low that he had to bend his head to hear her.

He stroked her hair. "You look just fine to me, baby. You never needed the mask you were living underneath. We'll get your hair cut and buy you some clothes, then go places you've only dreamed of, Kel. You can come to the States with me. You said you had your passport."

"In my purse, wherever that might be."

"I have it," interjected Reese.

"Kiss me."

"What?"

"If I don't look bad, then kiss me."

Branson kissed her so lovingly on the lips that they seemed to become one right there in front of Sage and Reese both. All at once, he tasted the blood from when she bit her lip.

"Time for us to leave them, Sage. Let's go look at our room." Reese said glancing around Branson's hotel room. For a second, she thought it should have been her in that bed. "We'll be next door if you need us," she said, heading towards the door.

He turned his head towards the pair as they left.

"Thank you. Both of you. I am forever indebted to you, Marshal. And Sage, it's nice to have you back in my life again."

"Nice to be back… Dad," she said, and leaned down to her father and kissed him on the cheek.

Reese smiled and opened the door.

"See you in the morning, Kane. Kelly," and Marshal Reese Wade made her exit. When they had gone, Kelly snuggled into Branson as he kissed her again and again, they lay down on the bed. For five minutes, they held each other until finally, she dozed. He closed his eyes, and for the first time since his wife's death, he found a sense of peace. The evening took on shade and the bedroom filled with colors from the streetlights.

An hour or two passed, and Reese quietly opened the bedroom door. She looked in and saw the two of them lying there. How she wished she were the one in Branson's arms, and how strong her jealousy was becoming toward Kelly.

Quiet as a mouse, still feeling like an intruder, she moved through the room and closed the long, red curtains.

Branson opened his eyes and whispered to her, "Thank you."

"How is she?" came the subdued reply.

"She's sleeping soundly now. There's been no more bleeding. Kelly needs to eat. Have to get her some soup or something. Said the hamburgers made her feel sick. Could you see if the hotel has a kitchen?"

"And you, what would you like to have?"

"I already have what I want. Both of the girls are safe. Just get something for Kelly to help her regain her strength."

"Sage okay?" Branson asked.

Reese nodded.

"Don't leave her. She needs you. Would you have done that for me?"

Before he could answer the question, Kelly moaned in her sleep. Reese saw the look on Branson's face as he watched the girl open her eyes. If he could have gotten to Walker, he would have killed him with his bare hands.

"By the way, I saw the news on TV. Seems they said that persons unknown abducted a girl and a couple of agents from the hospital. A fire was blamed for causing the diversion. You're good, Branson, damn good."

"Thanks."

"Only problem is they'll be looking for us."

"Walker's people will. But Buchanan will know it was me. The television report was only a cover."

"How do you know that?"

"Because he knows how I operate and he'll look the other way. He'll figure I know what I'm doing." He smiled at her.

"I'll go get some food."

Three days they spent holed up in the hotel. Three long days and two nights. When Branson slept, the charge was put to Sage or Reese. Wade hated her shifts. On the third day, Kelly was more lucid. She sat up in the bed so that Branson could get some food in her. Sitting on the side of the bed, he spooned soup into Kelly trying to give her a little at a time.

"Steady on there, Kel. Don't eat so fast."

"I'm hungry and I'm a growing girl. Or hadn't you noticed?"

"Oh yeah, I noticed."

"Where we going? Back to your place? We have to fly or drive down?"

"Slow down there Kelly. You're moving a little fast. When you wake up, you wake up don't you? Which question would you like answered first? We're going to drive. Soon as you're fit. Couple more days. I'll get a car. Sage went with Wade to buy us some more clothes. You all need something to wear. Wonder how they're making out there? They should be pretty safe out there long as they stick together."

"Well, Wade hates me. And Sage, she'll bring me back something like she wears," she grimaced.

"Stop it. You two better learn to get along if you're going to live under my roof."

"We're doing what?" She stared at him and almost choked on the soup.

"You're both coming back with me. She'll have the spare room, and you and I the other bedroom. Come on now be a big girl and keep eating."

"You mean it? I thought you were just saying that before to change the subject or something. But you really do mean it." She reached up and touched the 'S' hanging round his neck. "I'll do right by you. I won't ever let you down. You can teach me to be what you want. To dress right and speak properly." Her eyes met his.

"You already have done right. And I don't care what you wear. I have a feeling for you, Kelly Walker, which I definitely shouldn't have. It's even one I can't seem to understand."

"Why not? Because I'm so young? What if I said I had a feeling for you, too? Would that be wrong? You knew I did back at the compound. When you made love to me, it was different. Not like the Johns I knew. But that's all behind me. Is it behind you?"

It hit him hard. "Yes. Now come on, eat."

He was having a hard time getting over her past and what she had become. But what she was, his daughter was, too; so, what was he supposed to do about it. Just then, Sage came through the doors with Reese following behind her.

"You awake, then? We brought you some clothes."

Sage set the packages on the bed. Branson helped her open them. One by one, she pulled the garments out of the bags. Her face was a study. Jeans, a sweater with a high neck, underwear, and some flat shoes.

"Told you," Kelly laughed, almost choking.

"Yeah, you did, darling. You did."

Branson held up the sweater. A dull brown... definitely not Kelly.

"What are you two laughing about now?" Sage asked. "I got what you told me to get, only I got more like I wear. Oh, I get it... very funny. Sage-type clothes, not Kelly clothes." She was beginning to warm to Kelly. "I got myself some things, too, and a pair of black jeans for you, Dad."

That irritated Reese even more. She could sense a closeness creeping in between the two younger women, which was managing to crowd her even further away from him.

"You used all my cash then? Did you spend that whole damn two hundred dollars I gave you? You leave me anything? I hope to god you did. Will you sit with Kelly while I go and pick up a car?"

He rose from the bed, kissed Kelly, grabbed his jacket and left the room.

"I'll take the packages back into our room, Sage. See you in a while."

When she had gone, Kelly turned to Sage.

"Ouch," she cried.

"What's wrong, Kelly?"

"Hurts when I laugh!" She held her chest.

"Kelly, can I ask you something?" Her tone was very serious.

"Sure, long as it's not about drink or cocaine. No allowed to do or talk about them anymore. Your dad's orders."

"No, neither of those things." Sage sat down on the side of the bed and played with the end of the blanket. "You won't just string my dad along will you? What I'm trying to say is... well, he loved my mother. I know what I accused him of doing; but he did love her. You've seen the chain round his neck. He thinks a lot of you…and I don't want him hurt anymore." She dropped her head.

"Listen to me." She moved her body nearer to Sage. "I ain't no saint, I know that. But Kane is good to me. He got me out of that place, he protected me, and I'm not about to let him down. I know he has some feelings for me. And I also know I'm young. I want to tell you something, but you have to promise not to tell him. You've been nicer to me lately, like well - maybe you don't hate me so much now. I'm gonna trust you with the secret. My feelings are running deeper. I fell a little in love with him, and the last few days made me realize that. You won't tell him, will you?"

"No, I won't. You have my word. Just make him happy again," Sage said, putting her hand on Kelly's.

Outside the door, someone else heard. And someone else hadn't promised not to tell him or anyone else. Reese turned away and went back to her room.

"Hi, girls. All set. We pick the car up tomorrow. They didn't have one 'til then. The place is right across the road from here. Where's Reese?"

"In her room. Why?" his daughter, Sage, inquired.

"Aw, probably nothing. But when I was outside, I saw her on the street at a pay phone. Listen, Sage. Don't tell her when we're leaving, okay? We'll just go, the three of us. It's not fair to involve her anymore. I think we'll leave earlier than we planned. We can get the car anytime after six o'clock. Wake up early in the morning, okay? Don't wake her, but listen for me. I'll tap on your door."

He moved to the window and peered through the shades.

"If that's what you want. Think I'll call it a night. I'm kind of tired. All that shopping." Sage was beginning to understand her father's ways, and didn't question his instincts anymore. She turned to Kelly, and for the first time, when she smiled at her she meant it. Kelly waited until Sage left.

"Something's wrong, isn't it? Is it Wade? You don't trust her anymore, do you?"

"No."

"Because of me?"

"Partly. Buchanan told me that she went undercover with Stratton. I'm beginning to wonder how undercover; and, yes, partly because of you, too. You want to take a bath or something?"

He sat on the bed by her and stroked her hair.

"That would be nice. I could put on that lovely nightshirt that Sage bought for me and we could watch some TV," she said with a smirk.

"Your father won't give up, especially if he knows where we are. If Wade is double-dealing chances are they know now where we are. She knows we can't be touched here. Too many people in the hotel. She will have told them we are leaving the day after tomorrow. We'll be gone by first light." Sliding his arms underneath her, he carried her into the bathroom and closed the door behind them. He left her nightshirt in the bag.

CHAPTER 10

The sunrise over Brisbane was stunning. Branson watched it from the balcony chair, where he could see the lamplight dimming and the day heralding a new life. Sitting in a bathrobe, he sipped coffee and smoked a cigarette. He glanced back into the bedroom and could see Kelly sleeping. It seemed a shame to wake her. Another few minutes wouldn't hurt. Last night, he had bathed her and they'd made gentle but meaningful love. Washing Kelly had aroused him, and she had enjoyed it. He kissed her, and the sexual tension heightened until once more intimacy brought them together. She was so young and yet so much of a woman. It was a good feeling. If only all mornings could be like this one. He set the cup down and went inside the room.

"Kelly, darling, wake up. We have to go. I'm not sure it's safe to stay her any longer." He sat on the bed while stroking her hair. "If Reese has, for some reason, betrayed us, Walker will send people soon." And he paused. Maybe it wasn't Walker. Maybe she had called Stratton. "Come on, baby. Let me help you to get ready."

Kelly interjected, "I'm feeling a little stronger now. I can try to get ready myself, but thank you for being… well you know, ready always to help me like you are."

Branson looked at her to see if he felt like she was going to be able to get dressed on her own and said, "I'm gonna run over and get the car. It should be there by now. I'll wake Sage on the way. Need to get her in here and ready to go with us."

Kelly nodded. She wasn't quite awake but had started getting out of the bed.

He tapped lightly on Sage's door. His bleary-eyed daughter peeked out.

"Get your things together and come next door. You can shower in our room. If Reese wakes, tell her you're going to help Kelly while I sleep some…and hurry," he whispered and gently closed the door. The hotel was still quiet. Branson made his way outside, crossing the road to pick up the rental car.

Kelly waited for Branson to return. While getting dressed, she and Sage had decided to turn the television on to one of the local stations. They couldn't believe what had come on the TV. He slipped into the warmth of the room.

"Kane," Kelly said as he entered the room again. "I think you need to look at what is on the news. Oh, my God! Look at the television."

The volume of the set was low, but the picture was clear. Branson sat down on the bed and within a second or two of watching, groaned. Walker's picture flashed across the news. They just said he's out on $500,000 bond. Kelly's father, the bastard, was out of jail. Shit, this was only something a good attorney or a crooked judge could arrange. For a couple of seconds, Branson couldn't breathe. He didn't hear the door open.

"Isn't that…?" Sage asked.

"Yeah, sure is," replied her father.

There was a fire in his eyes as his mind raced. Branson knew as soon as Walker got out he'd try to get to Miles Stratton. Stratton was Walker's way out, and Stratton was also the first person Walker would tell that the infamous Mr. Kane was a cop if Reese hadn't already divulged that piece of information. Right now, he was relying on Reese's feelings for him clouding her judgment, just a little.

"Sage, you ready? Come out of the bathroom and help Kelly get dressed while I get the things together." From his bag, he pulled the .38 that the bartender had lifted for him.

"Where'd you get that?" Kelly asked.

"Does it matter? We need it for protection and it's not traceable… it has never been used." Branson pushed the gun down inside the back of his jeans.

Stumbling out of the bathroom, Sage was frantically pulling on her clothes and trying to help Kelly at the same time. She began to get a little frustrated.

"Dad, can you help me with Kelly?"

He pulled the sweater over Kelly's head and zipped up her jeans. Catching the look in her eyes, Branson tried to ignore it. It was one of hopeful expectation.

"Got your things? Sage, if you'd carry Kelly's too, that would be help-ful for us to get out of here faster. Let's go."

Checking the room one more time, he closed the door behind him. Branson ushered the girls down the stairs. Kelly leaned against him, and he supported her with his arm. Stopping at the hotel reception desk, Branson paid the bill in cash and added plenty to thank them for their cooperation. Thankfully, he carried plenty on him at all times. The car was parked outside, a green Mercedes.

"You girls climb in the back, and Kelly… be careful."

Within seconds, they were out on the highway, moving down the road at seventy miles an hour and rising. Branson drove fast. He was certain where Walker might be headed. There were only a few private airfields in that part of Brisbane, and Walker would have to wait to be picked up and taken there. He sped through the streets, hardly stopping for red lights. They were an inconvenience he didn't need.

"Slow down," Sage yelled. "This isn't doing Kelly much good."

"What I intend to do will make Kelly feel much better."

"Do you know where you're going?" Sage asked her father, feeling for the first time that he may be leading them into some danger.

"I think I know. I brought Walker here by chopper the other day to meet with Stratton. At the time, it seemed like their pickup point. Strat-ton met him here before going back to the commercial flight."

Branson made a left out on to a country road and stopped the car.

"Why'd you stop here?" his lover asked, finally lifting her head up from the back seat where she had been lying down.

"I thought you were dozing." He turned to Kelly.

"How the hell can I be anything but awake with you driving? You trying to kill me or my pa?" She grimaced.

"Yeah, and who was the one that didn't think of that last night in the bathroom, Kelly. Shit. Sage, I'm sorry I don't mean to blast the relation-ship under your nose." Why didn't he use his brain occasionally?

"Don't apologize. I can't pretend it wasn't a shock, but I have to get used to it if I'm going to be living with you guys. Actually, I do want us all to get along and get to know each other better."

Branson reached over and squeezed his daughter's hand. "We wait here."

"We're in the middle of nowhere." Sage looked out of the windows. "Why would we wait here, Dad? Isn't this crazy?"

"No! We are where we need to be! Now, we are all here together and we're gonna be just fine. You, little lady, just relax! There's an airstrip a couple of miles from here. If I remember right, this is the only road in and Walker has to come here."

Trees surrounded the road and it was easy to pull the car into the shade with an almost camouflage maneuver.

Sage whispered to Kelly, "I hope he's right, for all our sakes."

"Yeah," Kelly said lying down in the back seat. She leaned on the leather and within seconds, she dozed.

Branson closed his eyes. An hour went by. He wondered what Reese Wade was doing. She had to be the one who had betrayed him; not a pleasant thought if it was Reese. He was on his own, more or less. Buchanan would take steps against her. Betrayal was something that no department would tolerate. And yet, he felt guilty. His thoughts were rudely interrupted.

"Dad! Look! There's a car coming."

Looking in the rearview mirror, he could see behind them there was a black sedan. Branson started the engine of the Mercedes. No one would be looking for him in the car he was driving. He let the car get closer without reacting.

"You two, keep down. Sage, make sure she is safe back there. Cover her with something. Then, you slip down in your seat so they won't see you either."

The car got directly behind them and then went past. Instinctively, he knew who was in it. Using some discretion and some copy sense, he pulled out into the road and kept his distance. Reaching into the back of his jeans, he withdrew the gun and laid it on the seat beside him. The car, which was now in front, picked up speed. Branson did the same.

"You two. Hold on!"

Pulling alongside the sedan, Branson turned his head and looked directly at the passenger. Walker started yelling at his driver. Branson managed to think quickly and cause his car to bump the sedan. Walker first looked pissed; but after a few good car slams, he began to look terrified. Branson saw Walker's expression change with each metal screeching slam.

Walker looked over into the back of the Mercedes.

The second Branson saw this, he yelled, "Kelly, get down, damn it! What the hell did I tell you?" Kelly had lifted her head a little to see if they were going to crash. Fear was griping her. Although she trusted Kane she did not trust her dad, or his goons.

Branson swerved into the sedan. Its driver was not as experienced enough to do cop style battle. Therefore, the only thing he did was increase his speed to an unhealthy ninety-mph. Branson easily kept pace. Repeatedly, he sideswiped the sedan until the doors of the sedan were dented in the frame. Then he dropped back. The sedan picked up speed and the Mercedes fell behind.

"Dad, slow down! For God's sake, you'll kill us all."

Kelly almost sitting up again said, "No, he won't. Just let him do what he has to do. He has to get my Pa."

Sage glanced at her. There was an unmistakable glitter of revenge in her eyes. The same looks that her father wore. She looked away, disturbed, and in fear for her life.

Sick of the bantering, he decided to pursue again. Branson hit the bumper of the other car with a hard jolt, causing the sedan to swerve into the grass to a place where it slid down a muddy bank. This time, the jolting impact caused the engine to stall. The sedan came to a grinding halt. Branson slammed on the brakes, grabbed his gun, and leaped out of the car on a fast pursuit. He was running for "their lives!"

Sliding down the grass, he reached the car before anyone had time to move. The driver was out cold; blood was streaming down his forehead.

Branson spotted Walker and walked around to his side of the car. "You. Get the fuck out of there. It's just you and me." The second Walker opened the door; he moved to brandish the piece in Walker's face. "You think I'm just going to shoot you; right here, right now?

Oh no, that's too easy. Think again, Walker!" Branson took the butt of his pistol and slammed it against Walker's cheek, screaming, "Get out of the car you fucking goon! Now!"

"No," he replied shakily. He clutched his cheek. Blood seeped through his fingers.

"Get down on your knees and crawl. Move, you gutless bloody wonder." He half-turned his head.

Hearing a commotion back at the Mercedes, he yelled, "Kelly, get over here."

Walker looked up at his daughter, standing there supported by Sage. Hatred boiled, causing the girls to glare at Walker.

"Kelly, you won't let him kill me. Now will you? Remember me, I'm your Pop. I'm your blood." He groveled in the dirt. His pleading was pathetic.

"Mother was my blood, but you killed her just the same, you fucking bastard. And I'm not going to grow up like her, running from man to man at your request. Kane's my protector now. And he's gonna protect me against you and your fucking goons. Kane won't let no one like you touch me, not ever again." Her arm tightened around Sage's shoulder, as tears caressed her cheeks. She continued yelling at her father, "Blood ain't important to you. You never cared I was blood when you used me, now did you?"

Still pleading, Walker said to his daughter, "He's just a cop. Kelly, now think about it girl. What the hell do you need with a cop? Goddamn it, and I'm your pa and you need to come with me." He squatted on the ground.

"You ain't my pa, not a real pa. You never have been. What pa does his own daughter?"

Sage flinched. Kelly turned to Branson and looked him square in the eyes.

"Kane, you finish my pa however you want. Don't spare my feelings, 'cause I don't have any for that piece of shit," she said with a dead expression.

"You heard the lady. Get in the car." Branson grabbed him by the jacket. "Get in the damn car; in the front next to the driver. Put the seatbelt on." Branson surveyed the scene, with a bit of a smirk. "Been drinking have we? I see that you have bottles in the back." He grabbed a couple bottles and tossed them into Walker's lap. "Now you have them in the front. Celebrating, were we? Go on… keep drinking." Walker timidly grabbed one of the half-empty wine bottles and took a swig. "Now pour the rest down you."

Walker shakily tipped the wine down the front of himself.

"Good, that's good. Keep going. Pour the whole contents of the bottles down you."

Branson kept the gun on him. He waited for a few seconds, pondering the next move, savoring the moment. Sage watched in horror. From his pocket, Branson produced his lighter.

"Kelly," he yelled back to the girls, "You got a piece of material you don't want? Handkerchief or something."

She opened her purse and tossed a handkerchief down the hill. Branson caught it. He held the white cotton material over the flame. The tip caught light.

"This is for my wife and your daughter." Branson held the flame close to Walker's face. "One last thing. How could you try to kill Kelly? Your own fucking daughter?"

Walker looked up at Kelly. Her face was blank, in contrast to her father's face, which was contorted in total fear.

"Goodbye, pa," she said as she tipped her head and moved her hand as it waving goodbye.

Branson slammed the door shut. It locked into the bent and twisted frame. Branson held the cloth until it was engulfed in flames, then he tossed it through the open window onto the back seat.

"Goodbye, Mr. Walker. May you rest in hell."

"Don't do this! For God's sake. You'll pay in hell for this too, you son-of-a-bitch." Walker was still hysterical. He pushed on the door, which wouldn't budge. His arms flayed through the window. "Kelly, help me!" he screamed.

"Dad, don't do it!" Sage begged. "Let the man out. Please dad, for God's sake; don't have this murder on your hands too."

Kelly leaned back against the green Mercedes. She watched her father do everything he could to free himself from the burning car. The dark nights of terror flooded back through her brain. Walker's face contorted in total fear, his hands pressing against the door. He banged on it. He tried to squeeze out through the window, but he was too fat and stuck in the frame. The back of the car was lit up, and smoke billowed out.

Sage let go of Kelly, who walked a couple of feet from her and then promptly threw up. She could still hear her dad's screams as his life ended.

"You might as well stop trying to get out, you son-of- a-bitch. Your death is now!" Branson held the gun high, and he moved back to the girls. And then, it was over; the car disappeared in a ball of flame straight into hell; Kelly watched. She had watched her father beg, just like her mother had before he beat her. Now she saw the whole picture. Branson slid his arms around Kelly and she clung to him, with her eyes still fixed on 'the inferno.'

"How could you do that?" Sage moaned. "I don't understand you. In fact, I don't quite get either of you."

Branson turned to his daughter. "You never saw your mother lying in the morgue. This wasn't hard at all compared to that. This was an accident. You saw the car run off the road. Drinking and driving. You saw that, didn't you? Just ask Kelly. She saw the same."

"Kane's right. Just ran off the road. Poor folk just burned alive before we could get to them." Her eyes never faltered in their commitment. "Pity we couldn't help them, but they only had them selves to blame. When will people learn?" Her face was deadpan. The relief in her mind was overwhelming. She collapsed into Branson's arms. He picked her up and carried her to the backseat of the car.

"Baby, hey, come on. For you, you're safe from him now, it's over."

He stroked her face, and wiped away her tears of relief.

"Can we go to your home now? Can we do that? Please? I want to leave this god-forsaken place now."

"It's about five hundred miles, darling. The whole damn Gold Coast is in between. I guess we could fly, if you want to go that quickly. For you, I'd do that."

"No, just take time and drive. We can stop places on the way. I don't feel too good about flying." She shifted uneasily on the seat.

"You okay? Does it hurt?"

"Yes. It hurt's more than you'll ever know," she whispered.

Sitting beside her on the car seat, he leaned and asked her, "What, Kelly? What did you say?"

"Said I know it'll take a few hours, but can we drive?"

"Sure, whatever you want." He looked around for Sage. "Sage, I need to do something. Would you please come back here and sit with her? Do you hear me? Don't look at me like that, damn it. If you could have seen your mother…"

"You keep saying that, but now I'm looking at you… my dad… who murdered a man in that car."

"Actually that's the third."

"What?" She stared in horror.

"Walker is the third. Pierce and Stevens left for a better place."

"Stevens and who? You're no better than they are. You know that? Except you have a license to kill, but not to murder!"

"So you gonna turn your father in, Sage Branson? If you are, you better remember what I told you. You'll have me to deal with," Kelly whispered her threat to Sage.

Branson looked from one woman to the other. He was missing something. Kelly had become his angel… an angel on his shoulder.

But the look stayed on Sage's face, who didn't answer. Branson made a call to the local police and reported that a car had careened off the road and was now on fire.

"My name? Branson. Agent Kane Branson." He hung up the phone. "We have to wait 'til the police get here. They won't be long. Kelly, you know what to say, right? Just be silent, would you?"

She nodded. Sage sat down on the grass by the car.

"Sage? Sage, you want me to go to jail? That it? If you can't lie, don't say anything, right?"

No reply.

Kelly flashed her eyes at Sage and she turned to her lover. "Does she know what to do? I don't think she does, Kane?"

"She'll come through, won't you, baby? You are a Branson, and they look out for their own. Actually, you don't have to lie. You weren't watching, so you didn't see anything."

Sage knew what she had to do. This man Walker had killed her mother. Kelly had warned her not to cross Branson, and she had meant every word. It was obvious, even to Sage, that Kelly did indeed love her father. She would go to hell and back for him. The fact was, she just had.

Branson lit a cigarette. The rings floated on the air and escaped into the atmosphere. Sirens echoed over the hill. Branson turned to greet them. Kelly watched him. Something was wrong. She had been with too many men not to know. He looked different. The beard, maybe that was it. Maybe she liked him better without the beard. No, that wasn't what was different. Hate was consuming him with a different type of 'inferno.'

The cars stopped, but the flashing lights continued. Branson stepped away from the Mercedes. He pulled his shades from his jacket and hid his lying eyes.

"You Agent Branson?" asked the uniformed cop. "May I see your badge?"

Branson froze. Buchanan had his badge. Shit! Force of habit had made him say 'Agent'. He had the .38. He could produce that, but it wouldn't bear his serial number. What a mess. Another siren heralded a higher authority. The car stopped, and a man climbed out.

"Hey, boss," Branson called. "This officer wants to see my badge."

"Agent Branson is one of mine. He's undercover. He's also a pain in the ass; but, one of mine all the same."

Buchanan flashed his credentials.

"Sir, I'm sorry. I should have realized that. I just have to get some details."

"I'll do that, officer. Get that damn fire under control," said Buchanan.

"Yes, sir." The officer moved away.

"Thanks for coming just in the nick of time. How did you know I'd be here?" Branson asked.

"Not hard to figure out. When I knew Walker had made bail, I knew you'd go after him. We picked Wade up, so we kind of knew where you were the whole time."

"You know me that well, boss?" Branson questioned.

"Apparently," he continued. "Seems she was more undercover than even her own people knew. Wade was posing as Stratton's woman for some time, but she was also feeding him information. But for some reason, she hasn't yet disclosed your identity to Stratton. Making money both sides of the fence, though. She helped you by making sure Walker didn't know who she was. Lucky for her, that Stratton never mentioned her to Walker. Everything was going well for Wade until you came along. It was then that she took a liking to you and you didn't even notice her. Evidently, you had someone else on your mind."

Buchanan continued explaining to Branson, "When she called Walker's connections, she told them where to find the girls, but left your name out of her disclosure. In some strange way, she was still protecting you. She knew the airstrip you'd flown to with Walker. Guess you told her. I knew you didn't have any damn badge and thought you might need it. Branson's badge, well you know, I just thought about it, is all. I see you have the girls with you. You know you have a material witness, don't you?"

"Yeah, I know. But she came voluntarily. That go in my favor?" He laughed and pulled the shades from his eyes.

"You look like a man with a conscience. Want to talk about it? Or was it just an accident?"

"You better be off. Best ask my companions. I was pretty busy driving."

"Maybe I will. Or you can take the time to tell me the truth. Save me asking them and putting them through the details all over again. Probably wasn't a pleasant ride for them, you know. I can smell burning rubber from your car, and were those indent marks on that car before you rented it?" He glanced at the road. "The tire marks on the road tell a different story."

Branson looked his boss straight in the eyes. "An accident. Nothing more."

"Damn man, think about it. If you lie now, I cannot protect you down the road. That's the truth, right?"

"Yes." Branson stared straight ahead. He couldn't look Buchanan in the eyes.

Buchanan had been a cop long enough to know when someone was lying to him. In addition, he had known Branson long enough to see he was up to something, but wasn't coming clean about it just yet.

"Then I'll have to ask Kelly what she saw," Buchanan said, moving toward the car to approach Kelly. He sat inside the back of the car. "Miss, I need to ask you what happened here. Do you know who was in that car?"

"Yes." She glanced at Branson to see if it was going to upset him for her to talk to Buchanan.

Branson shook his head slightly.

"How do you know?" Buchanan asked.

"Saw them go by." She stared straight at him. "Was my pa and some of his goons. They seemed to be drinking and acting all crazy. Like maybe they were high on something."

"How do you know all that?" he continued.

"Know my pa." She almost gave too much away.

"Then what happened?"

"Car flew off the road, landed down there. Somehow it burst into flames."

"Somehow, Miss Walker? It wasn't helped?" Buchanan asked.

"Helped? What's that supposed to mean? The car was out of control. They were going too fast, as if they were in a hurry to get somewhere. The driver was skidding all over the damn road. Shit, they came close to killing us by hitting our car a couple of times. Did you see our car?" Kelly said, as she fiddled with the seat belt.

Buchanan noticed.

"You don't seem too upset for a girl that just lost her father?"

"Are you upset at losing him, a criminal like he was?" she retorted. "Mr. Buchanan, I need to get out of the car for a few moments."

"Why?" he asked.

She needed Branson's reassurance. Kelly was close to breaking and she knew it. Tears welled in her eyes.

"Kelly's upset and naturally so. Can't you let her be?" Sage came to her aide. "My father must have told you what happened. Kelly's still weak from that no good piece of shit trying to end her life. Now, we have to take care of her." She leaned in the car from the other door and encircled Kelly with her arms.

Branson stared at them.

With the car door still open, Buchanan kept asking questions of Sage. "And you, Sage. I'm sure the answer will be the same, so I won't even bother asking. You heading back to Brisbane or someplace else?"

"Planned on driving back to Sydney by the scenic route, unless there's anything else you need to know," Branson said while interrupting Buchanan's questioning of his daughter.

"Not right now. But make sure these girls stay with you. Kelly is still our witness, and the rest of the group is out there somewhere. Meaning you still aren't safe and especially here."

"I plan to do that. They won't leave me, neither of them. Kelly still needs care."

"Yeah, I heard how she's still so sick. Marshal Wade made that very clear. Apparently she was outside the door and heard what Kelly said."

"What she said? What did she say?" Branson was puzzled.

"Let's walk over to the scene." They strode side by side across the grass. "Kelly told Sage that's she's fallen in love with you. By the look on your face you didn't know she has, did you?"

"No," he whispered. "I didn't. I just thought…"

"Be careful, man. You're going to end up getting yourself killed over that girl. Shit, you know not to mix business with pleasure. Have you gone and lost your ability to stay a professional cop through and through? Damn, you are Branson and you're from Branson's Country. Are you gonna blow all that over a damn girl?"

"Nah, not me. I have a score to settle, remember?" He looked back towards his car. "Oh, I have a gun that should now belong to the AFP. Got it from a pub. Belonged to someone once."

"Keep it. Just give me the registration number from it before I leave here. I'll get it transferred. Go home, Kane. I know you planned on going after these guys, but think about it carefully. That was before you were reunited with your daughter, and before Kelly. Remember, she is under your protection."

"Did Kelly really say that?" He was having a hard time with the statement.

"According to Wade. When she heard Kelly tell Sage about loving you, Wade knew it was all over."

"Wasn't anything between Wade and me. I thought about it more than once, but Kelly was and is on my mind. What will happen to her? It's partly my fault."

"Your fault she sold them out? Don't think so," answered his boss.

Branson shrugged his shoulders and flicked his cigarette to the ground. He stamped on it as if he was snuffing out another life. Buchanan noticed it and thought he'd say one more thing to the troubled cop.

"Please, back off. Let the law do their jobs? Go home, make a life with that girl, if you have to… just back off is all I'm telling you."

"Are you saying I have to do this? You think she's a charity case for me? Goddamn, you just told me the kid's in love with me. But, I'm in my fifties and well, she's my daughter's age."

"Please, Branson, go home and stay there. I do not want to order you, and I don't want to arrest you. I have looked the other way, but you're making that harder to do. Leave the rest to us. It's our job." He kept stride with Branson.

"Your job? In the first place, if you had protected Kelly at the hospital, I wouldn't be in this fucking mess." Branson turned on his heel.

"Branson, don't you damn well walk away from me! Branson!"

He kept walking and climbed in the Mercedes.

"Dad, what were you arguing about with Buchanan? You look so angry."

Branson turned his head and stared at Kelly. "When we get home, you and I have something to discuss." Then he looked to the road.

Kelly could see his eyes in the rear-view mirror. He was glowering through the windshield. Branson swung the car out onto the tarmac, turning the wheel sharply and hit the highway doing 70. Anger showed through. Anger, and desperation to know the truth.

As his pace settled, Sage dozed with the motion of the car. The radio in the car was now playing a tune that seemed to be fitting for the day. "Killing Me Softly" by Roberta Flack was probably not just a coincidence.

Maybe it was an omen. Maybe he better make damn sure the rest of his plan kept them safe.

"Kane?" Kelly whispered.

"I said when we get home." Irritated, he stared ahead letting her know he was no longer in the mood to talk. He just wanted to think and listen to the song.

"You're not going to talk to me all the way to Sydney?"

"Yes, but not right now and not about that. Now please sit back, Kelly, and just listen to the song with me."

She lay back in the seats and sunk into an uneasy slumber. He could hear her breathing behind him. Looking at the gas tank, Branson noticed it was close to empty.

About an hour passed when he decided to wake them. "Sage, wake up. Help Kelly get up and out of the car. It's time we took a break at least to go to the bathroom, while I get some gas."

Kelly turned to Sage. "He knows I'm in love with him. It was for me to tell him. He won't speak to me. You told him. You hate me that much?"

"I didn't tell him anything, but I think I know who did. My roommate."

"Wade? How the hell would she know? Unless she was listening. Oh, my God. She turned us in because of that?"

"Isn't so much you she hates, as much as it's my father she wanted. Didn't you see it? I guess you didn't. You had other things to think about at the time. You need to pee?"

Kelly shook her head. She watched him pumping gas. He saw her watching him and stuck his head inside the car.

"It's a long ride back. You sure you don't need the bathroom? I can carry you in there."

"Okay." She relented because she just wanted him to hold her.

Branson finished filling up the tank and moved to her door. He slid his arms under her, looking into her face.

"Do you?" he asked.

"Do I what?" Kelly played with the lapel on his jacket.

"Are you in love with me?"

She lowered her eyes. "Yes." Tears dropped silently down her cheeks.

He cleared his throat. "Don't ever cry, whatever happens. Promise?"

"Promise." She let the tears flow down her cheeks as her arms were now around Branson's neck.

He kissed her cheek and got a slight taste of the salty tear. Then he set her down by the ladies' room. She seemed so frail, as she wiped away the tears with her sleeve. Kelly disappeared inside the bathroom.

He looked up to the stars. It was all wrong, all of it. None of this felt normal. He gnashed his teeth. Still two to go.

While he waited, he fetched food and plenty of Cokes from the store. Branson sat in the car and waited until his girls appeared back around the corner. They climbed back in the car. Kelly looked tired and pinched.

"You okay, baby?"

'I'm fine, Kane." Kelly rested on the leatherwork.

"Got some food. Not much, but better than nothing."

After the girls ate, Branson munched on chips from the bag. He handed some to Sage, but Kelly refused because she still didn't feel much like eating. The hotdog smells made her feel sick.

"How much farther, Dad?"

"Two or three hours, maybe four, and then we should see the outskirts of Sydney. You guys wanted to drive back. Would have been quicker by plane. You want to stay over somewhere tonight?"

Kelly wanted to stop right there.

"No, let's go on, unless you are tired. Can I sit up there by you? I'm not in the least bit tired, and I could help keep you awake," lied Kelly.

"Sure, baby."

She snuggled down on the leather seat next to him. Not thirty miles down the road, Kelly had fallen across him as he drove with her head propped on his arm. Time to rest for a while. He pulled over, shut the engine off and leaned back in the seat. He pulled Kelly to him and she murmured in her sleep. She felt warm to him, and how he wished they were on their own in the car. However, there would be time for that later. First, he figured he would like to continue getting to know her as a woman instead of a girl.

Branson hadn't meant to sleep so long. Nevertheless, when he awoke, it was pitch black and the road looked deserted. He looked at his watch, its face illuminated in the dark. Almost midnight. Damn and he'd wanted to be home by now. Slowly and quietly, he pulled back out onto the road, and this time he kept driving until he reached home.

Pulling in the driveway of his huge and rich, ornate looking apartments, he turned the headlight off. "Ladies, would you care to join me?"

Sage opened her door and climbed out. Kelly looked directly ahead.

"This where you live?" she asked in a slight shock.

The apartments were floodlit and looked good, even to him. It seemed a long time since he had been home. If ever he really gave up being a cop, he had this to fall back on. For once, he thanked his grandfather for leaving him some money. He'd invested well with this property.

"This is what I own."

"You mean the whole apartment?"

"No. I mean the block."

"The whole damn block? You own it? What the hell are doing being a cop?"

"Inheritance played a big part and I love…loved… being a cop," he said while digging in his pockets for his keys. "Normally I ride out the back door on the bike, but the Mercedes is too big to go inside."

"Come on, be serious, Dad. You don't actually ride a motorcycle, do you?"

"Sure do, baby."

He carried Kelly from the car to the door. Sage opened it. A spacious room greeted them, and in the corner sat his bike.

"Can I sit on it?" Kelly asked. "I'll be fine. I've ridden many times before."

Sage wandered around the room. "Great-grandpa left you money? And you bought this? Did my mother live here?"

"Yes, yes, and yes. We bought it for us to live in when retirement came. Well, it will be yours eventually… and… your mom loved it here. Said it made her feel young and she sometimes rode the bike with me."

"Then I won't sit on it…" Kelly moved away.

"Don't be crazy." He lifted Kelly onto the silver bike.

"Think I'll go find a room to sleep in; which one would you call mine?" Sage asked her father.

"Second door on the left."

She left her father and Kelly alone.

"Kelly, I have to know. Buchanan told me. Do you really mean it?"

She rested her hand on his shoulder and played with his collar. "Yes, I meant it. I've lost everything else, and I don't want to lose you, too. Will this change things between us? I mean, it's okay that you do not feel the same kind of feelings that I do. As long as I can share your life… and your bed."

He put his fingers on her lips. "Move forward." He climbed up behind her and encircled her waist with his arms. "I didn't say that I didn't feel anything for you. What I had said was that you should have your own life. Go meet some young guy, get married, have kids. Have a nice house and a man that works a secure job from nine to five each day. I am not sure I could give you that type of life. What I'm sure about is that right now is I can give you a place here with me. One of the problems will be though with me being a cop and all, you'll never know where I am. Kids, maybe we could have 'em. Who knows? You could give up drinking. And, like I told you, no drugs."

Branson stopped long enough to think a second and take a deep breath. He looked in Kelly's eyes and said, "But, Kelly, if I do make a commitment to you, then I don't expect to find you in anyone else's bed. If you can play by these rules, then you can live my life with me. Tell me now."

"You missed something. Do you feel anything for me?" she whispered.

"I feel for you. I care about you, yes, darling, I sure do." Branson looked almost embarrassed.

"Will you tell me what I want to hear, please?"

"You're so young, damn it. How the fuck can I tell you what you want to hear. Those exact words are just not easy for me after all I've been through in the last few years?" His arms constricted in anger. Watching Kelly's reaction, he could tell he had forgotten what all she had been through the last few years. He grabbed her and held her close to him.

"Tell me or I'll leave right now. And while we're on that subject, you give up smoking if I give up drugs. And we both stop drinking. That's my terms." She made a move to leave.

"Damn you, Kelly. All right, I'm in love with you. Happy now?"

She smiled at him. "Where's your bedroom? Or, is it our bedroom now?"

CHAPTER 11

The weeks passed in a blur until Buchanan came to visit. Even with Walker dead, Kelly wasn't safe. Not yet.

"Mr. Buchanan, how nice to see you. Dad's on the patio with Kelly. Would you like something to drink?" She was 'Miss Politeness' itself.

"No, thanks. How is he?" Buchanan stammered. "I mean…how's he really doing? He and Kelly. You think he's okay here? Maybe he won't go to the States."

"Sorry to disappoint you. He booked three seats for the weekend flight. We will be with him. Figures it's safer."

Shocked, Buchanan stepped out onto the balcony.

Dressed in blue jeans and a tight cream sweater, Kelly looked very different. Gone were the thick layers of makeup, revealing pretty eyes and fresh peachy skin. Her eyes were no longer filled with despair and her hair shone in the light.

"Kelly, nice to see you. You look a lot healthier. Branson, can I talk to you alone?"

He lounged back in the chair. "Whatever you have to say, you can say in front of her."

"She's a credit to you. And you look ten years younger. Kelly, I congratulate you. You're obviously good for my agent."

"Cut the crap. I'm not *your* agent. Just say what you want and stop this bullshit."

Buchanan sat down and pulled Branson's badge out of his pocket. He fingered it gently. "They want you to either take this back or resign. The department wants you back on a case. No half measures. They're protecting their own. You've seen the cops outside the whole time, right?"

"Yeah, I've seen them, for as much good as they'd do us. Stratton and King won't come here. I have to go to them." Branson stood up and looked out over the city, the lights catching his eyes. "Okay, you want an answer? Not a difficult decision. I resign."

Kelly stood up and slid her arm around him. "Don't do that for me."

"It's not for you, but for myself. I won't be dictated to by anyone. It's my way or no way."

"Then I'm sorry, Agent Branson. I'm afraid I must ask for the gun."

Branson held up his sweatshirt from the back of his jeans. "Here take it. Thing's a damn peashooter anyway. Got myself a real gun back inside the apartment."

Branson turned away. He had just lost his country, his small part of Australia, which was now his badge, his gun, almost everything; except for Kelly and his daughter.

He walked inside, found the whiskey bottle, poured himself a drink, and took it to his room.

"I need to go after him. Goodbye, Mr. Buchanan. We'll meet again."

Was this the same Kelly? All brand new, thought Buchanan.

She passed Sage on her way through the patio.

"Why did you do that?" Sage began. "After all the years he gave to you, and the busts he made. Doesn't that count for anything? He was actually beginning to be happy. Kelly is a big help to him. We all get on well. Why now? Is it because of his trip to the States?"

"Nothing to do with it. I tried to get the department to hold off longer. Your father is so stubborn." Buchanan tucked the gun away. "If he needs me, he has my direct line. And tell him I can't lie if I'm asked questions, not anymore. I know he killed Walker. We all know." Buchanan heaved a sigh.

"Goodbye, Mr. Buchanan." She escorted him to the door.

"He's taught you well. Just watch out for him. I may have been his boss, but he was also my friend." Buchanan looked sad at the prospect of losing him.

"By the way, what happened to Reese Wade?"

"U.S. marshal's office sent for her. Heard nothing since. Fortunately, it didn't have any direct results on the three of you." He opened the door.

"So where is she now?"

"I honestly don't know." Buchanan was only telling half the truth.

"Goodbye, commander," Sage said, closing the door behind him.

"Kane, come on. You don't need that. You made me stop. Said it goes for you, too."

She sat down on the bed next to him and removed the glass from his fingers. Slowly, he turned his head to look at her.

"You know I have to finish it, with or without the law. You understand what it's like to hate beyond question. Only you."

"I also know what it's like to love beyond question. You taught me that."

She took his face in her hands and put her lips on his. Letting her hands slide down to the edge of his sweater, Kelly slipped her hands underneath the thick wool. His skin was sensuous to her touch. Even more demanding was his kiss. There seemed to be a pulsating urgency in his manner. He pulled the cream sweater up and over her head. Her nipples became hard. His hand searched her body and took its time reaching down into her jeans. Kelly slowly unzipped his jeans and reached inside. He was hard and quivered at her touch. He pushed her down on the bed and moved down her body, kissing her tender skin. Like molten gold beneath his lips, he savored every inch of her.

Kelly could feel he had to be reassured and this was the only way she knew. She pulled her jeans off in her haste for him to be part of her. He slid into her and pulled her as close as two people could be. Her legs wrapped around his frame, and she kept him there. They both came together, a thing they had become used to doing. Branson held her down, a different kind of look in his eyes. He wanted more. There was something going on that she was not aware of, and something she intended to find out. Not just a lust for sex. Another kind of lust.

Sage hesitated at their door and then backed away. Kelly was looking out for him her way. Sage sat down in the living room, envious that Kelly had someone to love someone to hold. How she wished she had someone. Going to bed without a man was something she was beginning to hate.

The weekend brought rains to Sydney.

"What the hell are you two doing? We have a flight to catch. Just throw some things into backpacks, damn it. You should have packed yesterday. How much are you taking? We're going to be on the road, not in some damn fashion parade." He checked his tone.

"Ready, Dad."

Sage emerged with one huge backpack and a travel bag. Behind her came Kelly. She had on jeans and wore a jacket with a high neck, with hardly any makeup and her hair cut in a style that made her look several years older. It was much shorter and circled her face. Sage watched her father's eyes start at the top and go down Kelly's body. There was a satisfied smile on his face.

"You look terrific," he whispered.

"Thank you." For the first time in her young life, Kelly blushed.

"You should do that more often. It becomes you. You know we may just have to change your name legally to Branson, and I don't mean as a token."

"Dad?" She sounded more than horrified.

"We'll talk about it later. We're going to miss the flight. Come on." He ushered them outside and into a cab in the pouring rain.

"Could you repeat what you just said?" Kelly asked when they were in the cab. She was dazed and really taken off guard.

"I said we'll talk later, but it's an idea, isn't it?" He was still his dictatorial self, but shades of gray were creeping through.

"You mean, marry you?" She could hardly get the words out.

"Guess that's what I mean. I think it is anyway." His own statement confused him.

"Oh, my God." She was stunned. "Oh, my God. Yes!"

"What?" he replied.

"Yes, goddamn it. Yes, yes!" Kelly flung her arms around him.

"Don't you want to think about it? I mean the age difference is something to ponder."

"Mate," the cab driver yelled over his shoulder. "If I had someone like her to tell me she'd marry me, I sure as hell wouldn't question it. You lucky son-of-a-bitch."

In the half-light, he could see his future wife. He was a lucky man, all right, and he felt his first tinge of regret. Maybe Buchanan was right. He should give it up now.

Despite the rain, the flight left on time. There was a great deal of turbulence and both girls were sick. The flight was long. Kelly finally dozed on Branson's arm. He watched her in the morning light. She was pretty and she was his. But this insanity couldn't stop. He had to see it through whatever the price. Fatigue overcame him. His sleep was fitful and his nightmares real. Kelly woke and turned her head to look at him. Beneath the blond hair that swept across his face, a look of anguish appeared. She watched him toss in his sleep. How long would she have him? He awoke suddenly, beads of sweet running down his face.

"What's wrong?"

"Nothing. Just a nightmare." He wiped his face on his arm.

"That's the third time this week," she whispered.

"Keeping count, are we? How do you know that?" He looked curiously at her.

"I watch you. You didn't know that, did you?"

She smiled in a sad way that made his heart melt. He stroked her face.

"I wish…"

"What, Mr. Kane?"

"I wish we had had time to date. You know the old fashioned kind of way. There are a lot of things I have yet to learn about you."

She looked down at his jeans and laughed. "Bad timing for that, Kane."

They landed in Los Angeles, where the sun never stops shining. He was not carrying a gun. He would pick one up later from one of his connections. They cleared customs, but he turned a few heads. Kelly was getting used to that. They caught a cab to the hotel. Branson didn't want to be too obvious in his choice of locations, and the hotel was down in Santa Monica. Pacific Coast Highway held many memories for him. Sage had been conceived at Malibu on some wild bike ride out on the shore.

After checking in and dropping the luggage in the rooms, Sage went down to get a view of the beach. Branson stood on the balcony of the hotel looking out to sea. Two arms slid around his waist.

"What you thinking?" Kelly snuggled into him.

"Thinking we should rent a bike and take a ride down to Malibu." He pulled her arms tightly around him. "Damn it, Kelly. You always going to have this effect on me?"

"I hope so." She slid her hands down the front of his pants and she closed the balcony doors.

He managed to find a silver motorbike like his. The Harley fit comfortably between his legs. Good hunting bike and that's what he intended to do. He knew more or less, where Stratton could be found. He'd done his homework, and the AFP files were always complete. Stratton would be too arrogant to leave his own surroundings, even with the threat of arrest hanging over his head. Branson left the girls at the hotel and took off on his own. He assured them he would be back by midnight.

"Just be waiting for me when I get home, okay?" he told Kelly.

"Always," she'd replied and had crossed her legs in such a manner that made him almost forget why they were here.

He suddenly realized that was what frightened him the most. Being on the bike was like going home. He felt secure again. The power of the bike exhilarated him and the dangerous speeds drove him to the edge. Touching ninety, he felt the thrill. He needed it now more than ever. The timer on his dangerous lifestyle was running out. In Malibu, he found the house. He parked in an alley. All he needed was a quick look at the grounds. The gates were high and impenetrable. However, the tarmac driveway was remarkably short. He spotted Stratton's men stationed around the home. Stratton must be home. Even better, possibly, so was King.

Without warning, the gates opened. Branson ducked into the shadows. A stretch limo appeared from the side of the house. He leaned as far back against the wall as he could. He could just see the driver through the glass. It was King. He stopped at the main door. Stratton stepped out into the evening light. Branson would know him anywhere. He had an air about him. He straightened his suit and slicked back his hair. Miles Stratton was well known to the Hollywood set and its women. It was then that Branson made his plan. Stratton would know what the AFP wanted him to know. To Stratton he was still Mr. Kane. He hoped. Stratton could only know if Kane was a cop if Walker or Wade had somehow told him. What Stratton would know was that Walker's daughter had survived. So, too, had Kane.

He contemplated going over the walls. There was, however, another in, and that was straight through the gate.

"Kelly, you awake?" He turned on the lights as he climbed in beside her. She was warm and she smelled of fresh lavender soap.

"I was waiting for you. Couldn't sleep. I can see by the look in your eyes that your mission was successful. So when do we go?"

"What?" He pulled the sheets over him.

"When do we go in? That's why we came, right? You and I are going in all legal-like. Will I be Mrs. Branson before then?"

"How the hell did you know? I wasn't even sure until tonight."

"'Cause of what my father was. I watched him doin' things. What's the plan?"

"For someone so young, darling, you sure do know a lot. We're going through the gates. It's the only way. We'll find out once and for all what Stratton knows. When this is done, we'll fly to Vegas. Not until then will you become my wife. Not until this is all over. Come here." Branson leaned across her and turned out the light.

Kelly lay in bed, watching Branson dress. For a fifty-two year old, he sure was something.

"You want me to go with you?"

"Yeah, why don't you? We could drive along PCH." He tugged on his jeans.

Her eyes never left the contents. "What's PCH?"

"Pacific Coast Highway. A stretch of road that takes you to heaven on earth. Want to see it?"

"You'll let me ride with you?"

"Sure, let's do it."

She dressed quickly before he changed his mind.

"Where you guys headed?" Sage asked.

"Bike ride to heaven," Kelly said.

"The way my father rides, that's possible. Be careful, Dad."

"I always am. Just going to show Kelly a few landmarks. Then we have to make some plans. Sage, you have to be in on those. They include you. Be back in a little while."

He pulled on his leather jacket, and handed Kelly a sweater. This was the Californian winter.

Secured on the bike, Kelly wrapped her arms around his waist.

"You ready?"

"As I will ever be. I've ridden before, you know."

Sure she had, but not with him. He powered the bike up. It vibrated beneath him and he felt her arms tighten around him. As the sun rose across the ocean, Branson took on the speed of the highway as though it was his own turf. His second home. He could feel the wind in his hair. His helmet hung from the back of the machine. Life once more had meaning. He went eighty up the highway and rode close to the machine. Kelly was firmly attached to his back. The day had started cloudy and mist hung over the ocean. Today was a special day. It was Kelly's birthday and she thought only she knew. Branson brought the bike to a stop.

"You can open your eyes now."

"Weren't closed," she pouted.

He smiled. He'd felt her grip tighten as he changed gears. She climbed from the back of the bike and walked to the edge of the sand. She turned in the half-light, her body silhouetted in the rising sun. Branson wanted her more than he wanted anyone in his life. He swung his leg across the bike. This had been his and Sage's place. Now it would be theirs. He took her hand and led her down to the inlet beneath the road. It was shaded from the street, and a small fissure of water trickled out into the ocean. Only early morning seagulls disturbed the lapping sounds that the gentle waves made as they hit the shore. Kelly was about to speak, when he put his finger on her lips.

"Don't speak, don't break the spell," he whispered.

Branson sat down on a rock and pulled her onto his lap. She could feel his hardness underneath her.

She whispered softly, "Here?"

"Right now."

Slowly he pulled her jeans down and undid his. His hands cupped her breasts.

"Happy birthday, little butterfly. Happy birthday."

"How... how did you know?" she stammered.

"Your passport."

"Kelly, if you want a child, it's okay." Tears streamed down her face and she looked to the sea for comfort. The love in her heart roared in her ears. Branson took time to enjoy her.

"Did I say something wrong?"

"No," she answered. "Nothing wrong. Just wonderful."

"Oh. Well, it's the truth. Whatever you want to do. Like I said, we'll go to Vegas and get married," he replied.

"All I want is you. Remember that." She looked into his face. "Don't go getting yourself killed. I know what you dream about, Kane. Your nightmares are too real. I know what you dream." Kelly touched the lines on his face.

"How the hell do you know, Kel?"

"Because you talk in your sleep." She pushed the hair from his eyes.

"Since when?" He paused. "What did I say?"

"About your wife...how much you loved her. You just called her Sage Jay. I knew on the plane that there was something about you that was different. 'Specially when I found out you were a cop. I took you back to my pa's place because you said you would protect me. And you're good, baby, the best. But I needed someone, too. Someone for me and someone to get to my pa."

He started to laugh. "You used me. A kid used me," he said, and bounced her playfully on his knees.

"Oh, like you didn't use me! But then, things happened. It wasn't what I expected. I had wanted to turn Pa in for some time. I wanted to be free from all the problems, and I knew you had feelings for me. Anyway, I hoped. I was fed up with my life, but if you hadn't come along, I don't know if I would have gone along with this witness thing. Then things got all screwed up and I really began to hate him. And you happened, Mr. Branson."

He listened intently. She called him Mr. Branson. He was on a pedestal because he had saved her life.

"Now we have each other and you brought me back to the real world. Not anyone else, just you." He kissed her.

"Race you to the water!"

They both scrambled to their feet. Kelly pushed Branson back down to get a head start. "Hey!" he hollered, caught a little off-guard. He jumped back up and dashed to the water.

Then she wasn't a child anymore. He watched her standing on the edge of the shore, her feet kicking the waves, her hands holding back time, a picture of innocence… in his eyes.

"You win. But, we must go. There's a lot we have to do," Branson said.

He kept the same speed as before going back down the highway. He didn't feel her hands squeezing so tightly now. She trusted him all the way. They pulled up alongside Stratton's home.

She whispered, "This it?" She looked amazed as she viewed the mansion.

"Yeah. Take a good look. We're going in through those gates, one way or another. And Sage is going to be on the inside."

"Can she do it? I mean play prostitute again?"

"I don't know. But he'll recognize you. Anyway, I couldn't let you take the chance."

"But you would your own daughter?" she questioned.

"That came out wrong. No, of course not. All she has to do is pretend. Chances are he doesn't know who I really am. You can be my lover. He already knows that. He'll know the AFP took the compound. He sure as hell knows about Wade. She was playing both sides of the fence. Depends how much she has told him. My guess is we'll be safe for a while. He'll wonder why we're here without the China white. I'll tell him as the bust went down, you and I got out…some excuse we were outside making out… anything. I need a job and somewhere for us to live, not so far from the truth. He told me that if I ever needed one to look him up, so that's what we'll do. I need a job, specially as we have a baby on the way."

"A what?" She stared at him.

"He doesn't know how long we've slept together. You could be. You gonna go along with this?"

She flinched. "Yes."

"Good girl. So let's go back and tell Sage the good news."

"Yeah, let's." She could not wait for that.

"You're going to what?" Sage stood in the room screaming at her father. "And Kelly's going along with this insanity? You," and she looked at Kane's lover, "I hoped, could make him see sense. And you want me to do what? I don't believe you would ask me to be picked up by him. Are you serious? You are, aren't you? Dad, this is going too far. It's too much to ask. And you, Kelly, you haven't changed one bit." She slammed the door behind her.

"Sage!"

"Let her go," Kelly said. "What did you expect? She was just getting used to us and then you spring this on her? I could have told you it would happen. We'll just do it alone. You don't have to have anyone on the inside. And if worst comes to the worst, I can manage him also."

"The hell you will! I told you, no one else would touch you. We'll get around it somehow. Tonight, we'll go out on the town. I know most of the hangouts down here. He would not stray too far from home. We will find him and I'll offer him my services. He won't check me out 'cause Walker did that and my passport is the only ID I carry. Doesn't say a thing. You want to go eat?"

"What about Sage?"

"She'll get over it. But, for now, she's out."

At seven, they left the hotel. Sage sat in her room and sulked. She'd thought about what her father proposed and she couldn't do it. Therefore, she was out.

"Can you climb on the bike in that?"

Branson looked at her outfit.

"You wanted me to look convincing, didn't you? Sage's kind of clothes won't do that. I kept this skirt and just lowered the front of the T-shirt. Thought it looked good. Knew you would appreciate it. High heels are easy to ride in. Come on, let's go, before we both change our minds."

Clubs were common in Santa Monica, especially the kind of clubs that Stratton would frequent. By nine, they had found Stratton's Mercedes parked behind Coco's Place. King was standing, smoking a cigarette, beside the car door. He flicked ash onto the floor. Branson pulled around and parked the bike. King saw him dismount and squashed the cigarette. He was immediately suspicious of him and the girl.

"Don't I know you?" King asked.

Branson pulled off his shades. "Probably." His accent gave him away.

"You're the guy from Walker's place. You flew the chopper that day. What the fuck are you doing here?"

"Your boss told me if ever I need a job to come look him up. So, I need a job."

"Since when does a hotshot like you need a job?" he jeered.

"Since I lost my partner," retorted Branson.

"Who's the girl?"

Even better. "Walker's daughter."

King looked her up and down. King was tall and well dressed. Quite a catch if he were on the right side of the law. She smiled, but not too much.

"Is she available?"

"You touch her and I'll kill you. She's pregnant."

"That figures. Kane, wasn't it?"

"Right first time, sonny boy. Now, let's go see your boss." He patted King on the side of his face.

"You arrogant bastard…"

"Problem, King?"

Miles Stratton emerged from the club. His gray suit shimmered in the light. He was immaculate. Branson pondered a second about how good it would look colored red. Women surrounded him.

"No problem, boss. This man wants to see you." King stepped back.

Stratton looked surprised. "Thought all Walker's people got busted." He was on the defense and then he saw Kelly. "What were you? Too busy to be caught? Ms. Walker, my pleasure…and apparently his."

"She's pregnant with his kid, needs work," interjected King.

"Really? And just how did you not get caught?" asked Stratton.

"Just like you said. Too busy." He ran his hand down Kelly's backside and left it there.

"And Ms. Walker, how do you feel about your father's demise? Heard he died trying to get to me. In fact, he called me, but the line was so gar-bled all I could hear was 'get me out'. I figured he was trying to tell me who betrayed him, but I couldn't quite hear. You happen to know who that would be?"

Branson's hand tightened on her butt. "She was with me, you know, when we got the news. Cried some, but I gave her something to take her mind off it."

"Yeah, I bet you did. I could use a man like you."

The offer stands. You have experience, you fly choppers, and you know what China white tastes like or Walker wouldn't have gone into partner-ship with you."

Branson nodded.

"Okay, we'll give it a try. Got your things with you?" He looked around for transportation and saw the motorbike.

"No. Back at a motel, down the road. Didn't know if there was any-thing to find here."

"For you, yes. You can bring her if she makes you happy. Only want happy men working for me."

"With you…" corrected Branson.

"Whatever."

"One thing, Stratton…she stays mine. Not any little playmate for your friends."

"Agreed. Be at the house at eight AM sharp. They will let you through. Goodnight."

Stratton watched the pair walk away. He saw Kelly's skirt ride up as she mounted the bike behind Branson. He turned to his man. "Follow them. It's too much of a coincidence they turn up now."

They were dismissed, but they were in. They pulled out of the lot and headed down the road. Branson decided to collect their luggage later. He found the worst motel he could, got the keys, and headed back towards the bike. Kelly hovered, her eyes darting round the parking lot. Branson turned the key in the lock and let him and Kelly in.

"You think he's on to us?" She dropped her purse onto the tawdry covers.

"Don't think so. He's just being careful, checking us out. I'd do the same." He looked through the shades and saw the car outside. "Good job we didn't go back. I'll call Sage and tell her to stay low. We'll pick up some clothes in the morning. You got your passport with you?"

"Always, just in case."

"Smart girl. Nothing we can do but stay here. They can't find anything about us tonight. In fact, they won't find anything at all. I'll leave Sage a message, then we'll hit the sack."

"Not tired," she said, leaning across the bed.

"Who said anything about sleep?"

CHAPTER 12

Branson slept with one eye open. When he was sure the car had gone, he went into the bathroom to make the call to Sage.

"Where the hell have you been? I was worried sick about the two of you."

"You were? Now, that surprises me. Exactly what was it that worried you?"

"Just because I wouldn't play, doesn't mean I don't care about you," Sage replied, not really answering her father's question.

"Were you worried about me, or both of us?" asked her father once more trying to find out if she had started caring about Kelly.

Sage paused on the line. "Both of you. It's just really hard. She's going to be your wife. I'm not sure if I can actually treat her as a mother type figure."

"Don't look at her like that. Look on her as a friend. I don't think she even knows what friends are because of the environment where she was raised. Kelly only has me and one day I won't be around." Branson sat down on the side of the dirty bath. The tub had days of scum and someone else's body grime on it. The shower curtain hit him in the back and he pushed it away.

"Don't say that. Don't even think it. Anyway, you're too damn obstinate to die."

"Well, maybe. Anyway, just lie low. Get room service and don't under any circumstances, go outside. If they suspect that you're my daughter, then we will have immediate problems. Do you understand?"

The door opened and Kelly entered clad in a shirt and rubbing her eyes. "Thought I heard your voice."

"It's okay, baby. Go back to bed." He put his arm around her.

Sage said, "So, Dad, when are you going?"

"First light. Just stay put. If you don't hear from us real soon, don't

worry. However, I promise we'll be in touch one way or another. Sage…
I love you."

"Love you, too. And, Dad…tell Kelly to be careful."

"I will, and thank you for that."

He hung up the phone and picked Kelly up in his arms. At six, they
showered. At six-thirty, they were gone.

"There must be some damn store nearby where we can grab some
clothes, even a drugstore. This is California, the ever-open state," he yelled
over the roar of the bike.

"Look over there on the left. Some sort of store," she replied.

Kelly was waving her arm towards a Sav-On drug store.

He saw it and pulled into the lot. "I'll stay here with the bike. Go get
whatever you need, and you know what I need. Here's my credit card.
Just charge it."

He straddled the bike waiting for her. He didn't see anyone around.
He pulled out a cigarette. It was too early for normal folk. She emerged
with a bag full of goodies.

"What did you buy?" He pulled the bag open.

"You told me to get what I wanted and things for you, too. Hope I got
the right size."

"How the hell did you know what size to get me?" He pulled a black
sweatshirt, socks, and T-shirts from the bag.

"I know you very well." She was glowing.

They were the right size, right color…perfect.

"And what is this?" He fished out a piece of black material.

"Something for me to sleep in."

"And how much sleep do you think you're going to get wearing that?"
His eyes gleamed. "Okay, it's seven thirty. Let's go. Don't want to keep a
man from his destiny, do we?"

"You decided how to do it yet?"

He tossed the half-smoked cigarette down and stomped it out. "No."

They arrived at the mansion. The gates opened and Stratton's men let
them in.

"Nice bike. Park it around the back. Boss is waiting for you."

Branson did as he was told. They walked around the drive to the door.

"Kelly," Branson whispered, "did you put my passport under your
things? If they see the whole name, it's going to make him more suspicious. Not that he would find anything."

She gave him a quizzical look. "It's well hidden, but your license? Doesn't that say…?"

"No, it doesn't. Only Kane. Kept it from when I was undercover."

An immaculate Miles Stratton greeted them. He wore a well-tailored cream suit and shades. "Mr. Kane and the lovely Kelly Walker. You've grown up since the first time we met. Nice to see you. Come in and sit down, and we'll discuss a few things."

Kelly looked at her lover. His face was as stony, almost expressionless, as the marble floors under their feet. Kelly had never seen such a house. There were high ceilings, couches that she'd only seen in magazines and men at every turn. The place was a fortress. They were in, but she wondered how the hell they were going to get out.

"Drink, Ms. Walker?" Stratton asked smoothly.

"I'm pregnant, remember? And he wants the kid."

"Kane, for you?"

"Whiskey." He narrowed his eyes at Kelly.

It was bittersweet and went down in one go.

"Another?"

"Not while I'm working. I like to keep a clear head. What did you have in mind for me?"

He hated this pretense, this bureaucratic power and being subservient, especially to the likes of this man. But he kept it hidden well behind his practiced façade of indifference.

"Would you two like to see the house and the grounds? The bedrooms may interest Kelly."

Branson stood up. "Let's get this straight. Kelly doesn't do that anymore. She's my woman." He paused for effect. "Forget it. We're out of here. There are plenty of other people who would know what to do with talents like mine. Let's go, Kelly."

"Kane, I was just…"

"I know exactly what you were doing."

He took Kelly's hand. Branson was playing close to the edge. She stood alongside him, small and pretty, and Miles Stratton's leer was more lustful than ever. Pregnant by Kane or not, Stratton still wanted her.

"Okay, so be it. King will show you to your room. I need to make a call, then meet me out by the pool, without the girl." He dismissed them with a wave of his hand.

Branson turned the key, locking their door. He searched the room for bugs. The bedroom was clean. "Fuck. I never figured he'd want you again. Sage would have been a better distraction. Think your pregnancy just took a new turn. Tomorrow you get morning sickness, you hear. Sage Jay was sick after two months."

"I'll be fine. Just go down and meet him. I'll lock the door behind you."

When he left, she moved to the window. She stared out over the grounds. The ocean loomed in full view and looked big and sprawling. It had now become Kelly and Kane's special place. Being sick in the morning shouldn't be hard to do; nevertheless, she still had to run often to the bathroom to throw up.

"So, Kane, you want what kind of job? Walker thought highly of you. For now, a bodyguard suits me fine. What's your aim like? King, give him a gun. A .45 suit you?"

Branson took the gun and checked it. Was Stratton testing him?

"Let's go outside. I practice out here sometimes. Doesn't make the neighbors too happy, but who cares about that?" Stratton had changed into jeans and shirt.

The gun handled well. He aimed at the target and emptied all the chambers. King went to look for the holes in the target, expecting to find the paper in tact.

"One hole, Mr. Stratton. Others must have missed," he sniggered, pulling the paper from the twenty-feet away target.

"Tell him to take a closer look." Branson smiled slightly.

"Bring me the paper," ordered Stratton.

It was one hole, all right, one huge hole.

"So, I'm convinced. You're a crack shot. Either a cop or a hit man. Which is it, Kane? Which one are you?"

"Care to find out?" Branson was quick on the turn.

"Already know. You have some reputation down under. How many times did you make a hit? Ten or eleven? Walker must have been a small fish for your line of work. Were you planning to take over after him? Or was there another attraction?"

It had worked. The AFP had done their job. They'd covered his back and made him a future. Mr. Kane was real. The less Kelly and Sage knew the better. As far as they knew he had resigned; and, to the outside world, his past never existed, except as Kane.

"Yeah, I wanted his operation and what better way than through his kid. And, yes, I did kill him. He was in my way. Maybe I'll do the same with you."

There was a pregnant pause. Then Stratton laughed.

"Go ahead - try." He laughed again. "By the way, keep the gun. I have a job for you tonight. Nah, don't worry. I won't touch the girl. You have my word."

Stratton's word was gospel, until he changed his mind. He gave Branson all the instructions he needed to know for now.

"King, show him around. I'm going to take a nap," Stratton said, sitting down in a chair next to the Olympic sized pool.

It was warm in the sun and he dozed. Kelly watched Branson from the window. She'd seen him hit the target. He was deadly and now she was scared. He had no regard for life other than hers, and Sage, and that's what scared her the most.

A banging on the door disturbed any thoughts she had.

"Kelly, unlock the door. It's me."

She let him in and looked at his expression. "You're doing a job for him, aren't you? I saw you outside. You're like some trigger, waiting to be released. Kane, let's get out of here," she pleaded.

"Can't, darling. You know that." He checked the gun.

"Yeah, I do. I just hoped…"

"What?" He was edgy.

"Nothing." She turned away from him. "So, when you gonna do it?"

"Tonight. Some guy he wants removed. Giving him crap." He put the gun down the back of his jeans. It was more of a part of him than clothes.

"How you going to do it? Don't you think he'll be a tiny bit suspicious if you don't kill the person?" She sat down on the bed.

Branson sat down next to her. "Who says I won't?" He watched her eyes. "There's ways around it. You okay? You look pale." He rested his hand on her face. "You've changed in such a short space of time. You look different, you speak differently, and there's something else. The bullet wound's not bothering you, is it?" His concern showed.

"No. It's been a strange few weeks. You came into my life, my pa… and now we're in a whole new country. Wish we could stay here. I like what I've seen so far. Better than home."

"Really? You've only seen a little bit of it. Perhaps we'll be able to see more after Vegas."

"I'd like that. Kane, it's not just me that's changed. You have, too. But never mind that. Now, what time do you have to be ready?"

"At seven. I'm gonna take a nap. It's going to be a long night. Why don't you get out that purchase from the store? You know… the sleeping thing."

"Thought you wanted to take a nap?"

"I do, baby. With you."

Branson stood in the entrance to the door and eyed the contours of her body under the black silk sheets for a moment, then left. He had no idea how to get out of this killing. Perhaps the guy wouldn't show. He had the misfortune to meet King on the stairs.

"My boss wants you."

"I'm on my way. You can see that. You coming with us?"

"Yeah, not that it's any of your business."

"Don't like me much, do you, Mr. King?" Branson leaned on the railing.

"You're an arrogant son-of-a-bitch. Think you're smarter than me. Well, just because he gave you tonight's little job don't prove a thing, mate. It's just a test for you."

"First, it wouldn't be hard to be smarter than you. Second, I'm not your pal, and last, you're in my fucking way." He paused. "And I know it's a test."

King blinked and moved. Neither of them noticed Stratton at the bottom of the stairs.

"You two going to stand around all day?" Stratton asked. "Both of you get over it. You're going to work together and that's that. Let's go. King, get the car."

"Yes, boss." He turned on the step. "Not finished with you," he whispered to Branson.

"You never started," replied Branson, and swaggered down the stairs.

Branson knew Stratton wanted him where he could see him. He knew he checked out clean enough and came up with the right credentials, but still.

It was fun riding in the limo. Branson joined Stratton in a drink. Just one, as it was better to keep a clear head. He noted Stratton's expensive suit, then looked down at his own clothes. At least his jacket and boots were real leather. The driver of the black stretch limo hesitated at the lights. A motorcycle cop drew up alongside with his light flashing.

"Goddamn. Wonder what he wants?"

Stratton's window went down. "Anything wrong, officer?" Miles Stratton was calm and very smooth.

"Back light's blinking, sir. Maybe one of you two guys needs to take a look at it."

"King, keep the engine running. Kane, you go."

Branson stepped out of the car following the officer round the back of the limo. He looked for the offending light, but there was none.

"Don't see anything wrong with it, officer," Branson said projecting his comment towards the large and stern looking officer. "Something else we can help you with?"

"Under the back of the car. See, sir?" He forced Branson to bend with him. Then he whispered. "Target is a plant. You're under constant surveillance. Okay to shoot."

The officer checked the other light. "Have Stratton's house under surveillance also. We can hear, and see, everything that goes on in that house. Your girlfriend's safe. So is your daughter. Boss from your department has her and they are safe here in the States." He straightened up. "Seems to be working okay now. Must have been something I saw in the reflection. Thanks anyway, you guys. On your way then, sir," he said pointing his stick towards the front of the car while speaking to Stratton.

The cop mounted his bike and, with a backward glance, he left Branson standing.

Branson got back in the car. How long had they been watching? More bureaucracy. It was great. They were watching out, as long as they didn't take over the whole damn operation. Stratton lit up a cigar. The Cuban aroma was strong but pleasing.

"What the hell was that all about, anyway?"

"Got me," replied Branson.

The destination wasn't revealed until they arrived at a private club down on the strip. The limo pulled into the drive and a valet opened Stratton's door. He stepped out of the car, adjusted his tie and brushed down his suit. Branson followed, zipping up his leather jacket as he went. The club's bouncer opened the doors and let the party in. Nothing Miles Stratton did surprised Branson anymore. Of course, Stratton had his own table, one he had reserved for years.

"I need a drink. Kane, go order for us: Scotch on the rocks and a beer for King." He said, "By the way, tell them to put it on my tab."

Branson sauntered away.

"Still don't trust him, boss?" King sat across from Stratton on a hard-backed chair.

"Not yet. We'll find out in a few minutes, though. He's much too arrogant to be a civil servant. But if he's so good at what he does, we'd be smart to use him anyway. We can always get rid of him later."

On the way back towards the table, Branson sang out, "Drinks coming up."

He sat down opposite Stratton and peered at the two Americans. How easy it would be to shoot both the bastards and walk away. But, that wasn't the plan.

"Not drinking then, Kane? You want a woman?" He laughed. "Nah, guess you have one to go back to now."

"I told you that I keep my head clear when I'm working. No drinks and no women. Not this kind, anyway."

Branson looked at the hookers. They didn't remind him of Kelly anymore.

Stratton looked at his watch. She was late.

"Something wrong?" asked Branson noticing that Stratton was acting nervously. "Looks like you are waiting for someone."

"I am… And there she is now!"

Branson stared in total disbelief at the door. There in the doorway, removing her coat stood Reese Wade. She shook her long brown hair, smoothed her dress and walked confidently over to the table. Stratton stood up. His companions did the same. He took Wade's arm and kissed her on the lips.

"Mr. Kane. This is Reese Wade, my girlfriend." He smiled.

Branson wanted to vomit. He put his hand out to her instead, "Pleased to meet you, darling."

When he touched her hand, he felt how cold and clammy it was and wondered if it was because of Stratton or because of his being there. Although he could sense her nervousness, she still showed no expression on her face.

"You working for Miles?" she asked him matter-of-factly.

"With him," Branson replied sarcastically.

"Ah," and she turned her back on him. "Sorry I'm late, Miles. Had some paperwork to finish. Didn't think I'd be this late. So, you all started without me?"

"Of course. We were just educating Mr. Kane here in the ways of American clubs. Reese, why don't you go dance with King? You know I like to watch you dance."

"Fine by me, Mr. King. You ready?" she asked.

King stood up and offered her his arm. Gingerly, she took it. They moved to the dance floor.

Stratton turned to Branson. "I found out the other day that US Marshal Wade has two strings to her bow."

Stratton watched Branson's face.

"You look surprised, Mr. Kane."

"Pretty good-looking for a US Marshal, wouldn't you say?" That was the only line Branson could think of using at the time.

"She is, and she came in very handy. Always kept me informed, 'til lately. I think she has someone else. Problem is, I don't know who that someone else might be. Marshal Wade keeps disappearing on me. I know with her job, she has to spend time away, but I am not sure why she spends so much time away. Mr. Kane, I want you to find out why that is; do a little investigating for me. Now, if you don't like the answer," he paused for effect, "you take her out... your way."

Branson said nothing. Even with his brain in overdrive, it was now clear what Stratton's plan was. Had his showing up caused bad timing for Wade? He pulled his cigarettes out and lit one up. Inhaling deeply, he sat back in the chair. Wade had to have known this was going down. The cop said the house was under surveillance, so Wade knew Branson was doing the hit.

"You sure you want to do this?" he asked Stratton. "Killing a federal marshal isn't gonna sit too well for me or my reputation either." He took another drag.

"On the contrary, your services will be worth a fortune." Stratton seemed to have an answer for everything.

Branson looked at the dance floor and at Reese hoping to God she did have on a vest. Stratton finished his drink and said, "So, Mr. Kane, what's your price? Name it." Stratton leaned towards Branson.

"Piece of the action here in the States. A nice setup for me and Kelly." He couldn't think of anything else that fast.

"You got a deal. We'll discuss details later. Enough of King dancing with her; it's now your turn. Attractive man, like you, must know how to dance. Take her for a spin. Then, I think we should all go back to the house. Have a nightcap. Much more private there."

Branson squashed out the cigarette, stood up and moved to the floor. He whispered a word or two to King. Stratton watched each move he made. King returned to his seat and Branson took over where King left off. He took Reese in his arms. She glanced at the table and saw King talking to Stratton.

"You told him the deal?" asked King.

Stratton nodded.

"You got an ulterior motive, Mr. Stratton?" King inquired.

"I want Butterfly back and this woman here out of my life. She's trouble now and she'll only be more trouble down the line."

King scowled at him. "He'll kill you if you touch Kelly."

"He can try."

"He'll succeed, Mr. Stratton."

"If he does try, he'll live to regret the day he was born."

Reese pouted her glossed lips. "Pretend you're having a good time," she said while they danced.

He had his arms around her. "Am I missing something here? What I don't understand is why you slept with a man like Stratton? He's scum and you know that. Besides, why did your department let you carry on in this line of work? Most of all, why the hell did you come here tonight? You had to know what he had in mind?"

"Could ask you the same about Kelly? Why are you carrying on? Maybe I don't think she's such an upstanding citizen either. Sorry, that wasn't nice."

She kept her arms tightly around his waist… she didn't want to let go of the man she had spent such a long time wanting. "Always did wonder what it would be like to be in your arms. Now I know. Lucky Kelly." She paused. "I wasn't working both sides like you thought. Well, maybe a little. I was always under-cover with Stratton. That's how we got the info to your government. It was going well. They were to send the agent in, you, get the witness, Kelly, and break up the ring. Stratton was never suspicious, until I met you; and until he wanted Kelly back. I'm in his way. Easy… he gets rid of me. He thinks you'll be picked up for killing a cop, and he gets Kelly. What he doesn't know is who you are. I never told him. And you know full well why I didn't. We have watched everything in the house. I have to disappear. I knew what was going down tonight. However, I also knew it was you making the hit. So, voila, I'm in safe hands. I did call Walker's people, but you left. Then, I saw you all leave that morning.

Sage walks loudly. But it worked. You got what you wanted. You all did. You got the push you needed."

"Wade, you do have a vest on under there, don't you?" Branson asked her as his hand slid on her back. He still couldn't feel the vest.

"It's slim-line; always supposing you shoot me in the chest and not in the back," and she pressed against him. "Feel it now?"

"Stop it. Right now. Your boyfriend is watching. You want him to think it's me that you know? He's already suspicious. Stratton believes you were gone too long from him." He held her tightly. "I love Kelly, Reese. It took me a while to know how I feel, but it's true, I love her. If I ever said anything that you took… well, you know. And now, that we have to go back to Stratton's and I have to *kill* you, I'll do it in a way that I can dispose of your body. The house overlooks the water. Maybe I won't have to shoot you. Maybe I can push you and you will just fall in the water. Accidental drowning, they call them. Just you make sure the news turns up your death as an accident."

"That's all settled. My death will be an accident. I guess we better get going. Kane, I never, and would never, give you away. You have to believe that. Walker's contacts were supposed to get Kelly, only you got out first. I'm glad, really. Jealousy is an ugly virtue." She hesitated. "Be happy with her, Kane. Just be happy. Promise me." She looked up into his eyes.

"I promise you. Where will you go? Stratton has to believe you are dead, or you will never be safe. One day you will hear on the news of Stratton's death and you will know that you can return to a normal life. Just listen and wait for that news. Don't come out until then or you'll be killed also."

He took her hand leading her back across the floor handing her back to her destiny.

"So, let's get back home. Reese, is your car here?" asked her boyfriend.

"No. Took a cab. Thought you'd have the limo. I need my coat, though. I'll get it on the way back from the ladies' room."

It was just the excuse that Branson needed, and Reese had supplied it.

"Mr. Kane, your opinion?"

"She's gonna try and take a hike."

Stratton nodded. Branson turned, walked through the door and out into the night.

Reese peered through the tinted windows of the stretch. She could see Branson's reflection in the glass. His face was stony and expression-less. The act was good. If she had to die by anyone's hand…

Stratton's limo pulled into the driveway. Stratton's home. Branson's new turf.

"Kane, why don't you go and get your woman? We'll be having drinks on the patio." Stratton was still giving the orders.

"She's probably asleep. You know, with being pregnant and all. She gets a little sick. Think I'll just leave her where she is."

He couldn't bring Kelly downstairs. Kelly was clever enough not to give the game away, but it was too much to keep track of and be preg-nant. He needed to get Reese on her own near the top of the hill; and this was easier than he thought. Stratton had begun to act as if he could read Branson's mind.

"Reese, you want to take a walk with Mr. Kane while I make a call?"

"Sure, always glad to be with an attractive man. See you in a while, Miles," she said, leaning forward to kiss his cheek.

Kelly watched from the window. She'd heard the limo pull in. Across the floodlit lawns, she saw Branson walking up their walkway with another woman. She opened the window to get a better view and real-ized it was Reese Wade.

Kelly's mind began putting two and two together. She saw them walk to the edge of the property. She knew what was over the side of the ravine. A sheer drop and ocean. *Oh shit*, she thought, *so this was the hit*. Stratton's own girlfriend, Reese Wade was going to take the fall. Fear shot through her. Kelly began to wonder how could the department let Branson kill another cop. They disappeared from her view, and she heard the scream. Kelly put her hands over her ears and ran inside the bathroom.

Branson shoved Reese as hard as possible. Sliding down the bank, Reese kicked rocks into the water. She grabbed handfuls of tree branches and pulled herself to safety. Branson pushed his hands in his pockets and walked back up the lawns. Stratton was waiting.

"A drink, Kane? You look like you could do with one. I didn't think you'd go through with it…not a woman and certainly not a US marshal. I'm in your debt."

"That you certainly are, Mr. Stratton. That you are." Branson downed the drink in one go and left them standing on the patio.

In the bedroom, he pulled off his clothes and climbed in bed and snuggled up beside Kelly. He turned away from her in disgrace and stared blankly at the wall.

"God, what have I done?"

"Kane?" she murmured.

"It's me, darling. I'm sorry I woke you."

She leaned over him. "What did you do?"

He kissed her.

"You've been drinking?"

"I killed a woman."

He couldn't tell her the truth. Better if she didn't know.

"I know. I saw you. I had hoped I was dreaming."

"You saw me? How?" and he looked at the open window.

"I was standing over there and I saw you with Reese. Did you really kill her?"

There was no reply.

"Kane, did you?"

Still looking away from Kelly, Branson said, "Tomorrow we have to do what we came here to do and get the hell out."

Kelly never slept that night. His nightmare was becoming a reality, and he cried out in his sleep. She held him until he was calm, his body soaked in sweat. When he was sound asleep, she ran to the bathroom and once more threw up. Now she was sure. Pulling a blanket around her, Kelly sat and looked out at the ocean. A lot of trouble and a little bit of pregnancy was causing Kelly to long for Australia. At nine, he awoke.

"Kelly? Where are you?" he called out, panicked.

"Right here, where I'll always be. Maybe it was all a dream, right?"

"Nightmare, Kel. It's all a fucking nightmare."

Stratton made his announcement in his office when his men had gathered. They had the TV on. The broadcast said that a body had been found on the beach. They listed the name and showed the picture, ruling it an accident. Branson was in the clear.

"Okay, listen up. Mister King, are you listening? Good, then I'll continue. Last night I gained a new partner. Mr. Kane. He took care of our US Marshall for us." He put his hand out to Branson. "Very good, Mr. Kane. It wasn't even ruled a possible homicide." He said the last sentence with some reluctance.

Stratton was one step ahead of the game. Branson had just passed the test but he knew to continue watching his back. He was now secure in his position with Stratton, but he hated that. Did Stratton want him set up for Wade's murder like she said? If it was him, Stratton had failed. Who else hated him that much? Buchanan crossed his mind. But he was undercover for Buchanan. Wade had said that she didn't give his identity away. Still, Branson felt that Stratton knew something else and it worried him.

He listened to Stratton drone on. A notion began to flicker in his mind. Why didn't Sage want to be a player? She'd never met Stratton. Or had she? She could have seen the setup in the house. The cop said she was under guard. How much under guard? She was away from home for a very long time. And, when he finally found her, she was working in the Walker compound.

Was his only daughter the informant? His gut tightened. There was no one else that it could be… maybe his own flesh and blood was his worst enemy. The AFP had a spy in their midst and there was nothing he could do about it. If it was Sage, when had she turned? There were just too many things to review. Maybe he'd think more about it all in the morning. Maybe he'd talk to Sage… maybe not. Nevertheless, he had remembered the look in her eyes as he set fire to Walker's car. It was beginning to add up. Sage hated Kelly for taking her mother's place. Then another thought dawned on him. Sage might have known Stratton all along. Had she tipped him off personally? Had she told Stratton that Branson was an agent? He had a feeling that in the next few minutes he was going to find out.

Codename: Sage, was beginning to sound like the perfect description, even more than he'd ever imagined.

CHAPTER 13

The silence was deafening. An outsider… now a partner… simply not your normal, everyday happening, a policeman killing another policeman. King certainly wasn't happy when he heard about Reese's disappearance and possible death. What King really wasn't happy about was that Branson might in some way be involved. Stratton, on the other hand, seemed to be playing by the rules.

"So, you got what you wanted real fast. Did you know she was government before tonight? One or two things just aren't making sense, something just isn't adding up… Mr. Stratton thinks the fucking sun shines out of you."

Branson looked King straight in the eyes. "Does he? And you, what do you think? You want to step outside and finish this line of questioning; or, are you going to sit back and take it?" He had to squash King's fears before he confided them to Stratton.

"I'll see you later. Just you and I, we are going to meet up someday. You understand what I am telling you? You be ready, you hear?"

"I hear you man. I'll be ready. You can bet your life on that." Branson turned away. He wanted the confrontation, and the sooner the better.

"Mr. Kane will be flying out with me this afternoon," Stratton said. "I have some business to attend to and we need to get it done soon."

Stratton was clever. If he did know anything, he wasn't letting others in on it. Keeping as many facts to himself as possible had always been his strategy. The good news was, at least, that Sage hadn't given him away after all. This afternoon, Stratton thought he would find an opportunity to get rid of Branson.

"Kane, you be ready at two. I think the girl needs to stay here. Looks like something might be bothering you. You feel like sharing what the fuck's going on with you?"

"First of all, you should know that I don't normally go around killing females."

"Guess not. Now, I really have to trust you. Seems that is my alternative at this time," Stratton said and then began changing the subject.

"That wasn't all Walker told us that day. Said someone was a cop. Too fucking bad he's dead, or we'd ask him. Anyway, I think now, that maybe he meant Wade wanted to see me hang. Did you ever meet her before last night, Mr. Kane?"

"Did I look like I had? Did she act as if she knew me? Think about it man."

"Nope. I guess you're right. Well then, welcome to Stratton Enterprises."

With Stratton taking him at his word so easily, Branson began to believe Sage had not betrayed him. Wade had told him the truth. She had never given him away.

"At two, Kane, let's meet out by the chopper pad."

"Yeah, right. Whatever you say. I'll be there."

He climbed the stairs to the room that he shared with Kelly. At that very moment, he heard her scream. Branson tried the door. It was locked. He braced himself against the railing and kicked in the door. Once the door flew open, he got a sight of something that would break any man's sanity. King had Kelly pinned to the bed. Her clothes were torn. Kelly herself was trying to wriggle free of the bastard goon. When she heard the door fly open, her head twisted to the side and she saw Branson. A small amount of relief came upon her face.

Branson lunged at King, screaming, "You fucking bastard!"

After he pulled King from her, Kelly huddled up in a fetal position. Branson grabbed King by the shirt and began slamming his fist into his face and then his stomach. He pummeled King anywhere he could reach. Finally, King fell to the floor. Branson's boots connected with his face. Blood spurted from King's nose. Branson didn't give King time to come around.

"Kane, no, stop! For God's sake, stop." Kelly climbed from the bed and grabbed his arms. The love she had for him caused her to care more about his safety than her own. "Please, don't act like them. I am okay. It's not worth it. Kane!"

Stratton and two men burst through the door, pulling Branson back. King lay battered and bloodied on the floor.

"God, get that piece of crap out of here." Stratton turned to Branson. "You, clean up and meet me downstairs. Shit, King was the one who warned me not to touch her. Said you'd kill me. Guess he should have listened to his own advice."

The two men tried to hold Branson. However, he shook himself free of their grasp. There was blood on his hands and clothes.

"You condone this kind of behavior? You think this kind of shit serves any purpose? Why can't you control your own men? Do you believe I will put up with this crap?" boomed Branson.

"No, of course not," Stratton said. "Are you okay?" he said making the mistake of leaning toward Kelly. Branson grabbed his arm.

"One step closer and I'll kill you, right where you stand!"

Stratton ceased his move and said to Branson trying to lighten the angry atmosphere, "I believe you would. That's why you're so right for this kind of work," laughed Stratton as he left them to console each other.

Branson knelt near Kelly's knees, placing his head in her lap.

"He set me up because he knew what I would do. Stratton sent King up here to test the water. I'm so sorry baby. God, I wish this hadn't happened to you. Now, neither one of us is safe in this damn place. I'll help you get your things together. We're leaving." Branson went into the bathroom and washed his face and hands. Coming out, he said, "Kel, did you not hear me? You need to hurry, darling, let's get your things into that bag. We're leaving right now."

"We can't."

"The hell we can't. Next time, you won't be so lucky. Maybe I won't be so lucky either. If they hadn't stopped me, I might have killed the bastard."

"I can deal with Stratton. It is you I'm worried about, and that's because you're changing, and not for the better. So you made a hit? It's not the first time and if this all keeps up, it may not be your last. However, all of this does seem to be getting to you. Kane, I am beginning to believe that I'm in your way. You're too busy protecting me. I should go. You stay. I'll get out of your life…"

He faced her, and laid his wet hands on her shoulders. "What kind of crap is this? You're not going anywhere without me, you understand?"

"I'll go where I want. Who the hell, do you think you are? You are not my keeper. And why the hell are you so angry with me and with yourself?"

"It's not you that I'm actually angry with, it's me. Satisfied now? I'm pretty sure I killed Reese…"

She sat down on the bed, moving some of the covers out of their way. Kelly put her hand in his and saw his worried brow. "My God." Her brain raced on.

"Sage…where is she?"

"Probably safe, which is more than I can say for us. King suspects, and if he goes to Stratton… I need to get you to safety. I cannot deal with this anymore. The more I kill, the more I want to kill and the hate grows. It's not going away. Now I'm a fucking cop killer just like the… All that I seem to think about now is how I want anyone connected to this dead. What the fuck is wrong with me? I seemed to be obsessed with all of this."

He slumped down on the bed beside her. Obsession had wrung him dry.

"Believe it or not, I understand," she said. "The day you killed my pa caused me to be able to understand how you might be feeling right now. I hated pa for what he was. I also hate him for all he's done to me and to my mom. Mom used to say, 'Be careful what you wish for' and, my God, she was right."

Kelly rose from bed and grabbed his sweater, "Here, change your sweater. That one's got blood on it."

Kelly helped pull Branson's sweater up and over his head as he lay back on the bed. Kelly leaned over him and said, "I'm not going anywhere. I didn't mean to get angry with you. I was trying to make you see sense. I'm scared, mixed up and now I have a strange feeling about it all."

Staring at the ceiling, he said, "What kind of feeling?"

"Don't know, just strange, and it involves us. One way to describe this feeling is to say that it is as if you might be hiding something from me. If I ask you a question, will you tell me the truth?"

"If I can."

"If you can or if you want?" Kelly retorted, getting frustrated with him. She was trying to talk honestly, and now it felt as if he might be starting to give her the run around again.

"Same thing."

She let it go. "Are you still undercover, working for the AFP?"

He paused. Thank God that was the question. "Yes, Kel… but I've been trying to figure a way out of having to do that."

She took his face in her hands. "I won't leave you, but one day, you will leave me."

"Never." He shivered.

She pulled the covers up and over them. The two of them lay in each other's arms. Branson began staring at the ceiling and the thought came to him that this was not part of his great plan. Both of them slept for awhile, but restlessly.

At two, Branson went downstairs and bumped into a waiting Stratton. Branson had locked Kelly in the room and taken the key with him. Stratton approached him.

"Change of plans. The whole thing has been moved to tomorrow instead. I seemed to have lost my appetite for today. You want something to eat?" He ushered Branson towards the dining room. On the table were salads and steaks. The smell of meat filled the air.

"No, not hungry. How's King?"

"He'll make it."

"Pity." Had he said that aloud? Stupid move.

"Listen, about what happened upstairs. Doesn't make any difference to me," Stratton said.

Branson could have laughed. He was already sure that it didn't make any difference. Stratton was probably thinking Branson was a crack shot, would kill government agents, and had a thing for the girl. Branson was playing right into his hands, or so he thought. Branson was letting Stratton see what he wanted him to see. Gain his trust and then rip him apart… him and the whole damn house.

During the early part of their conversation, Stratton inquired, "How far along is Kelly?"

That caught Branson off guard. "Six weeks."

"You going to let her keep the kid?"

This was interesting. "Sure, why wouldn't I? You have something else in mind for the baby?"

"I know a family who would buy the kid." Stratton lit up a cigar and puffed on it with a cruel grin.

Branson wanted to shove the cigar and the grin way down his throat. "Actually, I'm thinking of marrying her."

Stratton almost choked. "You're what?"

"You heard me right." He sat down in the wicker chair and looked out at the ocean, suddenly feeling back in control.

"Butterfly Kelly and you? After as many men as she has fluttered to, seems like you'd want a different type of gal, is all." He was not amused and hid it well. "What an odd combination. Well, hell, as long as you've picked her and you ought to know what you want, why not have the wedding here? This weekend. My gift. After all, you did do me a favor. A big favor."

"Fine, great idea. Why not this Saturday?" retorted Branson, hoping to see Stratton react with a stall. He would have preferred being in control of his own wedding, but why not go with the flow.

"Why not? The rest of the day is yours. Go tell Butterfly the news." He dismissed Branson.

Stratton slammed his half-smoked cigar into the ashtray. He hadn't just rid himself of one woman, only to let Branson still keep Kelly.

After Stratton's comment, Branson decided the term "Butterfly" annoyed him. He climbed the stairs and as he unlocked the door, he thought he heard her crying.

Having recently gone through a scare with her, Branson got a rush of adrenaline causing him to hurry in the room. "You okay? Baby, what's wrong?"

She was standing at the window, her hand on the pane. When she heard his voice, she closed the window. He came up behind her, circling his in her arms.

"I have some news. How'd you like to get married on Saturday?" he asked, kissing her neck.

Kelly whirled around and looked Branson in the eyes. "What are you saying? Do you mean it? Yes! God yes, I'll be your wife, now, tomorrow or even Saturday."

"Stratton is gonna set us up and make it our day. It will also be a perfect day to blow this place to kingdom come. All we have to do is to get the message to Buchanan. I am hoping he can see and hear. My mobile phone is back with Sage and our gear. Man, the son-of-a-bitch just handed his head to me on a silver platter."

"You're serious, aren't you? Are we really going to get married? Here?" She was excited at the prospect of being Mrs. Branson.

"Yeah, darling. Not my choice of a wedding location, but it's at Stratton's expense and this way, he'll see you leave with me." His tone was jubilant. "And both the bastards will die on Saturday, which will just add to my day. You, my sweet little butterfly, are going to make the rest of it." He drew the shades.

For Stratton it was a novelty. There had never been a wedding on his grounds before. He had three days in which to organize it. He wanted this wedding to be legitimate, through and through, bought and paid for by him. It would give him credibility. It wouldn't give him the girl; he had lost Butterfly Kelly. Maybe, just maybe, he could do something about that fact.

Buchanan, who had heard about the wedding, set up some devices so he would be able to filter through Stratton's monitoring system. Better safe, than sorry. "Never seen anything like this. He's going through with it and letting Branson take Kelly."

Sage sat with him. Her father was really going to marry Kelly. Sage watched him walk around the house and inspect the grounds. All of the downstairs was covered with security. Door attendants were in four locations. Surveillance couldn't have been better, only the bedrooms were untouched. She was also beginning to know and understand her father better. Most things seem to be falling in place, all except for Wade. "Dad's growing his beard out." Sage said while looking a little embarrassed.

"You've begun to love your dad very much, haven't you?"

"Yeah, guess I do love him more every day, without even realizing it. He scares me some. I hope he knows what he is doing."

"You mean with Kelly? Your father's a pro. He knows exactly what we expect of him."

"That's what worries me. He never told us that he was still working for you."

"That's what I mean by calling him a pro."

Kelly slept very little the night before her wedding. She'd watched the arrangements of the wedding being made as the days wore on. In a trance, she had eyed the preparations. She saw Branson grit his teeth and bear the way Stratton was treating him more like a servant than a colleague. Not having control of their own wedding was bothering both of them. Kelly watched it all, knowing it was killing him.

Branson's nightmares became more frequent. Instead of Sage Jay's name, he cried for Kelly. This troubled her. She still saw the lust in Stratton's eyes when he thought Branson wasn't watching. Mostly, she tried to stay near the bedroom as much as possible. If Branson ever saw it…

There was a knock at the bedroom door. "Kelly, open the door. I want to talk to you about something." It was Stratton's voice.

"Go away. Kane's here and we are busy." She yelled back, holding her hand on the lock.

"No, he isn't. He's downstairs picking out a suit for your fancy wedding. Brought something for you."

"As long as it's not in your pants."

"Same old Kelly. No, it is not that. I'm not as stupid as King. Just wanted to see if you were okay. You don't have to marry him. I can give you much more than he will ever be able to give you. Besides, we are more your kind. He's different than you are Kelly."

Not wanting to cause more problems than necessary, she pulled her robe tightly around herself and half opened the door. "I doubt that. He gives me everything I want. This man respects me and he is the only one that ever has." She peered through it.

"Well, just remember you have an option." He tried to put his foot in the door.

"I said, go away. I want Kane, not you. I…"

"You what, Kelly? I assume he knows you slept with me?" Stratton placed all his bets.

"You can bet that he knows. He knows everything there is to know. We have had long talks, you know. Now, go, before he comes back and he makes a better job of you than he did with King."

"Hmm. Don't think that's going to happen. I brought you this," he said handing her a package.

Shutting the door, she laughed in his face and said, "Oh, Miles Stratton, you have no clue!" She dropped the unopened gift in the trash bin.

Standing in the shower, Kelly wondered if she and Kane would ever get out of the mess that they were in alive. She slid her hands slowly down toward her stomach. Why did he have to pretend she was pregnant? Why had he said she could have a child? Why did Branson do anything?

Kelly pulled a huge white towel off the rack, dried her body and lay down on the bed. On the closet door hung a dress, one that was more befitting for a movie star in Beverly Hills. The dress was long, strapless, slinky, totally not her. White was its color; was she worthy of wearing white? It was easy to slip in and out of when in a hurry and they probably would be. Studying the dress, she realized that the skirt was going to be in the way of the getaway plans. The skirt would come apart from the top if she tore it hard enough. That gave her an idea. Not the ideal thing to wear under a wedding dress, but very practical: a pair of racing shorts and white snakeskin boots. Her veil was long, so she could pull her hair up underneath it. One tug and the skirt would come completely off. Satisfied, she looked in the mirror and it was at that moment, she decided not to wear too much makeup. Not bad for Kelly Walker. Not bad that was, until she saw Branson.

Unlocking the door, he stood framed in the doorway. Dressed in a tailored gray silk suit, gray shirt, tie, and shades, he shot a look her way that sent sparks through her entire body. A quick thought occurred, which she even faster wiped from her mind. However, he continued to stare.

"'Scuse me. Looking for a girl by the name of Kelly. Last time I saw her, she was twenty-two and a scrubby little thing. Man, I don't see anyone like that around here."

"She left some time back and I don't know where she went, or if she will ever come back. Will I do?" She fluffed the dress.

"Oh, you'll do very nicely," Branson said with a wink.

"Where did you get that suit?" Kelly said, smoothing the lapels of his jacket.

"Like it?"

"God, yes. You are even more handsome than you were when I first met you; and, it was then that I wanted you first."

He slipped his arms around her. "Got your passport on you?"

"Yeah, you want to see where I put it?" She put her hand on the neckline of the dress.

"Yes…no!"

"You got your passport and gun?" Kelly slipped her arms around him and felt the gun in the back of his pants.

"Let's get this show on the road. Say goodbye to this room. We won't be back here."

Kelly was not sorry to be leaving, but she regretted leaving the oversized bed and the splendor that went with it. She'd miss the breakfasts in bed and the lavish bathroom. However, nothing lasted forever. He helped her down the stairs, realizing that the back of her dress was definitely a problem. He stepped on it twice.

"That dress has to go…"

"Don't you worry, it will. You just worry about whatever it is you worry about and… I'll look out for me."

"I'll worry for you, baby. Just stay close to me, okay?" He patted her backside as she continued down. "Remember, nothing will happen 'til after we're married. Then, the fireworks will start. The explosives are set to go off. Kel you and me - hell, let's just start our marriage off with a bang too, what you say?"

"Sounds great, Kane. I'll see what fireworks I can cause for you. But, back to the other thing you just said, I have wondered where you go in the early hours. In fact, I thought maybe you were leaving me for another woman. How long you been planning this one?" Kelly wrinkled her nose at him.

"Sure, that's me. Bouncing from one bed to another. Sorry, that was in bad taste. Just doing what I do best and I have been trying not to worry your pretty little head about it all. Stratton had plenty of useful little gadgets in his basement; and now he has one more."

Kelly was about to ask one more question, but Branson opened the doors to the grounds. She looked at the lawns decked out to perfection. Tables with white silk cloths on them were placed strategically in the center of the huge lawn. A dozen roses placed in the center of each table. They had chosen a different color of rose for every table, along with an orchestra that played on the terrace. She gasped. "Oh, my God, this is beautiful. It's wonderful. Thanks to Mr. Stratton," she laughed. "He's not going to be happy when we ruin all this. Think Buchanan knows what's going on or what is about to happen?"

"He knows. He's just waiting. Bike's around the back and it's ready and gassed. Not sure how you're going to get on the bike in all that garb." He looked at the dress.

"Easy, I've got some shorts on underneath. One tug on this waistband and it just leaves the top. Accomplished, aren't I?"

"Very!"

"Mr. Kane and Ms. Walker. How nice you look." Stratton gave Kelly more than an admiring glance.

"You seen King?" Stratton asked while looking around the lawns. Miles actually looked human today. Sporting a jet-black suit and the usual shades, his air was not quite so confident. He wasn't used to losing.

"He's kind of in knots right now," Branson said, walking away with his bride-to-be.

"In knots? What did you do, Kane?" Kelly asked sliding her hand in his.

"Let's just say that the basement is a good place to cry. No one will hear him. I chained him to the wall. Right now, his new job is inspecting the plumbing. You know, I could have sworn I saw a few rats down there beside him!"

"Won't you ever stop?" she chided.

"When the job is done. I didn't kill him, if that is what you are thinking. I just left him there to visit with a few of his kind. Sad, really. Should have been out here enjoying the sun. This way he will learn not to get in my way." He laughed at his own joke.

"Pity he'll never see daylight again, or you. Darling, the hour has come now, it's two. Time to get married, ready or not."

"I'm ready to be yours forever, how about you?"

"Yep, let's do it. I think they're playing our song."

The wedding march echoed around the grounds from top-of-the-line speakers. The wedding was all going to be legal. Stratton stood up for Branson and that in itself made Stratton almost choke. Didn't make Branson too happy either. The world's finest drug baron as his best man. Well, he'd get over it. And the best was yet to come. Stratton had plans to make Kelly a widow, and very quickly.

Branson kept a watchful eye on everything around them. Glancing at his watch, he noticed it was two-thirty. At three, the timers would detonate and they needed to be safe, needed to be near the bike. Looking around at the different men, he wondered how many of them were caterers, federal, or how many might be local cops. He wasn't quite sure whom Buchanan was working with in the States; but he knew LAPD for sure.

The ceremony was quick, but simple. Kelly blushed when Branson kissed her, and Stratton's displeasure was apparent. She threw her rose bouquet in the air. Somewhere on the lawn slow, melodic music played. Branson knew none of Stratton's guests.

"You want to dance, darling? Let's hold each other and look like we are the happy couple on our way to the honeymoon. Be ready, baby. In a few more minutes, the gates of hell are going to open. When I take your hand, run. Pull the damn dress off if you have to, but be ready to run fast. There will be no second chance."

Branson held her tightly in his arms. She felt small and frail as she clung to him, moving slowly to the music. With each dance step they took, the place they were going to take off from got closer to them. Branson focused on Kelly and the events about to take place. Stratton's movements caught Branson's eye.

Stratton was doing much more circulating than was necessary. It seemed as if he was up to something; but then Stratton was always up to something. Branson glanced back towards the bike, which stood ready and waiting. He looked at his watch.

"You're making me nervous. Stop it," Kelly whispered to him.

"I just wish you didn't have to go through this portion of our day. I could do this part better on my own. If anything happens…"

"Nothing is going to happen to me. I'm more worried about you. Damn this veil. It keeps getting in my way."

Branson reached up and pulled it away from her hair. When he moved the veil, his strong hand touched her cheek. "Feel better?"

Her beautiful face softened as she said, "Yeah. Kane, there's something you should know…"

From behind them came a noise so deafening that she trembled in his arms. Instantly, smoke began pouring from the basement windows. People began to scream as the smoke billowed onto the lawns.

"This is it, baby. Don't lose hold of my hand," Branson said loud enough for Kelly to hear over the noise. Feeling her hand tighten around his, he looked up and noticed Stratton. He pulled the gun from the back of his pants and held it by his side. Their eyes met.

"You-son-of-a-bitch." Stratton's voice was loud and clear.

"Let's go." Branson said while pulling her toward the bike.

From every side, came the sound of explosions. It was beginning to seem as if the explosions were not going to stop. Guests scattered in every direction. The caterers and valets all produced guns. The bust was going down.

The newlyweds raced across the lawn. As she ran, Kelly started to pull the bottom of her dress from the top.

It stuck and still they reached the bike in record time.

"Kane, I can't get the damn skirt to come off!"

"Well, I intended to take it off you anyway. Didn't have such a public place in mind for your undressing." He pulled hard and the skirt cleared revealing her second set of clothes. "Nice shorts. You should have just gotten married in those," he said with a wide grin on his face. Swinging his leg over the bike, Branson said, "Come on, Kel, get behind me."

"I'm trying…" She stepped out of the circle of material with relief.

"Kane!" A deeply distraught Stratton fired a shot making sure he hit his mark.

Branson took the bullet in the leg. Still, he started the bike. Kelly had slowed him down just enough to be caught. Scrambling onto the bike, she threw her arms around him, but noticed blood seeping through his suit leg. Her hand grabbed his shoulder and she looked at him as if he was crazy for them to be leaving with him hurt.

"Don't worry about me," he yelled. "Just hang on."

The pain was intense. His leg hurt like hell, but he couldn't let it stop the planned massacre. Branson fired back, hitting Stratton in the arm. The wound didn't stop Stratton either.

"You better run, Kane. Don't you worry though; there'll be no place for you to hide!" Stratton yelled.

Branson made a move to dismount from the bike, and then remembered his wife. "Come after me, Stratton. Let's just finish this once and for all. Your henchman is already dead. First one to blow."

Stratton saw red and started walking toward them. When Stratton got within twenty feet of them, Branson put the gun back in his pants and powered the bike. He gunned it straight out of the gate and down PCH… He headed for the canyons. He knew that Stratton would follow. A black sedan pulled out behind them. Branson glanced in his mirror. One man sat at the wheel, and Stratton sat in the passenger side. He figured by now, that King had found his way to hell and he hoped it had been a slow death. The chains would have held him fast in the basement. Only one more to go.

Kelly's breath touched his neck. Realizing she was probably scared, he decided that he needed to do something more to create their safety. Coming the other way, he saw the unmarked car with its headlights flashing. Buchanan and Sage were in the back. He checked the road behind him.

"Hang on, Kel," and with a sudden swerve, they crossed the line and headed the opposite way. Branson veered in front of the oncoming car, which came to a screeching halt. Buchanan leaped out.

"You damn fool. You trying to kill yourself?" Then he saw the sedan on the opposite side of the road.

"Take Kelly!"

"What?" she screamed at him.

"Just get off the goddamn bike. You stay with them 'til I get back. This has to be finished once and for all, for everyone's sake."

"Don't leave me," she begged and tried to grab his arm.

"Buchanan, hold her."

Sage jumped from the car and rushed to them. "Dad. I love you. Please, damn it, do not do this. Dad…" and her voice trailed away.

He was gone. Kelly fell against Buchanan. She looked up into his eyes.

"I married him and I had a wedding present for him. A real nice one."

Kelly turned to Sage and whispered in her ear.

The bike powered to seventy, then eighty. His jacket whipped in the wind. He was being reckless to the point of stupidity, but the job had to be done and he had to hurry. Stratton was right behind. Buchanan could have had Branson tailed and Stratton picked up, but that was not the Branson way. Branson didn't stop until he hit the canyons. He made a right turn into Calabasas National Park. He kept on going knowing the car could only go so far. Advantage Branson.

He slowed and pulled behind the trees. Hills blocked him on the left and thick bushes were on the right. It was an ideal location. He looked at his leg and noticed that the gray trouser leg was running red and fully soaked with blood. The hit had been worse than he had originally believed. Ripping off his tie, he wrapped it around his thigh to stop the loss of blood. Still, it seeped down. Branson pulled off his jacket and opened the buttons of his shirt, more ready than ever to kill. Checking the gun, he made sure he was ready. Leaning on the bike, he waited and tried not to think of his new wife. Kelly only clouded his thoughts.

Stratton's sedan rounded the corner. When he climbed out, he said, "You got the balls to show yourself, Kane, or whoever you really are?"

"Before I kill you, I'd like to introduce myself," Branson's voice boomed. He stepped into the light. "The name is Branson…Kane Branson. That mean anything to you?"

"Branson is some hotshot cop from down under. He wouldn't get himself into this mess. I know his reputation. How do I know that's you?"

"You know. But do you know why I'm after you?"

"Don't have a fucking clue. Only know that it's going to end right here and right now."

"Oh, you can bet your life on that! Remember a woman you raped and murdered back in Australia? She was my wife!"

Stratton's face turned ashen. The cool and calm Miles Stratton was finally ruffled. "So just what do you intend to do about it? Just shoot me down dead? There are two of us and there's only one of you. This may be America, but it isn't the OK corral."

Branson pulled his gun up higher and aimed at the driver. Without any hesitation, he pulled the trigger. The man dropped to his knees, clutching his arm.

"Now there's only us." Branson had no compassion.

"You cold blooded son-of-a-bitch. You just going to let him lie there wounded?" Stratton looked at his man. He backed towards him.

"You want me to kill him? I can do that." He aimed the gun again. "But you need someone to take care of your body before the buzzards get you."

Branson began to feel strange inside. He glanced down again to look at his leg and noticed that the bleeding had increased. Stratton saw it and then, moved forward.

"Got you good, eh, Branson? Whereas, you just scratched me. That pretty wife you got there caused you to be distracted long enough that you missed your aim."

"Don't move, you bastard. I will not miss twice. My reputation came because I am a good aim, Stratton. I'm sure you have friends who will chase me back to Australia. However, that can't last forever. They'll get over you and move on past. But you…you have to die right now. And no, I don't plan to shoot you. In fact, I have a better idea. Maybe I'll take care of you like I did your pals, Walker and King. Dying isn't enough for you. You need to suffer, the way my wife did. Get moving." He motioned with the gun.

"What?"

"You fucking heard me. Get moving! This may not be the OK Corral, but back behind those trees, if memory serves me, is a movie set. That is where you and I are going. I know the layout better than you do. I used to hunt here. Again, I'm going to try my luck."

CHAPTER 14

"Can't you do something? Go out there and stop this!" Kelly yelled.

"He doesn't want that. Branson has to do it his way, or it will never be over." Buchanan released his grip on her.

Leaning against his car, tears streamed down her face and she shivered in the afternoon sun. Buchanan looked at the girl. Wedding dress top and shorts: an odd combination for a bride. He slipped his jacket off and draped it around Kelly's shoulders. She played with the ring on her finger.

Sage felt a sudden surge of sympathy for Kelly. She'd seen her mother go through similar circumstances with her dad. Other than Kelly being younger, it seemed near the same. She had just told Sage her secret.

"Dad will be fine. You have to believe that. He'll come back for you. He always comes back…and you have something very precious to tell him."

Kelly shot her a look and shook her head.

"You have something for him, Mrs. Branson?" Buchanan asked.

The words hit her hard. "I wanted to tell him…how much I love him, that's all," she said, toying with the band on her finger again.

"Let's get you into the car so you can change your clothes. You need to be ready for him when he returns."

"Ready? How the hell do you know he's coming back? How do you know he won't end up getting himself killed? For God's sake, send someone after him. At least some backup." Kelly was becoming hysterical.

"Okay, you win. I'll send an unmarked car after him. I have a pretty good idea where he'll go. He used to hunt around this area some years back," Buchanan said while pointing toward the canyons. "Back in there, is a movie set. It has been closed for some time. I'll have someone go by and take a look in there. But remember, it was your idea. Why are you so afraid he might die? Think he's losing his touch?"

"No, but he has a bullet in him already," Kelly cried.

"What?" Buchanan was taken by surprise.

"Stratton shot him in the leg. Branson winged him back, but Branson was bleeding. I thought you saw the blood."

This changed things. Branson out for blood was one thing; however, Branson losing blood was another.

"Get in the car, both of you." Buchanan ushered the two girls towards the car. "Kelly, is there something else you have to tell us?"

"No." She looked at the ground. Sage put her arms around Kelly and said, "Tell him. If you don't, I will."

"But, you said you wouldn't," she pouted.

"I lied."

"Okay, but you have to promise not to tell Branson. At least let me have a chance to tell him first. Promise?"

Buchanan could clearly see why his agent would be attracted to Kelly.

"I promise," Buchanan replied.

"He made me pretend to be pregnant for Stratton's sake. But it's no lie. I am." She smiled as though she were the very first woman to ever be pregnant.

"I had a feeling that was it," Buchanan replied putting his arm around her shoulders.

"You did? I'll tell him my own way. I just don't want to lose him."

"You won't," Sage said. "He'll be back. My dad always comes home."

Branson looked at the bird circling overhead. The blood didn't stop seeping through his pants. The heat was causing him to dehydrate. Trying to deal with the strangeness of the heat, he pulled his shirt off. If he could get over the rise with Stratton, they would be at the set.

Miles Stratton knew Branson had the gun pointed right at him. Branson's reputation preceded him, but a handicapped leg burdened him. He also knew Branson had nothing to lose, except Kelly, whereas he had everything to lose. Stratton stumbled over a hill and down below, he noticed a ranch.

Branson squinted in the sun. With a piece of torn shirt, he wrapped his head to sop up the sweat. The rest of the shirt, he threw away. Stratton yelled back to him.

"Hey, Branson, what the hell do you think you're gonna do when we get there? My guy will radio back for help. You should have killed him when you had the chance." He laughed insanely. Branson heard the fear in his laugh.

"Look up, Stratton. See that bird? He's circling over the car. Does that tell you anything?"

"Shit!"

Branson laughed. "Just another few feet, *Mister* Stratton, and you can see what your future holds. See which way you would like to die. Pierce, his remains are scattered around the universe. Stevens found his way onto the end of a rope. Walker was much more interesting. That one actually burned to death in his own car. King died at your place. Let's just say he was hanging around. Now you get to choose… so long as I get my way, and you suffer first. Just keep going into that chapel over there. Somewhat of a change for you…chapels."

Stratton could hear Branson loud and clear. Even injured, he couldn't take Branson. He hoped to God that his man had called for help.

Branson, following Stratton at a consistent pace, waved the gun at him. "There, get yourself to that door and then get down on your knees. Might want to say a prayer while you're there."

The well-structured chapel had shafts of light beaming across the floor. Movie set props lay in the corner, which seemed well used, and long discarded.

"Realistic. Man, this is just how I remember it. I used to hunt here. I spent a lot of years working undercover over here in the States. Didn't know that, did you, *Mister* Stratton? Oh, by the way, I'm tendering my resignation from Stratton Enterprises." He motioned with the gun. "Sit by the altar. See if God will forgive you before you die. Soon the sun will go down. That is when the fun really starts. You good at being hunted or only being the hunter?"

Stratton was perspiring, and it wasn't caused by the heat of the day.

"Think about what you're doing. You'll be killing me in cold blood, but I guess that doesn't bother you, does it? After all, you did kill a federal agent…and a female agent, at that. Guess you'll stop at nothing to get what you want."

Taking a breath, he stared at Branson for a moment to see what type of reaction he may get. When he could see that Branson was not even a little nervous, he continued badgering him, "And what about Kelly? Didn't you say she was pregnant? What's Butterfly going to do without you? Look at you now; you're bleeding badly. Is it really worth losing your life to get back at me?"

"Yes. Now sit down and shut the fuck up. Start praying that you die quickly. Pray that I think with my heart and not with this gun." Branson sat down next to the pulpit. Stretching his leg out in front of him, he noticed a small trickle of blood finding its way to the boards under him.

"Why don't you just shoot me? I know you can kill in cold blood. Oh, I forgot," he said smugly, "I'm not a woman." Stratton eyed his captor.

"If you're trying to make me angry, you're succeeding. But no, you'll get a fair shake."

"Who the fuck do you think you are anyway? Rambo?"

He laughed. Overhead they heard a chopper and Stratton took the opportunity to make a move. Branson's eyes quickly narrowed.

"Don't even think about it. They won't see us. Why do you think I brought you here? Sure the hell wasn't to cleanse your damn soul."

"Won't they send someone after you?" Stratton questioned.

"Probably."

Stratton was desperate to make conversation. He was playing for time. The shafts of sun had begun to fade. Shadows filled the chapel instead. No one had found them.

Back down the track, Buchanan's men found both vehicles. They called in. Buchanan's reply was for them to wait there. He knew where Branson had gone. He'd give him until dusk. Then, LAPD would go in and try to find him. The chopper was scouting the location. It was Branson's turf, a tiny patch given back to him in respect for his late wife.

"On your feet," he said to Stratton, sounding as if he had full authority. "Time to die."

Feeling as though his life was truly slipping from his grasp, he looked up into Branson's face. "No."

"I said on your feet, you-son-of-a-bitch, or I will shoot you where you sit." He pointed the gun straight at Stratton.

"Do it!" he baited. What the heck, it may be his last effort to stay alive.

Branson moved the gun up and he was dead on track for the forehead. He placed his finger on the trigger.

"No, stop. I'm up see, can't you see, I'm up." Sweat poured down his face.

"Get going. You have ten minutes. I'll be so close behind you, you'll feel me breathing."

"I'll just head back for the car," Stratton bragged.

"Good luck, 'cause you'll never find it in the dark. And, Stratton, by the way, I am as good at hunting, as I am at killing women. You might just think about that. Got something else for you to contemplate… if I don't get you, the mountain lions will. You may live around here, but you sure ain't no country boy. Go!"

Alone, Branson turned to the altar. "Hell, this isn't a real church, but it's as good as any. If you can hear me up there, forgive me for what I'm about to finish."

Stratton thought he knew the way back. He didn't, and the light had almost completely vanished. Sweating profusely, he went the way he thought he should. The route he happened to pick only led them deeper into the canyon. The long grasses impeded him and shrubs caught on his expensive suit. Stratton dispensed with the jacket and tie. Along the way, he had pitched anything that held him down. Branson picked up the jacket and the tie. All Stratton was doing was leaving a red-hot trail for Branson.

Branson's eyes were fierce, and even in the dusk, he could see that Stratton wasn't far ahead. The only obstacle was his throbbing leg. The bullet had to be removed. He should have pulled it out back at the chapel, and now he risked the chance of it festering. Now he was in severe pain.

"Okay," yelled Buchanan. "We have the local boys in the area. Let's go get this bastard once and for all. I gave Branson the time he needed. If his wife's right, he may need our help. Let's go." Buchanan, in his usual manner, was setting things in motion.

Kelly showered and changed her clothes at a local hotel. Sage sat on the bed waiting for her to finish.

"Some way to spend your wedding night, sitting with your stepdaughter and two cops, neither of them being my husband," stated Kelly as she towel-dried her hair.

Sage could tell that Kelly's voice was trembling. She wondered why Kelly wasn't crying. "You know you can cry and not be ashamed. Dad wouldn't mind and maybe you've been brave too long. Both of us have. I miss my mother, Kelly, but my dad really does want to be with you. And, you're not so bad, you know. Maybe we can be friends."

"I'd like that very much, really I would."

Almost as if she had needed Sage's permission, Kelly broke down in tears. Her lips quivered and her eyes turned red quickly. Sage enveloped Kelly in her arms. The cops discreetly turned away from them. Inside, Sage had a strange feeling that her father wasn't coming back. And she felt as if Kelly might be feeling the same way.

Stratton was losing ground fast. He began to run and fell, tearing his clothes. Still he ran with even more determination. It was quiet. In fact, a little too quiet, which bothered him. All he could hear was his own breathing. His breath was labored.

Branson was close behind him. The pain in his leg was almost unbearable, but this fact alone would not stop him. Branson could track in the dark. He'd done that type of tracking before. Besides, Stratton left plenty of clues. Branson shivered in the night air. How he wished he'd said goodbye to Kelly and not just left her on the side of the road. His loneliness caused him to see her image in the sun. How pretty she looked. He shook his head; maybe he was becoming delirious. Strength played no part in this little game. Willpower was what was keeping him going. The gun hung by his side. He hadn't quite figured where to shoot Stratton, with the four bullets he had left. Each shot needed to count.

They were heading through the canyon and out the other side. Branson knew there was a road and a five hundred-foot drop. Still, he needed to reach Stratton before he got that far. Branson stepped up the pace.

Stratton hurried on, his legs torn by brush and his face hot. Suddenly, he heard a noise, sounding as if they were near cars. They must be near the highway. Somehow he had doubled around and gotten them all the way back to the canyons. It was very dark. Headlights could be seen in the distance. By now, Branson was fifty feet behind Stratton. The headlights hit Branson full on. His body gleamed in the light. Stratton turned his eyes away, and he saw Branson behind him.

"Come on you stupid son-of-a-bitch. Make your play, Stratton," yelled Branson. "Head for the road. You can make it. Over there, try going in that direction… it is one hell of a drop into the riverbed. If the car doesn't get you, the drop will. I can't lose. Go for it." Branson was breathing hard.

"You won't get away with this. I have friends in other countries. You'll be on the run the rest of your life. Even the AFP can't protect you."

"I'll take my chances." He neared Stratton, gun in hand. "I said go. You're acting as if you didn't hear me. Maybe you'll be lucky, and the car won't kill you. You've got a fifty-fifty chance," he said raising the gun.

"For God's sake, don't do this! This kind of killing would be cold-blooded murder."

"Man, am I glad you recognize that fact. At least you have a chance, unlike my first wife. She had no chance. Now did she?" He asked, while aiming his gun. Branson's first shot went straight through Stratton's arm.

184

"God almighty! You're a crazy cop."

Stratton grabbed his arm. Blood gushed from the wound. As he gripped his arm, he became dizzy and slid down the grassy bank. He stumbled onto the road straight into the path of a car. The car, seeing him at the last second, swerved on by, blaring its horn. Stratton fell completely flat onto the dark road, covered in blood. The bleeding did not appear as if it would stop anytime soon. Branson ran down the grassy knoll after him.

"You're going to stay right where you are. I'll be by the roadside, and if you move, I'll shoot you from here." Branson shook his head because his vision was becoming blurred.

Stratton jumped up and tried to run.

"That's the spirit. Just what I told you not to do; but just what I wanted."

Branson began to lose focus. Sweat poured down his face onto his chest and back. Stratton climbed the barrier into the dusky canyon. He could see the decent in the half-light. Branson was behind him. In the background, he could hear sirens. The car that had passed them by must have reported the incident. Time was slipping away. It was then that he heard a scream. Stratton was falling.

"Help me! I'm going down. For God's sake, help me. You can take me back. I'll plead guilty. I don't want to die like this. You're damn a cop, why don't you do your job right."

Branson found Stratton hanging onto the rocks by his arms. He couldn't retain a grip with the injured arm, though he continued to try. Stratton's feet were slipping on the grassy stones beneath him. Branson towered over him like the angel of death.

"Help me," Stratton begged, even his eyes seemed to be pleading.

Branson stepped forward and his foot touched Stratton's fingers. Standing there at that one moment, he had the power over the life and death of this one man for sure. The siren was getting louder. Kelly's voice was also in his head. He could see her in the sunlight calling him home. Branson was with every death that went by, becoming just like them. He was also drowning in his own nightmare.

There was a bright light and someone called his name. It was a man's voice. Still he had the power over good and evil. His boot pressed on the fingers. Stratton screamed. Then Branson blacked out.

"Over here. Get the paramedics down here. Branson! Kane, can you hear me?" Buchanan held his friend's head. "Get the hell down here, move it!"

"Sir, there's another body down a ways. I'll take a closer look," yelled the officer.

Branson came to, and when he became aware that it was Buchanan, he said, "I got him, boss. I got him. We're free."

He shook with cold and fever. Still, he tried to move. The pain in his leg made him flinch and groan. It was searing and unconditional.

"Don't move. You're not doing too well, my friend. I didn't ask you to take on this assignment to give up your life, just to do your job. We have to get you to a hospital soon. You've lost way too much blood for us to wait any longer."

Branson, even now, thought of his new wife and murmured, "Kelly... safe?"

He hesitated. "She's fine. Some way to spend your wedding night, playing Rambo."

"You're not the first one to point that out to me." Branson turned his face toward the sky. "As long as Kelly's fine, then I am fine. See Buchanan, I kept my promise to Sage Jay, and now I have another promise to keep. You get us out of here. Back home, where we'll be safe. Stratton's dead. Now I am even closer to being sure that we are safe."

"Yeah, sure. Back to Australia, soon as you're fit to be traveling, that is. First things first. For God's sake, where are those guys?"

Then Buchanan's blood ran cold. He watched as they brought Stratton by, covered in blankets. He saw his arm move.

On the ambulance ride to the hospital, Buchanan rode with Branson. He had no idea what he was going to tell Branson. Why couldn't Stratton just die? He had to get Branson back to Australia right away. Stratton had far-reaching fingers. Sometime, some place, he would be waiting for Branson and his family.

The cop in the motel answered his mobile phone. "Where are they? She's here, and so is his daughter."

Kelly jumped up from the chair, knocking it over as she rushed to find out if her husband was dead or alive. "Did they find Kane? Is he..."

"He's alive. Now, let's get you both to the hospital so you can cheer him up a little. I got a feeling he'll be real glad to see both of you."

"Told you my dad would come back. Are you going to tell him?" Sage grabbed jackets for them both.

"I'll tell him later. He has enough to think about right now. He just killed another man."

"No, ma'am." The cop interrupted. "The bad news is Stratton is still alive. Found him a few feet from your husband. The bastard was still breathing."

Kelly stared at the cop. "Does Kane know?"

"We'll find out at the hospital. You ready?" he replied.

She grabbed her purse. Sage was right behind her. They climbed in the police car. With lights flashing, they sped through the streets hitting speeds as high as ninety did. Kelly stared out of the car windows wondering what she was going to say to her husband. Branson would never get over this failure. She knew him well enough to know that he would just make a new plan. How could she tell him he had a child on the way? Stratton would tail him until he killed him and, maybe even, her. Even worse, maybe he'd wait long enough, that he could come after their child. How could she tell Kane now?

The hospital ER had been alerted and they were ready for them. Branson came in unconscious. Loss of blood had taken its toll. His breathing was labored, causing them to fear for his life. The bullet had been easy to remove; keeping him alive was something else. On the operating table, things did not improve a great deal. Branson was not as strong as he needed to be. He suffered a mild heart attack. Buchanan and the girls arrived as they announced 'code red.'

"What's going on here? Where's Kane?" Kelly asked while screaming in the lobby. Running door to door, she looked for him.

"You relatives? You his daughters?" the doctor asked them.

Buchanan flashed his ID. "This lady is his wife, and this one's his daughter."

"Where is he? I want to see him." Kelly rushed to the ER door that the orderly had told them he was assigned. She peered through the glass, tears streaming down her cheeks and her forehead showing creases of worry and fear.

"You can't go in, not yet. Before you go in, I need you to sign a piece of paper. We need your permission, just in case." The doctor was matter of fact and this only aggravated Kelly's and Sage's worst thoughts.

"In case of what? You mean in case he dies? Oh, my God. He's going to die?" Kelly wrung her hands.

Buchanan pulled her back.

"Is he?" Sage asked Buchanan while holding onto Kelly's shoulders.

"The heart attack was mild, but he's lost a lot of blood. The bullet's been removed. The rest depends on how strong he is. Your dad needs the will to live."

"Heart attack? Last thing we knew, he'd only been shot. When did he have a heart attack?"

The doctor addressed Buchanan's question. "Just a few minutes ago. The trauma of the whole event and the loss of blood were just too much for him. But, now he seems to be responding a bit better. We'll know more about his condition in a little while. Just take a seat." He turned to Kelly. "Mrs. Branson, come with me. Let's get that paper signed."

"I have to see Kane. Buchanan, tell them. You have the power." She pushed the hair from her face revealing tired and frantic eyes.

"Calm down. You're not helping matters by getting so upset. I know this is hard, what with you two just recently getting married, but you need to be as strong for him as he was for you. We'll get the doctor to bring the papers here. That way you can sit down and I'll get you some coffee."

"I don't want any damn coffee!" she screamed and turned to the doctor. "Let me see him or I will make the biggest stink you ever saw in this god-damn hospital."

"Okay, okay. You can stand at the back of the room. Make no noise. The nurse will fix you up with a gown. But remember, you go near him and you're out of there. This is serious business and is no place for an upset wife to be making a scene. I want you to keep your husband's health in mind while you are in there. Promise me that, and I will let you go in for two minutes," replied the surgeon.

She nodded and handed Sage her purse. They opened the doors to ER. Almost instantly, Kelly was able to make contact with Branson's face... she just simply stood staring deep at his eyes. He lay there, on the operating table, with wires attached to his chest. Branson's face was pale and he was breathing through a tube. His uncovered leg and thigh were bandaged heavily. This was her husband. She wanted to run over to him and tell him that everything was going to be ok. Kelly wanted to tell him of the child they were to have. Nevertheless, the only direction she moved was down to the floor, in a faint. They carried her out.

"She passed out when she saw him. I don't want her in there again. She's in the next room," the doctor said. "Go in and see Kelly."

It was a long night in the waiting room. Kelly was ashen. Sage fetched coffee then fell asleep on the seats. Buchanan covered her with his jacket. Kelly sat like a statue.

"You okay?" he asked.

"Fine."

"Want something to eat?"

She looked at him as if he was stupid. "No, thank you. Not hungry." She paused. "He will make it, won't he?" she said, her expression softening.

"He'll make it. You can be sure he won't leave you, not now," Buchanan replied. He looked tired also. These events were taking a toll on the older man.

"Where did they take Stratton?"

"Down the hall. His condition isn't as serious as we would have liked it to have been. He's got police around him. Why? Thinking of finishing what your husband started?"

"Something like that. If I don't, Branson will…at some point."

"That's what worries me. It would be best if the three of you were back in Australia, maybe go into hiding. But I don't think that's going to sit very well with our boy."

"Oh, he'll want out of here, but not into hiding." She shook her head at Buchanan's suggestion. Kelly leaned back against the wall and waited. Watching the hands of the wall clock tick by, she waited as one, two, and then three hours passed. Daylight protruded through the window. The sunshine began to brighten up the outside world but Kelly's world was going to remain dark until she knew that her husband was mending.

At five, a doctor appeared in the hallway. "You can see him now."

"Is he okay now?" Kelly asked anxiously.

The doctor nodded. "As okay as can be expected. After all he's been through; he is in better condition than we would have thought he would be at this time. Don't stress him in any way, he needs to rest."

"Thanks, doctor." Kelly glanced at Sage. "Can she can come also? She's his daughter."

"That's okay."

Kelly took hold of Sage's hand. She was trying to be strong for both of them. She knew what to expect and Sage didn't. Buchanan looked at her. He knew why Branson had married this girl. She, like him, had guts.

The entire room was clinical white. They saw the machine attached to his heart, its rhythmic lines pulsating up and down. A sheet covered his lower body and his leg was propped up on pillows. Branson, heavily sedated, appeared healthier than he had when Kelly had seen him in the ER room. Kelly felt Sage's hand tighten around her hand and the faintness felt as if it was returning.

"That's just so they can monitor him. Make sure he's okay. If you want to sit by the bed, I can stand for a while," Kelly said to Sage, turning toward the doctor.

"That's right, isn't it? That machinery is just hooked up to him in order to monitor any changes?" She nodded her head slowly at the doctor while pointing at the monitor.

"Absolutely. The strain of surgery brought on the mild attack. You need to sit down?" He watched her closely.

"I'm fine. Just been a strange time in my life. Does he know he wasn't the only one to survive?" she asked tentatively.

"No, he hasn't regained consciousness. Why?"

"We don't want him to know yet that Stratton did not die."

They were left alone. Kelly watched Branson's chest rise and sink. She wanted to crawl in the bed with him. She sat down on the sheet.

An hour later, Buchanan decided to check on his friend. He found them as close as possible. Kelly sitting on Branson's hospital bed. Kelly's hand stretched out to Branson, Sage propped up in the chair. Buchanan closed the door and gave them back their privacy.

"Well, well. You must be the boss of the man in there." Stratton's voice was full of contempt. Handcuffed to an officer, he stood in the corridor outside Branson's room. "Better get him as far away from me as possible, both he and that little tramp he married. You may have charges against me, but my attorneys will get me off those charges. Couple of days and I'll be out of jail. See if I'm not right. He should have finished me off when he had the chance. Now maybe, I'll get to finish him. You give him a message from me. Tell him, wherever he goes, I'll be waiting. And tell him that I've had both his wives. Both of them were good. You can also tell him I said I'll have the girl again unless he leaves me alone."

"Why, you bastard. I should finish you off, as a special present just for him." Buchanan moved towards him. He thought better of it in front of the LAPD. "We'll make the charges stick his time."

"Want to bet?" Stratton laughed as he was led away.

Buchanan was angry at his lack of self-control. He walked to the door and stepped inside. How was he going to tell Branson that all his efforts yesterday had been in vain?

CHAPTER 15

Branson came around slowly, blinking a few times to clear his vision. His first glimpse was Kelly, her hand stretched across the bed to him. He grasped for her fingers and she awoke.

"Hello, little butterfly," he murmured.

"Kane." She slid across the sheet to his side. "I missed you. Don't ever leave me again."

Sage opened her eyes and gently closed them.

Kelly's tears fell on his hands. He stroked her face. His breathing seemed strained.

"I'll be fine. Please don't stain that pretty face of yours. Sorry I didn't make it back for the honeymoon, but we'll have time for that later on when you get me out of this place." He glanced at the machine monitoring his life. "Did something else happen other than that son-of-a-bitch shooting me?"

"You had a mild heart attack. Doctor said it was to due to the loss of blood and all that exertion. Did you have to go and play Rambo, like Buchanan said you were doing? I need you Kane and want you to get well. You have to rest for a while."

Now, where had he heard that term before?

"Rest with a pretty wife like you around? You're joking, right?"

"Shush. Sage is asleep and we wouldn't want to wake her." She blushed.

He liked it when she did. "Where's Buchanan? I need to talk to him."

"Doctor's orders. Don't get yourself too excited and others aren't supposed to cause you to become upset either. So, you just lay back and get some rest. You're so pale even that gorgeous suntan of yours is fading."

"Yeah, and you'd know about that, wouldn't you?" He laughed and almost choked on his own joke.

Sage opened her eyes, glad to hear her dad's voice, but not exactly thrilled that Kelly was there. She would have enjoyed having a moment or two of privacy with him. "You gave us some scare, Dad."

"I didn't know you cared," he said in a whisper.

"Now would you go and say something like that? You know I care about you. In fact, I love you and want you to be around for a really long time." She sat on the bed and buried her head on his chest.

Kelly stretched her arm around Sage, and the three of them were one. Buchanan, glad he had not barreled in, coughed discreetly.

"Come on in, boss," Branson whispered. "You can see I have my hands full."

"Yeah, I noticed. Man, you are one lucky guy. We need to get you back home. Doc says you can fly out of this place in the next few days. A special plane will take the three of you. Everything's covered." Buchanan finished closing the door and sat down on the bedside chair. Kelly stood at the window drinking a cup of coffee the nurse had brought for them earlier. At the moment, she did not care that it was cold.

Branson, still trying to get a clear picture of what all had transpired, felt suspicious. He looked at Buchanan. "Why the rush?"

"No rush," lied his boss. "Just thought you'd want to go home."

Buchanan looked at the monitor that had been set up and felt glad that this cop had not had to die like to many others. The heart rate blips increased. Nervously, he rose from the bed and chose a chair instead.

"Don't lie to me after all these years. Stratton's not dead, is he?" Branson turned his head to one side. "That son-of-a-bitch. I was sure he went over the side when I…"

"He did. Unfortunately, his clothes caught up on some branches and he survived," Buchanan said with some hesitation.

"Where is he? No, I don't want to know right this minute. Get my wife and daughter on the next flight out of here. Then we'll make sure I follow."

"The hell you will," Kelly said. "Till death us do part. That's what we said, and that's what it means. Till death, so I am staying with you. I am tired of you telling me that you are going to take care of me and then you up and go somewhere. This time, damn it, I am staying by your side."

"You are one scrappy little woman. You think you can boss me around?" He rose slightly from the mound of pillows.

"Yes, that is what I am and you love it." She leaned down to kiss him feeling vulnerable and an unfamiliar aching feeling.

Buchanan could see the pain in his eyes. It wasn't over, not by a long shot. One giant step forward, and two small steps back.

"You know, we can't go home. Some other place, maybe. Listen you two. He'll come after me." He looked up at Buchanan. "Bet that's what he'll be thinking, right? So we need a plan."

Buchanan nodded while noticing that Branson seemed to be too calm, his face unreadable. He doubted the girls noticed.

Branson said, "Why don't you and Sage go get me some ice chips?"

"Both of us?" asked Sage. "It does not take two to fetch ice chips. All you have to do is press that buzzer and the nurse will bring them to us like she brought the coffee."

"They need to talk," Kelly said to Sage.

To her husband she said, "We'll be back. In the meantime, don't go and get yourself all worked up and stressed out, you must remember that."

He waved his hand to them as they shut the door. They did as they were asked.

"You're in pain, aren't you?" his boss asked.

"Yeah. You could say that. They can't go with me. You know that already. How serious was my heart attack?" He asked, with pride, but all the while straining his head to look again at the monitor.

"Mild. How did you know the bastard wasn't dead?"

Buchanan was curious.

"By your quietness. Anyway, I feel well enough to get out of here. I have to think of the girl's safety. Kelly, especially, won't leave me, so I have to leave them without them realizing that is what I am doing. I expect you to help me, for their sake."

"Are you crazy? You think you are going to magically disappear out of this room?" he gestured the fact with his arms.

"No," he leaned back on the pillows grasping the rails once again, "I think I'm going to die."

"I'm getting a doctor. The medicine is making you crazy." Buchanan turned for the door.

"That's the only way. If Stratton thinks I am dead, I can go after him."

"And what about your wife and daughter? He'll pursue Kelly because he said that he would get her back and…"

"And what? He can't go after her if she's in your protection. Stratton

can try, but you can stop him. You can push the papers to get him extradited out of the States, once and for all. Make sure that if he gets back to
Australia, he is nowhere near my girls," Branson said while moving his
body. The grimace on his face was immense and Buchanan saw a flinch
begin and Branson grab the hospital railing to hold himself in an upright
position. In addition, he realized that the pain wasn't all physical.

Suddenly, Nurse Clair, with her baby fine plaited hair pinned to her
head, came into the room and frowned at both of the men. With years
of experience, she knew when one of her patients was getting upset. Her
little mouth tightened and then twitched in anger. She administered the
prescribed medicines and then shot a glare their way that caused a silence
in the hospital room. The nurse picked up the silver tray, which clanked
against the railing as she removed it. This broke the silence. Buchanan
and Branson watched her leave never having said a word. Her hip pushed
the room door open; she turned back and gave them one last stare, and
left with that look of 'I'll be back.'

Buchanan looked over to the windows without curtains and said, "You
just can't do it. We'll find another way." He knew Branson was right,
though.

"You know there's no other way. Tonight, get them to go somewhere to
eat. Then we'll make it happen. You can work miracles. You know what
to do to make me look dead. And don't give me any crap that you don't,
'cause we did it before. Several times."

"But…"

"But, nothing. You want to do it so that it's for real. 'Cause all I have
to do is pull this plug." He rested his hand on the wire.

"For God's sake, man. Don't do this and get yourself killed. You're a
legend and one that we need to stay around for awhile. We'll tie Stratton
up long enough for all of you to be safe."

"This is me you're talking to, not some damn rookie. What's it to be?"
Branson held the wire tighter.

Buchanan sweated. "Okay, have it your way. Tonight we'll get you
away from here. Kelly will go crazy. You know that, don't you? You're all
she has."

"She's young, but she'll find another man." He looked away.

"You fool. You stupid fucking bastard. All right, tonight. Make the most
of your day, my friend. And God forgive you for what you are gonna do
to Kelly." He stared blankly at Branson.

"He already did."

Branson's head turned toward the door as he heard the footsteps coming down the hall.

"Want more ice chips? I brought you as much as you can eat," Sage said.

"Great daughter you have," said Kelly and licked one of Branson's ice chips. "She knew I wanted to be alone with you. I need you, Kane. We can go home soon, right? Well, somewhere together, anyway?"

"Sure, baby. Here, climb up on the bed beside me. Let me hold you close to me."

She did not have to be told twice. Kelly scampered up on the tan hospital blanket feeling closer to a man than she ever had.

"You still not wearing anything under your jeans?" he asked his wife staring into her eyes, which seemed to be softer than he remembered them.

"No." She looked into his eyes.

"Great."

Branson slid his free hand into Kelly's jeans.

She dozed in his arms. The IV was restricting but he had managed to make love to her, and the pain in his leg was almost unbearable. He looked out the window at the sky. It was bright pink. He stroked her hair and watched the sun go down on the American shore. Never again would he share moments with Kelly in this foreign land.

A gentle tap at the door interrupted his thoughts. Buchanan stuck his head around the frame. Keeping his word with Branson, he asked, "Kelly, want to go out to eat with Sage and me? We'll go somewhere fancy."

"Kane, you mind if I go eat?" asked his wife. "I am kind of hungry, and fancy sure does sound tempting."

"No, baby. I'm not going anywhere. But I would like a kiss before you go."

"You just had…" She blushed.

Sage didn't hear her as they started for the doorway.

Branson creased his eyebrows and then motioned Buchanan to take his wife out of the room, and away from him. She did not notice.

"I'll be waiting for you." He let her go.

Buchanan ushered them down the lobby. Branson watched the door swing closed as he lay back on the bed. If he were going to do the job of getting rid of the trash, he'd do it his way. He waited until he heard their footsteps move away from his hospital room door and then pulled the wire from his body.

Passersby heard him cry out in the next room. Doctors and nurses came running. Nurse Clair was one of the first persons to arrive only to find her patient dying. It wasn't hard to cause a heart attack. She had seen the stress his visitors were causing him.

Branson had heard code red and that was all. The small group hadn't gotten to the hospital lobby, before they heard his alarms beeping. Kelly, whose hand had been on the elevator door when she heard the sounds, was the first one back up the hallway. Instinctively, she knew what had caused the noise. Sage was right behind her.

"Let me get through here! Get out of my way!" she screamed. "I'm his wife."

The room door flew open and she ran to the bed, tears flowing down her cheeks. Looking first at him and then at the doctors and nurses standing around him, she yelled, "Kane!" She shrieked long and loud and Buchanan grabbed her flaying arms.

"There was nothing we could do, Mrs. Branson,"

Doctor Weir said to her, "He has had a massive heart attack. I'm so very sorry."

She stopped. Realization set in quickly. Branson was gone. Fifteen minutes previously he had made love to her and everything seemed as if it would last forever for them. Unlike anything she had ever felt.

"You're sorry…you're sorry? He's dead and all you can say is you're sorry!"

Buchanan, in a fatherly fashion, held her tightly. "Kelly, I know this is horrible. I am still in shock from it all. But we need to stay together through this. Come on, think of Sage." He tried to hold her, but she would not be held. She pulled away from him.

"Sage is his daughter. I am his wife! I am the one suffering. Oh, my God, what am I saying. Sage matters also. I didn't mean that. Oh God, I wasn't even with him. I want to stay with him. Please just let me hold him one last time," she demanded. Tears streamed down her face.

"You don't want to do that." The doctor turned to Buchanan. "May I talk to you?"

"Yeah. Sage, you look after Kelly, I can't seem to get her to stop being hysterical." He motioned his men to stand by.

"Take me with you. I have to see him again. God, why didn't I tell him?

Now it's too late. Oh, God, Kane, please don't leave me. You're all I have."
She broke down and collapsed in the chair.

Buchanan, feeling torn between helping the girls and finishing the job,
sat down beside her. "Calm down. You'll lose the baby. I am sure that is
not what you want. Keep in mind, you do have something, you have his
child in you."

She stared into his eyes, giving him a look that was haunting. "No. I
can't lose his baby. Please, tell me what to do. Buchanan, you don't seem to
understand. He was the only man who has ever loved and respected me at
the same time. I just can't believe I won't be able to spend the rest of my
life with him. But, I'll stop crying and listen, I promise. Just tell me what
you want me to do." She slumped back on the chair outside his room.

"Stay here for a minute while I go with the doctor. I think it's okay for
you to see him again. Sage, I am so sorry about your dad. Good God, this
all happened so quickly. I was just sitting here and talking with the man.
Well, please sit with her. I'll be right back."

Kelly sat down, her face ashen. Tears streamed down from Sage's eyes.
She looked at Kelly. She had stopped crying. Her face was blank. Kelly
had become a woman, pregnant with Kane's baby, married and a widow
all in the blink of an eye.

Buchanan followed the doctor into the room. He stared at Branson.
There was no color.

"Is he really dead?" He was afraid of the answer.

"No, but he did pull his own plug. We did get to him in time. He's so
sedated that even his eyelashes won't move. He's a tough man. It had to
hurt like hell though.

Did I hear you right? His wife is pregnant?"

"Yes, and she didn't want him to know about the baby yet. He'll be okay,
won't he? Why didn't he just let us fake it? No, that wouldn't be him. If
she comes in, will she know?"

Branson's hand was clammy to the touch. "Is he supposed to be like
that?"

"Natural. She can see him for a second, but if she gets too close…"

"We need to get him away from here tonight. They'll get to him if we
don't hurry." Buchanan was trying to concentrate.

"Goddamn it, Branson? Why didn't you wait?"

"He can't stay like that for long. Sedation is only good for a few hours."
Doctor Weir had never had patient problems like this before and did

not exactly know that they were making the best decisions. He turned to Buchanan and said, "Depends on how his body handles it. Can you get him on a plane back to Australia in the next few days?"

"Yes and the girls should go back as soon as possible. We'll put them under our protection. I have a feeling that your other ex-patient is already on his way out of jail."

CHAPTER 16

Buchanan was right. Miles Stratton's attorneys had him out of jail by sundown and he was on his way out of the country on the next flight before Buchanan had time to do anything.

Kelly lay awake the whole night. Sleep would not come. When she looked at the empty space in her bed, she felt ice cold and she longed for Branson. How could he have left her? How dare he? Branson was the only one she had ever wanted as a husband. No other man would have been right for her. Why did everything she ever touched have to die? What would happen to their baby? Would Stratton still look for her, now that Branson was dead? She climbed out of bed and turned the television on.

The news reporters were informing the public about an accident at Malibu. AFP Agent Branson's face was on the news report. Stratton's picture was on there too. He was a wanted man by the U.S. Government. But he had left the country by his own means and just couldn't come back. All she saw was the man who killed Branson. Now the world knew who Branson was.

Kelly knew that she would go on for his baby. Branson would want her to do that. When she'd entered the hospital room, she had watched from afar. To touch him now would be to acknowledge his death. A truth that she could not accept.

Now she watched the news of his death on TV. She stared at the screen, as pictures flashed by of Miles Stratton who was now a man wanted by the FBI, among others…Kelly was among the others.

Sage found Kelly the next day, still mourning his death. Still watching. She hadn't eaten, or showered and was holding Branson's leather jacket. Sage packed their things and helped her shower. Kelly returned to the couch and sat down.

"You know you can cry, Kel. Dad would want you to feel your feelings."

"No, he wouldn't."

Branson had taught his new wife well.

Later that day, Buchanan sent a car for the girls, complete with an assignment of cops to watch after them. Everyone knew that they keep their best eye out on the girls. They teamed with the ones already outside of the hotel doors.

The Qantas flight sat on the runway at LAX. It waited patiently for its special cargo. Buchanan was at check–in. The girls were rushed through the runway under tight security.

"Has she slept at all?" Buchanan asked Sage worried about Kelly's appearance.

"No, nor eaten. She'll get sick if we don't watch her.

Where are we going?" asked Sage.

"To Sydney. We have protection for both of you, just in case. It's a safe house. I think Stratton is long gone and his threats to get Kelly back are empty. But we have to be sure. We will go from there to the funeral. By the way, your father left a letter with me in case anything should happen to him. Gave it to me some time ago. I…"

As he spoke, he saw the coffin arrive and glanced over at Kelly. There was no reaction. It was as though she had died with Branson. She had dressed in black pants and a long black jacket, and still she looked sexy. Buchanan watched her slowly walking. She was going through the motions. Sage put her arm around her. The last thing anyone wanted was for her to lose the baby.

First class seating was emptied and security was tight as Mrs. Branson, her husband, and his daughter took to the plane. Buchanan sat next to Kelly, placing her by the window, staring at the sun. She felt no warmth from it, but closed her eyes to dream and feel his arms around her. His smell oddly enough, felt close by. Her eyes held nothing except pain, but still she would not cry.

An hour into the flight, Buchanan purposefully went over to Sage's seat. "Are you alright?" he asked. She said nothing and just stared at him. He could see that she was not going to say anything about the way she felt. He continued, "Can't you make Kelly eat or get some rest? Look at her."

"I can't get through to her. Can't get in there. If only she'd let go and just talk about it." Sage's eyes were red.

"How are you holding up?" he asked seeing another opportunity to get her to talk about her dad's death.

"I'm fine." She rested her hand on Buchanan's. "Who is meeting us from the flight?"

"Deputy Lord and some of your father's friends. They will take you back to the safe house. Your dad's body will go back with us to Sydney. You remember Lord? He always liked you, if I remember right."

"Yes, he did. Dad was always trying to get me to date…" She stopped and broke down on Buchanan's shoulder.

He put his arms around her while she cried for several minutes. How he wished Kelly would do the same.

Sage moved and sat next to Kelly. The flight was long and tedious. Twenty hours was a long time to think, and that was all that Kelly could do. She reclined her seat and then she laid back, her eyes wide open. Sage dozed fitfully. Buchanan sat down at the rear of the plane. He was thinking of the girls, when his train of thought was interrupted.

"Sir, the pilot would like to speak with you."

"Thanks."

"You're welcome," replied the cop.

Buchanan headed for the cockpit.

"Message on the radio, coded for you."

Buchanan took the headphones from the pilot.

"Buchanan here."

"Thought I'd lost you all."

He turned away from earshot. "Where the hell are you? You were supposed to wait at the hospital until we got you out of there." He could not believe that Branson would have the nerve to call him on the flight. But then, one never knew what he would do next.

"I got myself out. What the hell did you tell that doctor? He sure was afraid of you when I left. What did you do, threaten his life?" He changed the subject. "Best if you don't know where I am. All I wanted to let you know is that I'm safe. I still have one or two loyal friends out here in Branson's Country. I'm tired and in pain, but safe. I did see you leave on the flight. I watched from a car."

"You did what?" He turned away from any overactive ears. "How the hell did you do that? And why did you pull the plug? You are not invincible. You might have killed yourself. Did you see Kelly? She's not doing too well. Hope you're proud of yourself."

His voice rose. The pilot looked at him.

"Not particularly. What did you want me to do? You protect Kelly and my daughter while I finish the job I started and botched. Anything happens to them and I'll come after you." He paused. "Do you have that letter I gave you?"

"Yeah, I have it. You still want me to read it to them?"

"That's a stupid fucking question. Why else would I give the damn thing to you? This part is the most important. Everyone has to believe I'm dead, or it will not work. The rest is up to you. Give me a good send-off. When the job is done, I'll get word to you. However long it takes to find him. Just make sure that you left money in that bank account along with a passport. You did do that, didn't you?" The line crackled and hissed. He was still in the States.

"Your cover is well taken care of and for the most part, you're safe. Try to bring Stratton back to us, and bring him back alive. Guess you heard he made bail the same night?"

"Yeah, I heard. I'll take care of this end. You look after my girls, especially Kelly. I…" he hesitated not used to his own emotions, "love her so much. Promise me?"

"You have my word."

There was a heavy sigh. "I'll be in touch."

"Kane? Kane, don't hang up? I need to tell you something real quick, it's about Kelly…"

The line was dead. Buchanan returned to his seat. Did Branson really know what he was doing?

Kale Bonner was his new ID. His picture was altered and it looked good. All Branson had to do was match himself to the shot. He had the time and he had the money, but the problem was that he didn't have Stratton. More than likely, the bastard was in Mexico by now. He had at least a two-day head start on Branson.

It was raining when the Qantas flight landed safely. The rain sounded like eggs frying in a skillet and seemed never to end. With all the emotional upheavals and the unceasing rain, Kelly had been airsick. She was pale and drawn. Deputy Lord waited with tears in his eyes. He had liked Sage for many years. He watched her grow up and knew his boss wanted him to date her. Now was his chance to look out for her. But he was not prepared for the woman she had become. She even looked like Branson, with her long blonde hair. Of course, her stunning figure was pleasant to him. He wiped his face with his hand.

Then he saw Kelly walking down the steps of the aircraft. Looking up into the rain, her long hair blew in the breeze. This was Branson's widow. She was just a kid, striking and determined, frail and yet strong. He saw the look on her face. Death haunted her.

"Mr. Buchanan," he shook his hand at the one interrupting them. "We have everything standing by. There are cars to take you to the house."

"Lord. It's good to be back. This is Kelly Branson. A very special person."

"Mrs. Branson, Deputy Lord. You have the department's deepest sympathy."

Kelly looked at him. "Thank you. Mr. Buchanan, can we go home? Back to Kane's place? I want to go there first."

She was so quiet, not like the Kelly he knew.

"We can stop by. Best if you don't stay too long. Stratton still has far-reaching fingers. He may just give up, though. Now that…"

He had never lied to a woman before now but honoring his promise was important to him. As they turned for the cars, they all saw the coffin. Buchanan ushered them into federal cars. Black limos flying the Australian flag. Lord drove them to Branson's place. The rain had faded into drizzle. It hid tears well. Lord opened the door for Kelly and in slow motion, she entered the apartment.

They all stood back and let her go. She saw the bike in the corner. She watched it shine in the lights. Running her hands across the cold hard steel, she could almost feel him. Her fingers lingered on the seat. Kelly climbed onto the bike and leaned down across the flag-covered tank. Her hands clung to the Harley. Sage clasped her mouth. Kelly turned her head toward them. Her hair tumbled down her shoulders.

"I'm not leaving here, not ever. This is Kane's place. He would want me to stay."

Lord admired her. He could see why his boss had married her. Buchanan moved forward.

"Kelly, you can't stay here. Not on your own, anyway."

"She won't be on her own," Sage said. "I'm staying here with her. It's my place too."

"You can't! It's not what your father would want. This is not safe," Buchanan said. "Anyone staying here is going to get killed."

"How do you know that? He would want Kelly and I to go on. I'll take care of her. She'll need me." Sage moved to her side, protecting her.

"I'll stay, boss, for a few days. Make sure everything's okay."

Lord took off his coat and laid it on the chair.

"I'll have someone stop by with your things. A whole squad of cops will be posted outside the apartment block. The funeral is the day after tomorrow. Sage, for God's sake, makes sure she eats. Both of you get some sleep."

Turning away from the girls, he said, "Lord, step outside with me." Buchanan lowered his voice. "There's something you need to know." Should he confide? Better that Lord knew. "Kelly is pregnant with his kid."

Lord turned white. "Branson? Did he know?"

"She wouldn't let me tell him. Kelly never got time to tell him when all this happened. It was part of the big scheme, only it backfired. I'll explain more in the morning when I call you. Right now, I'm tired." He ran his fingers through his hair. "So much has happened; I can't take it all in and keep it all straight by myself. This way, you know too, but you have to keep all of this a secret. Tell no one."

Lord returned to the room. "Where's Kelly?"

"Gone to her room to sleep. Did Buchanan tell you about her?"

"Yes. Pity your father didn't know. She's one hell of a woman. And how do you feel about the situation?" He sat down next to Sage on the couch and rested his arm on the back of it.

"Dad would have loved it. He did love her, you know. I thought at first, it was all a game. When I found out they were sleeping together, I wanted to die. I miss him and that girl in there provided him a reason to continue living. I owe Kelly. You see why I have to stay? She's the only connection to my father. Her and his unborn child."

He opened his arms to her and Sage sobbed in them. It felt good to have someone to share her grief, someone she could turn to when in pain. For Kelly, there was no one.

Dressed in black, Kelly waited at the door. She wore shades. Sage stood by her side. Buchanan had taken care of all the arrangements. He escorted her to the waiting car. Lord offered Sage his arm. Buchanan noticed.

The AFP turned out in force. A trail of motorcycles and cars lined the streets. It was to be full honors for such a hero. Their car pulled alongside the gravesite. Kelly stepped out. No one seemed surprised by Branson's choice of a wife. In her hand, she held a white rose. A white rose for death. Kelly moved forward. There was complete silence.

A hundred men stood holding their breaths. Kelly looked up to the skies and whispered his name. The mourners filed by his coffin, one by one, placing a white rose on his casket. She bent down and dropped the rose that she had held into the grave. When she stood up, she faltered slightly. As they lowered the coffin into the ground, Buchanan leaned forward and took her hand.

The pastor completed the ceremony, but Buchanan had his own dedication to share. "Kane Branson was one of my best cops. He knew his turf. I will miss him, but he will live on in our hearts. Branson…this will always be your country."

He felt Kelly's hand tighten on his and a shiver went hurriedly down his spine. Looking to the cutting, he saw a lone figure standing. The man was tall and dark-haired, with a moustache and beard. Buchanan blinked and the image was gone. Had he imagined it?

Buchanan handed Kelly the Australian flag. She cradled it in her arms. The wind blew her hair, and she closed her eyes. For one brief moment, Kelly thought she could smell the ocean and could see Branson riding down PCH. From behind the shades came tears. And she cried.

At that precise time, light years away, Branson stood on the beach at Malibu, tossing his old passport into the ocean. He heard the waves roar as his life floated away. From now on, he was Kale Bonner, until the score was evened. "Kelly!" He called her name over the roar of the ocean, fists clenched at his side, and then he turned and walked to his bike. It would be his home for the next few months. He had a lead, one he intended to follow. He could not go back to Australia until the job was finished.

It seemed senseless and painful to go back to Kelly. To be loving, he would let her find a life that he couldn't give her. He looked in the mirror on the Harley and a dark-haired stranger looked back. He was stern and severe. Dark did not suit his coloring, but it sure as hell suited his mood.

Swinging his leg over the bike, he powered it up and took to the road doing sixty, then seventy. He had a place to go and very definitely something to finish.

Buchanan had something left also. Pulling the letter from his coat, he realized that he was disobeying his friend's request by not opening the letter. He held the letter in his hand thinking that he wanted to hear from his man one more time. A time, for Buchanan, that would be a long time coming.

CHAPTER 17

The letter sat for months in Buchanan's desk drawer, and still he waited to hear from Branson. Kelly was near her time; nine months had gone by fast. She had never accepted the fact that Kane was dead. Sage became the mother hen. Deputy Lord was a frequent visitor to the apartment. Afraid that Branson would rise from the grave, Lord dated Branson's daughter in the old-fashioned courteous way of dating. Buchanan stopped by on a weekly basis.

"You look awful, young lady," he said, looking at the pins holding together the front of Kelly's jeans. "If it's money you need…"

"I like these jeans. The baby's giving me hell. At least, I can wear my old things and be comfortable. I polished his bike today. I just cannot part with it. I know it's crazy. When I see Sage with Lord, it makes it worse. Oh, they don't flaunt the relationship, but it makes me feel so alone." She sat down on the couch and held her stomach.

"I understand really, I do." It wasn't the first time Buchanan had come close to telling her the truth.

Buchanan watched Kelly turn to Branson's bike. Damn the man. Why was he staying away for so long a time? All it would take would be a call. However, the call didn't come.

The same day that Kelly went into labor, Branson finally located Stratton in Mexico. He had stopped for gas in a small town garage, and was following a lead he'd had for a couple weeks. He'd been dogging the same location for days, and today, his tenacity was about to pay off. Across the road a black stretch limo sat parked in front of a shabby warehouse. Two men appeared from the doorway. They shook hands. One scuttled back into the shadows of the doorway, while the other looked around, then got into a waiting car.

Branson couldn't believe his eyes. The tip had been worth the payoff. The person he had been trying to locate was now right in front of him.

Stratton would not recognize him now. His hair had darkened and was very long. His suntan had deepened because of the Mexican sun. The surroundings fit him well. Dressed in jeans and a T-shirt, he looked like any other bum on the road. After he pumped the gas, he sat astride his bike. The only giveaway was the snakeskin boots. Branson waited as the car pulled away and then he then followed at a leisurely pace.

Traffic was heavy. Branson hunkered down close to his bike. Man and machine as one. The car led the way; however, he stayed back until the stretch pulled into a driveway. At last, Stratton was his. Branson leaned back on the bike, the engine purring like a tiger.

"Time to die, Stratton. Have a good day, because this is going to be your last."

On the outskirts of Sydney, Kelly cried for Kane. Baby Star's birth was not easy. Kelly's labor was long, and she screamed for her husband.

Sage stayed close to her. Outside of the maternity ward, Buchanan and Lord paced up and down.

"So this is what having a kid is like?" asked Lord.

"Yeah, except this one now has no father." Buchanan turned away.

"You okay, boss? Something has been eating you for the last few weeks. It has to do with Branson, doesn't it?"

He looked startled. "What made you say that?"

Lord stood up and poured himself some water from the cooler. "You like some?" He handed Buchanan a paper cup. "One day, when you were out, your phone rang. I answered it. The line went dead. In fact, this has happened a couple of times. Yesterday, it happened again. Two hours ago, right before you called us to the hospital, another call came. You got some snitch that's found Stratton?" He peered over the rim of his cup.

"No snitch." Had Lord figured it out? "Probably a wrong number."

"They were long-distance calls. Not too many people call long distance repeatedly if it's a wrong number. I have to tell you, boss. After the first couple of times, I put a trace on the line. I thought this might be a dangerous crank after you. I'm sorry, but the trace came up positive. It was Branson's mobile phone number. Want to try explaining to me what is happening?"

Lord had been devoted to Branson, but how would he feel about being deceived? Maybe it was time to find out where his loyalties were, especially considering that Lord had recently become engaged to the man's daughter.

"How could that be? Could be a crossed number. Or someone else is using his mobile." He sipped at the water without looking up.

"Or…it could be Branson," Lord said to Buchanan.

"He's dead. We buried him. You know that."

"Yeah, right. Only you and the doctor know that for sure. We buried someone or something. But, who or what did we bury?" He looked over at Buchanan and then continued, "Branson's alive, isn't he?" he set the cup down.

"Don't you think he would have come for Kelly and his baby if he were alive?"

Lord thought a second and then responded, "Nope, probably not. Sage told me he didn't know about the baby. Plus, he doesn't stop until the job is finished. He's probably out there finishing the job he started and he's not on an official assignment. I'm right, aren't I?"

Buchanan's eyes gave him away. Why had he called after all this time? How could he have missed so many of Branson's calls? Could he be sensing Kelly's situation?

Tired of the Ping-Pong game, he started talking, but he tried to do it where no one could hear him or her. "Yes," he whispered. "No one can know, especially not Sage and Kelly. He had a vendetta to finish, and, even then, he may not come back. He doesn't believe he should give the girl any false hopes. She's still his wife, but he was hoping she would find someone else."

Lord almost choked. "You're kidding? Kelly? Find someone else? She is totally devoted to him. What was he thinking? Good God, doesn't he understand that she's still a widow mourning his death?"

"He doesn't. All he could see, when this all happened, was that he had to get them away to safety. He nearly killed himself in the process. He pulled his own plug."

"I knew it. All along I had this feeling." He hesitated and thought about what Buchanan had said. "Jeez. That definitely took some guts. But, then again, my boss always did have those. I won't tell anyone about this. After all, I'm a dedicated cop also. I respect him too much for that. Still, Kelly has a right to know he's alive. Maybe it's over."

His eyes teared and he wiped them away. Buchanan put his hand on Lord's shoulder.

"It's okay. Maybe he's calling with good news. If the call comes again, keep him on the phone. Tell him you know. Just please never tell him about the baby." Buchanan stopped speaking and listened. "What the hell?" Buchanan turned to the delivery room.

They heard Kelly scream again. In another minute, Sage burst through the door with joy in her eyes. She flung her arms around Lord's neck.

"I have a sister. She's so tiny and so blonde just like my…"

"How's Kelly?" Buchanan asked.

"She's doing just fine. Was touch and go for a little while." Sage followed up the update in a more subdued tone. "I wish my dad were here to see what he produced. He would be so proud."

"Yes, he would. Can we see the mother and baby yet?" Buchanan inquired.

"I guess so. I'll go ask," Sage said, then disappeared back through the doors.

"Goddamn, the man has a daughter and he doesn't even know it," Lord said. "That isn't right." Lord stared at the door as if Branson might appear any given second.

"You gave me your word." Buchanan looked tired and now the burden of knowing had been shared.

"I gave it and I'll try my best to honor my word. Doesn't mean I have to like it."

"Believe me, knowing only makes it worse," replied Buchanan.

Kelly held Star and looked at her. She caressed her fingers and toes, deciding she loved the little crease on her chubby little legs. Pulling the blanket tightly around her, she began to feel like Star's mom.

Sage sat on the bed and marveled at the tiny Branson in Kelly's arms. "Dad would be so proud of you, Kelly. And you, baby Branson look just like him, all blonde and oh my, those gorgeous blue eyes." Sage put her finger on the tiny person's hand.

Tears trickled down Kelly's face and onto his child. She closed her eyes and murmured his name. Her need for him had never been more desperate and seemed as if it would never end.

"Visitors," came a man's voice from the door.

Buchanan stepped round the entrance first.

"So what did you decide to name this beautiful little creature?" asked Lord somewhat sheepishly. Newborn babies weren't his thing.

"Star…I named her Star after the star we once looked at on the beach. One day, I'll explain to her why I picked her name to be that. At least I have his child."

"Dad would appreciate that." Sage cried.

Lord turned away. It just wasn't right. Branson should know.

Branson sat outside the house on the bike waiting. He wanted to be sure that Stratton was not just visiting. When he was satisfied, he left. He found a motel up the road. Even with his dark look, his accent still gave him away. An Australian, in this part of Mexico, would raise suspicions.

He picked up the keys and headed for Room 3 on ground level. The room reeked of cigarettes and cheap perfume. Dumping his bag on the floor, he lay down on the bed totally exhausted. The forty dollars a night he paid in advance was too pricey for this place. Now he would sleep awhile and then think of a way to dispose of Stratton. He longed to go home, a longing that had become deeper with each day. Constantly, he thought of her; he wanted Kelly. He pushed his thoughts to the back of his mind. Business first, and Kelly was better off without him. Still, he was curious about how she and Sage were. Twice that day, he had picked up the phone and called Buchanan in Australia. However, there was no reply. He'd try again in the morning.

Branson dozed. He awoke, feeling a little refreshed. Branson showered in something that looked similar to a bathroom. The door on the shower leaked and water seeped out onto the floor, and disappeared down a crack in the boards. He realized he hadn't eaten since the day before. Dressed in frayed black jeans and a rough-cut leather jacket, he walked to the front desk.

"Somewhere 'round here to find a steak?"

"Cantina down past la casa, *casa blanca*, uh, the big white house. Food, beer, girls?"

Why did every place he visit, offer him girls?

"Gracias."

His bike pulled out of the motel and blew past Stratton's big white *casa*. He parked the bike, pulled his jacket around him, and let his hair hang loose. Looking as much Latino as the Mexicans, he sported a look, which said, "don't mess with me". The cantina was not hard to find. It was crummy-looking, like the rest of the places nearby. Mumbling his order to the waitress proved easier than he thought, practicing his Spanish was interesting enough.

Two greasy tacos later, he sat back, wiping hot sauce from his moustache. The music got louder and the lights burned brighter. Branson began to wish he had stayed in the motel until suddenly, the door from the street opened; and, in the half-light, he caught sight of the object of his revenge. Branson stared, hatred burning in his eyes. The lights and music went unheeded around him, except for the searing bright light in his mind.

Silhouetted in the doorframe stood Miles Stratton with a cigar stuffed in his mouth and a girl on his arm, Stratton was again living his life to the fullest. Branson watched. His eyes never left the other man. Stratton sauntered across to the bar, then sat down and ordered drinks. Branson had a beer in front of him, which he made it last all night. He figured that Stratton had no clue he was being followed. Branson watched him laugh and flirt and thought the only thing Stratton should consider was flirting with death. He smiled to himself. That would soon be an option.

Around eleven PM, Stratton whispered in his companion's ear. They stood up, paid the bill and headed for the parking lot. Branson dropped money on the table and followed a good distance behind so that Stratton would never suspect he was being tailed. The entire time, Stratton was surrounded by other customers, which did him no good whatsoever.

He needed Stratton on his own. The only chance to grab him, seemed to be in the car or while he was in bed. Judging by the girl hanging from his arm, it was unlikely Stratton slept alone. Branson was sure he did not intend to kill any Mexican woman.

Branson sped through the night following the car. The silver machine growled. It was dangerous and lethal, like him. Stratton drove to the señorita's house. The trick was to get inside the building and then inside Stratton's head.

Stratton stepped out of the car, handing out money like the one it was growing on trees. He paid the valet, he paid the doorman, and he stuffed money down the girl's blouse. They disappeared inside the house. Branson didn't have that kind of scratch on him. He had the feeling Stratton was here for a spell. Time to go and get more money. He mounted the bike and drove back down the street slowly, quietly. No roar of engines. He drifted into the motel. The guests in the next room were anything but quiet. Music blared so loud; it could be heard in the parking lot. It reminded him of home. He banged on the wall and they banged back and turned up the music. Branson was changing clothes and he was trying to think. He climbed over the bed. Clad in jeans and a shoulder holster, he left his room.

"Turn the fucking music down." He banged hard on their door.

"Go fuck yourself," they yelled back at him.

Branson stepped back, and his boot connected with the green painted door. It burst the lock straight off and the door swung wide open. "I said turn it down. You gonna do it?"

"No." A Hell's Angel and his girl looked at him defiantly. Clad in leather clothes and tattoos, the young Angel posed no threat to anyone, let alone Branson.

Branson pulled the gun and fired one clean shot at the radio. "Now it's quiet."

"You bastard." The wayward Angel made a threatening advance towards him. His hand doubled into a fist. "Who do ya think you are, old man?"

"Don't push your luck, mate. Man, you Americans don't know when to quit." He aimed the gun straight at his balls and the tough guy wet his pants. "Bathroom's over there. Ma'am. Goodnight."

Branson walked back into his room and gathered his things. Pulling on a sweater, he left. In his temper, he had managed to blow his cover. He knew the guy might report the incident, Hell's Angel or not. From a block away, he watched the cops arrive. He had to move now, it was one a.m. Stratton would be back home, maybe. If the car wasn't at the big white house, he sure knew where to find him. He dug into his boot, retrieved his mobile phone, and flipped it open. It was evening in Australia. Lord answered. Branson said nothing.

"Branson? Sir? Boss, don't hang up. Please? It's me, Dan Lord." Silence, but no click. "I know it's you. Mr. Buchanan informed me. Well, I guessed and then he explained what went down. I need to ask you something. Sir?" He could still hear breathing on the line. "If you won't speak to me, I'll get Mr. Buchanan for you, but I want to tell you that Sage and I are engaged."

"You are what?" Branson yelled.

"It is you! I knew it." Lord was capable of emotions that even he wasn't aware that he had. "I want to marry your daughter. I love her, sir and she's in love with me. Mr. Branson, say something."

"No," was the only word that Branson resonated.

"No what, sir?"

"No, you can't marry my daughter. She isn't going through what her mother and Kelly did. I don't want my daughter married to some damn cop. You hear me?" His voice was deep, but crisp, clear and very much to the point.

"You can't stop us! You're not here." Lord was angry. "And there's something else you should know. It's Kelly."

"What about her?" Now, he had Branson's undivided attention.

Buchanan came in the room, hearing part of the conversation.

"Lord," yelled an irate Buchanan, and then he said, "Give me that phone and get out of my sight."

With the receiver in his hand, he asked, "Branson, you there?"

"What the fuck did you tell him for, and what's this about them being engaged?" Branson paused. "He was going to say something about Kelly. Is she okay? Has she found someone else?"

"Kelly has someone else in her life. She gave birth yesterday to your daughter." He paused. "Did you hear me? You okay?"

"I'm okay, but how is she?" His voice was barely above a whisper. "And the baby?"

"They're both fine. Baby looks just like you. Blonde, blue eyes. Kelly named her Star. Let it go Branson. Come back. It's not too late."

Branson choked on his own emotions. "Yes…it is!"

"Branson? Kane?"

To Lord, he said, "Goddamn, he hung up. Lord, get over here. You ever mess up like that again and your butt will be out of this department. You hear me? Personal feelings don't get in the way."

"He said I couldn't marry his daughter. Well, he's not here to stop us."

"So you told him. Why? To make him come back? And all you did was keep him further away. Get out of my sight. You just may have pushed him over the edge. Branson had called to tell us something. Now we'll only read about it in the papers. Good work, Deputy Lord."

"I didn't mean to…"

"I said get the fuck out of my sight!"

Branson sat back on the bike. Lord God, he had another child. Star. Trust Kelly to call her that. He laughed out loud. Now, more than ever, he had to make sure they were safe. He powered the bike and let it rip into speed. Concentration was hard. Finish the job and then disappear for good. No more communication with any of them. That would be hard, but maybe it would be best for all concerned.

He found Stratton back at the whorehouse. This time he had money, and he had balls. And he also had a gun. He paid at the desk, and picking up a girl was easy. Now he was in. Branson had never paid for sex, and he wasn't about to start.

As fortune would have it, the room he picked was next to Stratton's. He opened the door and let the girl in. The dark longhaired girl started to undress. He let her take her blouse and skirt off also. She had a good shape. Then he stopped her. Taking her by the hand, he led her to the bathroom door.

"Here's your money. Now go sit in the bathroom."

She looked at him as if he was insane. Branson realized that she didn't understand a word he had said. She only knew how to do one thing and that wasn't speaking English, let alone Australian. He showed her the door, physically put her inside and then locked her inside.

Branson also showed her the gun on the way in the bathroom. That she understood in any language. Sitting down on the toilet, she counted the hundred-dollar bills.

He slid out of the room and moved next door. Branson tried the handle to Stratton's room and found it locked. Nothing a good credit card couldn't fix. It was easy. Branson slid the card in the lock and it opened. He slipped into the room under the cover of darkness. After several drinks, Stratton became too occupied and relaxed to even notice someone looming at the end of his bed for several minutes. When he finally looked up, he didn't recognize Branson.

"What the fuck do you think you're doing?" He pulled the sheets up around him.

The girl tried to grab some of the sheet, but Stratton took most of it. Branson pulled the gun from the holster, moved to the lamp and turned it on. Stratton squinted in the light, his eyes adjusting. Stratton saw the tall, dark haired man. He blinked. It couldn't be. This was a damn nightmare. The hair coloring wasn't right, but he could not mistake the look on the man's face in front of him.

"Branson?" His eyes widened in horror.

"Right. I came to finish what I started." His voice was deep and full of intent.

"They said you were dead. You're dead! You're dead!" he yelled, his super-smooth composure lost.

"As you can see, I'm not dead. Now, get out of that fucking bed! I'd like nothing better than to just shoot you in front of this girl?"

"Where are we going?" His confidence was shattered.

"Gonna take a little ride. Man, oh man, how I've waited for this. Pull your damn pants on."

Stratton scrambled out of bed, his manhood limp. Branson laughed and then his expression changed.

"She speak English?" Branson waved his hand towards the girl.

"Yes, I do." She stood up, let the sheet drop showing her naked body bruised from the wear and tear of this man who was with her.

"You still at the same games, Stratton? You and Walker both liked to beat up on women."

"You will make him pay, señor?" she asked quietly.

"Oh, you can count on that. He won't be hurting any more women, as long as you don't talk."

"No, señor. He did this." She showed him the deep scars on her back.

Branson figured most of them were caused by burns from cigars.

"Let's go. You fucking bastard, can't you even learn to treat women decent? This is what in the end is getting your ass killed."

The girl watched, and as Branson pointed the gun at Stratton, the Mexican whore spat in Stratton's face.

Branson glanced at the dresser and the keys sat waiting. Branson picked them up. He stuck the gun in Stratton's back, ushering him down the back stairs. In the cold night air of the parking lot, Branson opened the car door, still with his gun aimed in Stratton's back.

"You drive," Branson ordered and climbed in the back seat.

"Where are we going?"

"Straight to hell," hissed Branson.

Stratton was sweating. He knew he was about to die. What he didn't know was how. He glanced in the driving mirror, watching Branson glare at him. Branson laid the gun on his lap and pulled something from his pocket.

"Now drive. Go. Out of here, make a left."

Stratton put his foot on the gas. The car moved on, faster at Branson's request.

"You won't get away with this. My friends will catch you." He shivered with fear.

"No one will find you. No one cares. Nor will they touch my family. You'll make sure of that." He passed his mobile phone to the front. "You call your *friends* and tell them you're feeling pangs of guilt. That it's weighing on your conscience. Suicide would be an obvious choice. Do it!"

He flipped the phone and handed it to Stratton.

"Before I do something, I'm going to tell you that I should have told you long ago." He half turned towards Branson. "Did you know your wife was doing drugs? Bet you didn't. Pierce used to go by her house, your house. He told us all he'd been supplying some dame…"

"I don't believe that… and I never will."

"Then don't. She was a regular party girl. Kill me and you will never know for sure, will you?" He spoke into the mobile phone. "Hey, Reynolds. Something I should have told you all long ago. That woman back in Australia…" Then he blurted the words out as if the person on the end of the call could help him. "I'm in my car and…there's a gun pointing right…"

Branson pulled the garrote over his head. It caught on the mobile and the phone dropped from Stratton's hand. He grabbed for the rope, but Branson was quicker. It slid down to his throat. Stratton lost control of the car. He tried to brake and, as he leaned forward, the cord became tighter. He couldn't breathe. His eyes bulged and the roaring in his ears was unbearable. All he could think of was survival. He pulled the keys from the ignition. The rope went taut. Branson braced his foot on the seat and pulled for all his worth.

"I don't care if I die with you. That's your mistake. You still killed her. Time to die."

With one last pull on the cord, Stratton gurgled. His eyes bulged and his tongue swelled in the orifice that he had used so often to condemn other men to death. He slumped down in the seat.

To the last man. Branson knew he was dead. He'd heard that sound before. The car slowed down. It was heading towards the ravine on the left side of the road.

Suddenly, Branson didn't want to die. He wanted Kelly. Now there was another reason to live: Star. He grabbed the phone, opened the door and jumped. The road came up hard to meet him. He saw the car sliding over the canyon side. He'd picked that road deliberately. In slow motion, the auto went down the hillside, twisting, turning, and exploding, as Branson knew that it would.

Branson picked himself up from the dusty road and turned around. He had the feeling Stratton had told him the truth. It was something he had to live with or bury, along with his past life.

He had a long walk back to his bike and a longer road to his new life. Getting out of Mexico was going to be harder than getting in. Stratton's friends would be watching.

CHAPTER 18

Kelly sat upright in bed and screamed. Sweat began streaming down her thin nightgown. Star woke and, in the next room, Sage grabbed a robe and rushed to Kelly's room.

As she pushed the door open, Sage asked, "Kelly, what's wrong? What is it?"

"Kane. He was walking down a long dark road. I could see him just as clearly as I can see you. And he called my name." Her voice was low and her eyes full of tears.

"He's dead, Kel. Dad's dead."

Sage encircled Kelly with her arms. Nobody heard the main door open. Dan Lord appeared at the bedroom door. He'd let himself in after his duty shift. He watched in despair, then swallowed hard. Remembering Buchanan's words, he turned away; but not before he heard what Kelly said.

"I saw him dead, but I didn't believe it."

"Do you now?" asked his daughter.

"No. And I never will."

Branson picked up his bike. At last, the nightmares were gone. He flew down the roads, the power of steel beneath him and the wind in his hair. He had his freedom, but did not know if he wanted to stay that way, or go back. Here, he had cover and a new identity. Once he stepped over the border, Stratton's friends would be waiting. Stratton could no longer get to Kelly. She was safe, along with both of his daughters, and he longed to see them all.

Branson stood by the edge of the ocean, weighing the pros and cons of each decision. He opened the mobile phone to call Australia, then changed his mind and tossed the telephone into the water. He watched it float away and then sink, along with his past life.

Buchanan and the whole department saw the news of Stratton's death on the international news program. At last, it was over. Both the AFP and the US Marshal's office closed the case: *suspect killed by person or persons unknown*. Only Lord and Buchanan had privy to the truth.

Reese Wade came out of hiding the same day that Stratton died. She had watched the news translate to Spanish in a small Central American town. Suspicions told her, Branson had completed the job. Only Branson had that style. She tried his mobile phone number; so did Buchanan. Both got the same message. It was not in service.

Buchanan sat down at his desk and opened a drawer. Was this the right time to tell Kelly there was a letter? Lord disturbed his thoughts by entering the room. "Saw the news. Is he?" asked Lord.

"I don't know." Buchanan shut the drawer. "This time I really don't know. I think he just walked away from his old life. At least now, you can live in peace; and, hopefully, him, too."

On the following Christmas Eve, Sage and Dan Lord walked happily down the aisle as man and wife. Buchanan gave her away. He figured it was time to let go of the past. Deputy Lord was no longer AFP, just as Branson had wanted. Plus, he had never gotten back on Buchanan's good side. Therefore, he enlisted with a PI firm in Sydney. Conveniently, Branson's apartment, in which they all lived, was nearby. Gone were his noisy neighbors. In were the Lords. Kelly held her daughter, Star who was growing fast. Long and lean like Branson, there was no doubt whose child she was. Kelly sat on the grass in the hot Australian summer sun. Dan watched her.

"Do you think Kane's here?" asked Lord, his eyes circling the guests.

"No. He would have shown himself," replied Buchanan.

"I'd hoped that he would come for Sage's sake, but mainly for Kelly. She needs to be happy. Sure is clear that is not going to happen without him."

"Maybe she is happy. Perhaps we cannot let go. She has her memories, and, even more importantly, she has his child. You go and be happy and promise to always look after his older daughter."

"Do you really have to think that? You don't have to worry about that, ever. I'll always look out for her. Branson was my hero. I told him that."

"I know. What I also know is that it is time for you to go and be with your new wife. Be happy."

Kelly walked over to him with her child in her arms.

"Mr. Buchanan, if I ask you a question, will you please tell me the truth?"

"If I can," he replied.

"If you can, or if you want?" she asked.

"Same thing," he replied.

She laughed. Where had she heard that before? "Is Kane really gone? Is he dead?"

Buchanan looked her in the eyes. Her deep round eyes ached for the truth. Moreover, right now, he didn't know what the truth was any longer. "The truth? I don't know. Was he buried in that coffin? No. But you knew that."

"You may find this weird, but…yes, I knew him. I understood what he did. How long has it been since you heard from him?"

"Right after you gave birth to Star. I thought he'd come back by now. After Stratton's death, I felt sure he'd call again. Instead, when I tried the mobile number, I found it was no longer in service." He pushed his hands in his pockets and looked to the skies.

"I'll still wait. For him, I'll always wait. There will never be another Branson."

Her hair shone in the sunlight. His child clung to her. Standing in the sunlight, that's where they would be, waiting for the last third of their family to come home.

Branson pushed the bike down the canyon side. It had served him well. There was a train leaving for Los Angeles in an hour. From there, he could take a flight to Sydney. This was his last attempt. He'd tried several times to leave. With each attempt, he became aware that they were still looking for him.

After trying different approaches to his disguise that failed, he went back to his old look. He stood in the motel room and cut off his hair to appear short with the blonde growing through again. He followed the instructions on the box of blonde dye. It worked and he finished the look off by shaving off his beard and moustache. He bought a gray suit and while he was out purchasing that, he'd had the passport altered. Money could buy anything, except freedom. He couldn't stay away any longer. Too many days and nights of missing them had to end. Seeing Kelly, Sage, and his new child was now his mission.

Branson walked arrogantly down the platform to the checkpoint and handed over his passport. The guard checked it carefully. Then, he opened the briefcase. If he was required to speak, he was dead. The guard handed the passport back without any problem. A respectable businessman was on his way home, his briefcase full of China white, his passport to freedom in this country. He sat down in the seat, quietly confident that he was going home. Maybe enough time had gone by, maybe they were all safe anyway. On the other hand, what if she had met someone else.

He disembarked at Los Angeles Union Station and caught a cab to LAX. He boarded the Qantas flight, minus the briefcase. At Sydney airport, he turned heads. He was a tall man with an awesome tan, who walked with an air of confidence and arrogance. Branson was back in his country.

The cab dropped him off outside his apartment. It hadn't changed and his key still fit. There was no one home and for that, he was grateful. A few minutes alone to let being home soak in were needed. Noticing a giant fir-tree, which stood in the corner, Branson decided to look the place over. All the presents were gone except one. A small box with his name on it hung from the holiday tree. His eyes kept scanning the room. Toys were everywhere; a woman's perfume lingered in the air.

Branson sat down on the old familiar sofa and opened the gift marked with his name. Inside the box was a chain. He lifted it out, and on the end of the chain, swung a silver "K". A note inside simply said, "To Kane, love Kelly." He undid the clasp and hung the chain around his neck. She had known he would come back for her.

Standing up, he went to the bedroom. This room actually meant more to him now, than ever. A child's cot sat by the bed. There definitely was no man in the house and this thought made him smile. In the corner of the large room sat his bike, polished and waiting. Running his hand down the side, he began to remember what day it was.

Branson couldn't wait for them to come home. He had a feeling that he knew where they would be and was willing to take the chance to see. Pushing the bike outside and onto the road, he straddled his legs over the sides of the silver-and-gray behemoth. It was good to feel his own machine again, the power stretching to its full capacity beneath his body. His suit jacket blew in the wind, and the sun streamed in his face. Today was the first day of a new year and even more important than that, his new life. Strains of Auld Lang Syne echoed in his head as he raced to see his family.

Leaving his bike at the cemetery gates, he walked to the clearing. He knew where they would have buried his casket. Down the slope, he could see his party returning home.

Buchanan was losing his hair; this made him smile. He saw Dan Lord holding his daughter's hand. Sage's stomach was swollen with child. She still looked like just a kid herself. Then he saw the baby on the grass, long blond hair down her back. Tears welled up in his eyes; these he wiped away. However, he could not wipe the thought from his mind of what he was going to say to her. In the sunlight, Kelly slowly turned her head. She was a woman, now, with long curly hair, not the kid he had known.

He walked slowly down the hill. He didn't know what to expect, what they might think about his return. Into the sunlight, he came, a quiet confidence surrounding him. His child saw him first. She looked at the man in the dark gray suit and shades. She crawled across in his direction, some kind of instinct making her go. Kelly, who had been looking down toward Star, looked up. "Star, don't go to strangers like that," she chided. She pulled down her shades and glanced at the man. "Oh, my God!"

Her legs were wobbly when she first tried to move, but in a second, she passed her child to Sage as she ran to her husband.

Branson stretched his arms out and caught her in midair, spinning them both around. They kissed passionately. All dressed in a black, short, tight, dress and exciting high heels, he looked at her as if he had never seen her before. Peering at her sexy legs, which were long and tan, he concluded that he was very glad to be home.

Sage gasped. "Dear God! Dad?"

Buchanan and Lord smiled at one another, and the rest of the party headed toward Branson. Kelly clung to Branson, tears running down her face. He slid her down to the ground and took her face in his hands. Then he leaned down, and kissed her hard again.

"I knew you weren't dead. I was sure of it!" she cried.

"Then you'd be right." He removed the shades. "But Branson's dead. The name is Kale Bonner, now and that would make you Mrs. Bonner?" he looked her up and down with so much love that Kelly could do nothing but stare at him.

"Whatever name is fine with me. I knew you'd come back for us and I told them all you would. I left your present on the …" She reached around his neck and pulled the chain from under his collar. "You found it," her eyes gleamed. "You like it?"

"I love it, and I love you so much Kelly. I couldn't stay away any longer," he said while holding her in one arm.

"And this must be Star." He gathered his child up in the other. Sage walked up to greet her father. He let go of his wife, and she took their child.

"Dad." Sage cried in his arms.

He stroked her hair, and held her there. He stretched his hand out to Lord.

"Before you say anything, you need to know that I quit the force. Got me a job working for a PI firm and it's pretty good. I love Sage too much to do anything to hurt this family, or you either."

"I know that." He turned to his boss. "Buchanan, you come to dance on my grave?" Branson broke away and stood by the plaque that signified his death.

Buchanan moved in beside him and put his arms around his friend.

"Hey, boss, didn't know that you were the emotional type." Branson returned the gesture.

"I believe this is yours?" He returned the letter to its author.

"Thanks for not opening it." He took out his lighter and set fire to the envelope. Deep down, he knew that in some small way, he was responsible for his wife's death. Now he had a chance to start over.

"We'll get you to some new location and make sure you have a brand new name. Best if all of you go. Dan and Sage, too. Sell your apartment block. Tomorrow would be a good day to start a new life. The AFP will make sure you're all okay. You have a lot to do and see. By the way, what was in the letter? I never knew."

"It was a note telling you what to do if the situation of my death ever really happened," he lied. "And we're not running. Not any more. We stay…all of us. I didn't come back to only keep running, or to run again anytime soon."

He stepped forward and stood next to his own grave. Branson stood alone. He knew now that he had been right. He'd come home a better man. The one he left behind was down in that grave. In the sunlit afternoon, he stretched out his arm. Kelly came forward and took hold of his hand. He whispered in her ear. She blushed and tugged on his jacket. Maybe not so different after all.

"I have something for you." He pulled a box from his pocket.

Kelly opened it, and from inside, she pulled out the chain that held the silver butterfly charm. She clasped it in her hand and he took it from her. Sliding it around her neck, he kissed her ear. Her eyes told him all

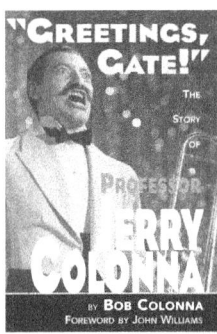

www.ingramcontent.com/pod-product-compliance
Lightning Source LLC
Chambersburg PA
CBHW072353030726
47505CB00014B/1808